Perfect Kisses

Perfect Kisses

SUSAN JOHNSON

SYLVIA DAY

NOELLE MACK

B
BRAVA

KENSINGTON PUBLISHING CORP.

h :om

BRAVA BOOKS are published by

Kensington Publishing Corp.
850 Third Avenue
New York, NY 10022

All Kensington titles, imprints and distributed lines are available at special quantity discounts for bulk purchases for sales promotion, premi-
ums, fund-raising, educational or institutional use.

Special book excerpts or customized printings can also be created to fit
specific needs. For details, write or phone the office of the Kensington
Special Sales Manager: Kensington Publishing Corp., 850 Third Avenue,
New York, NY 10022. Attn. Special Sales Department. Phone: 1-800-
221-2647.

Brava and the B logo Reg. U.S. Pat. & TM Off.

ISBN-13: 978-0-7582-0941-2
ISBN-10: 0-7582-0941-X

First Kensington Trade Paperback Printing: July 2007
10 9 8 7 6 5 4 3 2 1

Printed in the United States of America

CONTENTS

School for Scandal

Susan Johnson

Chapter One

Her pulse racing, Claire Russell pulled the hood of her cloak lower over her forehead, pushed her auburn curls farther out of sight and knocked on the door of the private residence. She dearly hoped the doorman wouldn't require an invitation since she had none.

She needn't have worried. After opening the door, the liveried footman merely nodded and bowed her in. Apparently, the guest list for the private masquerade was unrestricted.

Actually, Viscount Ormond was not so democratically disposed. His servants had been instructed to admit pretty ladies regardless of rank, but others were not welcome save if they carried a chit from him.

Claire knew nothing of the viscount's particular style of hospitality, but had she known, it would have only confirmed her jaundiced opinion of him. James Bell, Viscount Ormond, heir to an earldom that would soon be his if the present earl continued drinking to excess, was an unabashed rake, infamous for his dissipation and amorous pursuits. That he was, unfortunately, also famous for his vast wealth, stunning good looks, and prodigal charm was the reason Claire had come to this den of iniquity.

Her silly younger sister had fallen under the viscount's spell and foolishly labored under the illusion that his recent flattering attentions were genuine. Harriet viewed the viscount's gifts and posies, the strolls in the park when they'd chance to meet, and his billets-doux as a bona fide courtship.

Not that their equally foolish aunt, who served as their guardian, wasn't all atwitter as well that a peer of Ormond's rank and fortune was paying court to Harriet. As if a man of Ormond's dissolute repute was interested in more than an amorous fling with a frivolous young beauty like Harriet with no family of distinction and even less wealth.

Claire's cautionary warnings, however, had gone unheeded.

Her aunt's responses always followed a similar vein: "Just because you're quite on the shelf, my dear," her aunt would admonish, "is no reason to thwart dear Harriet's matrimonial prospects. Ormond is vastly enamored of your sister." Mrs. Bellingham would then smile smugly at Harriet as if giving her blessing to the union.

Harriet's comments had been less spiteful, but equally dismissive. "Now, Cleery, sorry as I might be that you were jilted by George Porter, you can't wish for me to suffer the same fate? And when I become viscountess, I shall be able to offer you any *number* of eligible men as suitors. Just think of it," Harriet cheerfully asserted, "we shall all live in splendor."

But illusory matrimonial hopes aside, Harriet's response to Ormond's masquerade invitation was the height of folly. Although, Harriet had slipped out tonight, Claire suspected, with their aunt's approval.

And now she, the only prudent member of their family, had arrived on the scene to save her sister from the viscount's sordid designs.

The sounds of revelry were readily apparent as Claire

moved up the stairs to the reception rooms—waltz music conducive to intimate contact, boisterous explosions of laughter, the occasional high-pitched female squeals gave evidence that the festivities were well apace.

As Claire came to rest in the doorway to the ballroom a few moments later, her very worst fears were realized.

The guests in their dominoes and masks were dancing in shockingly friendly embraces. Some couples were walking from the room hand in hand, in search of more privacy she didn't doubt. A tipsy young woman of the demimonde from her appearance was making a spectacle of herself, twirling wildly so her skirts flared high revealing her shapely legs.

Claire literally gasped as one young buck caressed his dance partner's breast right before her eyes.

Clutching her cloak tightly, as if it would serve to shield her, she nervously scanned the room, searching for her sister.

Neither she nor Harriet were so fine that either of them possessed a fashionable black domino, so she surveyed the crowd for a glimpse of Harriet's blue silk cloak. It was sky blue like her sister's eyes; it should stand out in the throng of black cloaks if she was still here. At the thought, Claire's heart sank.

What if she were too late?

What if the viscount's renowned seductive skills were already in play?

Her young sister would be ruined.

Claire stepped into the room, determined to brave the raucous crowd for the sake of Harriet's future. Threading her way through the throng, she avoided those groups most in their cups, dodged the occasional importuning hand, on two occasions offered such a forbidding look and set-down to lewd invitations, that the young men jumped back as if burned.

Her piercing gaze, sharp tongue, and air of command had it advantages.

Finally, just as she was about to despair of finding her sister, she saw Harriet and the notorious James Bell near one of the far windows overlooking the street. The viscount was leaning back against the narrow wall of the alcove, floor to ceiling French doors to his right, the ballroom to his left, and Harriet in his arms.

Her face was raised to him as though waiting for his kiss. Taking his cue, he did exactly that. He kissed her.

For so lengthy an interval that Claire was able to approach them unheeded.

"If you'll excuse me," Claire said, keeping her tone severe even as she grappled with the powerful impact of the viscount's outrageous beauty. "My sister is not allowed at entertainments such as this. Come, Harriet. I'm here to take you home."

The viscount had looked up lazily when Claire had first spoken, but had neither moved, released Harriet, nor altered his expression. "And you are?" he finally drawled, his heavy-lidded gaze surveying Claire from head to toe before coming back to rest on her face.

"I am Claire Russell, Harriet's older sister and I must *insist* that you release her immediately. It is wholly inappropriate for her to be in attendance here. As you well know, Harriet," she added, turning to her sister.

"Auntie said I could come," Harriet mutinously retorted, her pretty mouth pursed in a pout.

"Our aunt was no doubt mistaken about the style of entertainment." Claire refused to admit that her aunt would stoop so low in order to snare a man like Ormond. Although, from the viscount's sudden amused expression, she rather thought he already knew.

"Why don't I have a servant see your sister home," the viscount graciously offered, pushing away from the wall and easing Harriet back a step. "I'll take you riding in the park tomorrow, poppet," he added, smiling to assuage Harriet's frown. He lifted his hand in a negligent gesture and was immediately acknowledged by a footman, the man seemingly materializing out of thin air. "There, now, my sweet," the viscount said, brushing Harriet's cheek with his finger. "Jordan will see you home. And I shall call on you tomorrow at four."

Harriet glared at her sister. "You are ever so vexing, Cleery. Do go away," she pettishly said. "I *am not* a child you can order about!"

Ormond nodded at his footman and a look of understanding passed between them. "Now, now, don't chide your sister," the viscount calmly murmured. "She's merely concerned with the-ah . . . environment. And on second thought, I believe she's right."

"I appreciate your understanding," Claire replied, coolly. "Come, Harriet." Fully expecting to be obeyed, she turned to go.

"If you don't mind, Miss Russell." The viscount seized her arm with a quickness that belied his fashionable languor and pulled her back. "Perhaps you might stay a moment. We could discuss the–er—situation. Go now, poppet," he urged since Harriet gave no appearance of obeying her sister. "I'm sure your sister is anxious to ring a peal over my head." He smiled at Harriet to allay the sudden suspicion in her gaze. "I shall set this all right and tomorrow you and I will ride in Hyde Park. Would that please you?"

"Oh, very well," Harriet grumbled with the petulance common to women who were widely admired for their beauty. Ormond couldn't possibly be interested in Claire anyway unless he was a devotee of blue-stocking women which she very well knew he wasn't. And riding with him in Hyde Park tomorrow for all the world to see would be ever so delicious. She shot a fretful glance at her sister. "Cleery ruined everything tonight anyway."

"Indeed," the viscount said with a faint smile. His lashes lowered almost infinitesimally and taking his cue, Jordan stepped forward to escort Harriet home.

And a moment later, Claire found herself alone with the man reputed to be the most handsome man in England.

Nor could she honestly deny the designation.

In truth—any woman, not just an innocent like her sister—would be hard-pressed to withstand his brute virility. His dark, sensual gaze seemed to offer ravishment and pleasure in equal measure while his muscled form was conspicuous even beneath his fine tailoring and indolent pose.

Quickly taking herself to task, she sternly reminded herself why she had come to this debauch: To save Harriet from disaster. To allow herself to be even fleetingly captivated by a flagrant libertine like Ormond was inexcusable.

Overcompensating perhaps for her injudicious thoughts, she addressed him with rare hauteur. "We really have nothing to discuss, my lord. I certainly have no intention of ringing a peal over your head. I doubt it would do any good. May I only state, firmly and clearly, that I do not wish Harriet to become involved with a man such as yourself." Her duty done, once again she turned to leave.

And once again he stopped her, clasping her wrist lightly. "And what kind of man might that be?" he asked with a teasing smile.

She shook off his hold. "I need not explain the particulars to you, sir. Your reputation is one of long standing. Surely you know what you are."

"Would you like tea, Miss Russell?"

She was taken aback, by his invitation and the manner of its delivery. His deep voice was inexpressibly attractive—amiable and gentle as though she'd not just disparaged him, as though they were friends and social equals. Which they clearly were not. Reminded of the vast disparity in their stations, prompted as well to recall his reputation for charming women, Claire replied, briskly, "No, thank you."

"Sherry, perhaps."

"No."

"Ratafia? Women like it for some reason." His grin was

boyish. "I would dearly like you to stay and speak with me—about your sister," he added, as though in after-thought. "You're not afraid, are you?" he murmured. "I assure you, much as you may dislike me, I do not, I think, have a reputation for violence to women."

Nor would he have to, Claire decided, succumbing partially to his avowal . . . and perhaps to his great beauty as well. His black hair was artfully arranged in stylish disarray, his dark, heavy-lidded eyes were mesmerizing, his stark features were saved from harshness by his provocatively sensual mouth. Nor would he ever be judged effeminate even with his glorious looks, for he was all honed muscle and strength. Even elegant evening rig could not disguise the athletic power beneath the superb tailoring. She looked up to find his amused gaze on her, as though he was familiar with female adulation. "I'm sorry, I really must leave," she firmly said. Sensible by nature, she knew better than to trust an invitation from a man like Ormond.

"Let me see you home."

"That won't be necessary."

"Do you have a carriage outside?"

"No." He knew very well they couldn't afford a carriage.

"Surely I would be remiss if I didn't offer you safe transit at this time of night. We could find a duenna if you wish. I have a housekeeper somewhere on the premises."

Would he think her completely ludicrous if she refused such an innocuous offer? Was she indeed foolish to reject a ride home at this time of night? How much did decorum and propriety matter when she was at risk on the streets?

And he *had* offered a chaperone.

Perhaps his smile or his grand handsomeness—or perhaps his effortless charm—weighted her decision. Or maybe it was the simple delight she felt in having a man look at her the way he was . . . after so long. Whatever the reason she heard herself saying, "Very well. Thank you for the offer.

Truth be told, it was a bit frightening making my way here tonight." Terrifying in fact—the night streets of London were not for the faint of heart. "I confess I ran most of the way."

"You didn't bring a maid or manservant?"

"No." She hadn't dared; if anyone else knew of Harriet's indiscretion it could have meant her ruin.

"Ah," he said, softly.

"You know very well why." Suddenly aware of a strange, restive light in his eyes, understanding a chaperone from his household might not be completely trustworthy, she lied without a qualm. "I left a note for my aunt should something untoward befall me."

"I see. Very prudent, I'm sure. Does that mean I may dispense with rousing my housekeeper from her sleep?" He smiled, his gaze once again benign.

She hesitated, trying to reconcile her lie with his query. "If you give me your word," she finally said.

"Of course, you have my word. Shall we?" Crooking his elbow, he offered her his arm, fully aware she'd not defined the exactitude of what she meant by *his word*. Nor had he.

Chapter Two

The viscount's carriage was brought up with all speed, Claire was handed in, Ormond spoke briefly to his driver and then joined her. Sliding into a lazy sprawl beside her, he took note as she shifted in the seat to distance herself from him. Not that the narrow confines of the carriage allowed much distance.

"I have no grand designs on your sister," he offered, as though to assuage both her immediate and future fears. "Please rest easy on that score."

Her gaze was direct. "You and I both know your designs on Harriet are very much less than grand, so I shall not rest easy until you stop amusing yourself with my naive sister."

"And you are not naive?"

"Not in the least."

His brows lifted minutely. "Why is that?"

"I live in the real world, not in some fairyland like Harriet. Poor darling thinks wealthy, titled men actually marry women without family or fortune."

"It's not unheard of," he pointed out.

"Are you implying you intend to propose?" she silkily murmured.

"No."

"I thought not." Her retort was a blunt as his. "Now if

you'd tell Harriet as much, we could both get on with our lives. You would be free to pursue some other silly chit and I could stop monitoring my sister's activities."

"Even if I do what you wish, you may still find yourself chasing after Harriet." He chose not to say that the pretty little baggage had given him the impression she was more than willing.

Claire was not obtuse. She understood what he meant. "It's not Harriet's fault entirely. I'm afraid our aunt has been filling her head with impossible dreams. My sister is not fast and loose."

In his experience women of every stamp were inclined to be amenable when a title and fortune were involved. But the viscount merely smiled and said with deprecating good humor, "So it's not my charm that attracts your sister."

"Not exclusively," Claire said, smiling back at him for the first time, succumbing to his casual humility—a rarity in men of his class. "Although, surely you know that wealth is the prime allure in the *ton*."

"How is it then," he murmured, reaching out and shoving her hood aside so he could better see her face in the glow of the carriage lamps, "that you are indifferent to its attraction when your sister is not? Furthermore," he said more softly as he took in her delicate features, green eyes, and lush mouth with the critical eye of a connoisseur, "why are you so intriguing while your sister is merely pretty."

"Don't," Claire protested, pulling up her hood, purposefully resisting his flattery.

"Humor me," he murmured, slipping her hood off again. "I'm just admiring your hair. My mother's hair was the same color."

His voice had taken on a sudden gentleness and she remembered hearing the stories. How his beautiful mother and her lover had died in a carriage accident on the road to Dover—not that anyone blamed the countess for fleeing from her depraved husband. That the viscount refused to live with his father afterward was added scandal; he'd set up his own establishment though he was scarce sixteen. "It's an unfashionable color now, I'm told." She didn't speak of the circumstances of his mother's death, though the rumors had followed him. Nor did she wish to offer sympathy to a man like Ormond who had overcome his sorrow by availing himself of every vice and excess without regard for the females he'd ruthlessly discarded in the process.

"I find that the fashionable world is often in error." His voice, like hers, was without emotion, as though they both were carefully weighing their words. "Harriet tells me you've lost your parents, too," he said.

He spoke as if his father was dead, she thought. "Yes . . . four years ago. Our parents died of the putrid throat. We are wards of our aunt as you no doubt know—or rather Harriet is. I am not." Please, God, may she soon be quit of this carriage. His nearness was becoming disquieting.

"Harriet refers to you as a spinster," he said with a teasing grin—apparently untroubled by their close proximity.

"A very *contented* spinster." She refused to respond to his boyish grin, intent on retaining her composure. "Unlike Harriet, we're not all looking to marriage as our salvation," she pithily added, wishing him to understand that she was not as gullible as the other women who came within his scope.

"Then you and I should get along famously," he drawled.

She sent him a withering glance. "There is no you and I."

His brows rose in teasing rejoinder. "I could make it worth your while. My fortune is considerable—and as you previously noted, alluring."

"Not to everyone, my lord. I choose to earn my own way in the world."

"Good God. Doing what?" The only women he knew who earned their own way were in the demimonde.

"I have a school for young ladies."

"How commendable."

"A necessity. I don't wish to be beholden to my aunt."

"I see."

"I'm sure you don't. Men like you have never known privation."

"Or perhaps men like me—as you so censoriously remark—have known other kinds of privation." Overcome by an unexpected sense of sadness—raw as the day he watched his mother die—he looked away for a moment. He must be overtired, he decided. When had he last slept? He couldn't remember. Turning to his usual remedy for melancholy, he leaned down and pulled out a flask from under the seat. "Whiskey?" Uncorking the chased silver container, he held it out to her.

"No, thank you." A stiff, discouraging response.

Perhaps it might have been to others; Ormond took no notice. "If you don't mind," he drawled, already lifting the flask to his mouth. Draining it in one long draught, he took note of her rigid posture and murmured, "No need for alarm. I never get drunk." He smiled tightly. "In contrast to my father who has never been sober," he added, each word filled with loathing.

"I'm sorry." She made a small moue—reluctant to find herself feeling compassion for Ormond who would have seduced Harriet without a qualm.

"No, you're not." Corking the flask, he tossed it on the opposite seat.

"Rather, I don't *wish* to be."

"Because of Harriet."

"Of course. You would have dishonored her."

He didn't answer. He shrugged instead. "She wasn't exactly unwilling."

"She's young and stupid. You are neither."

"What do you want me to say? It's the way of the world." He shrugged again. "And I'm no saint."

"Just kindly stay away from her."

He held her gaze for a moment in the dimly lit interior, a willful fire in his eyes. "What about you?"

"I'm not interested."

Immune to the reproof in her voice, he said half under his breath as though trying to understand his aberrant impulse, "And yet, curiously, *you* interest *me*." He frowned faintly in an effort to grasp the incomprehensible. Fulsome blondes were generally his style, not this prickly, bluestocking with a disconcertingly direct gaze.

"Take heart, Ormond," Claire murmured, noting his frown. "I'm sure you'll change your mind by morning. Rumor has it you're fickle," she added, sardonically.

He laughed, her mockery pointed but true. "Touché. While you, I expect, only harbor the most sincere and lasting emotions."

"Is that not the way of the world, my lord," she replied, derisively. "Men play at love while women risk shame for similar activities."

"As you say," he murmured. So she was not a complete martinet when it came to the conventions governing women; she apparently took issue with the double standard. Before he had time to reflect further on that intriguing bit of information the carriage came to a halt. Glancing out, he saw that they had reached Mrs. Bellingham's. As his gaze returned to Claire he found himself saying something he hadn't said since his green youth. "May I kiss you good night?"

"No, you may not."

Was that panic in her voice?

Or something else entirely?

Attuned to the nuances in a female's tone and, furthermore, disinclined to be gainsaid, he lifted one brow. "Is that a challenge, Miss Russell?"

"It most certainly is not!"

Ormand's gaze was knowing, as though he understood that her outburst was not entirely indignation or umbrage.

Sliding upright from his lounging pose, he reached over and touched her cheek. "It's only a kiss," he said. "How can it hurt?"

"This is *exactly* why I don't want you near my sister! You toy with every woman who comes your way—without regard for anyone's feelings but your own! Ormond, don't be ridiculous!" she exclaimed as he lightly gripped her shoulders. "Ormond—for heaven's SAKE!" she heatedly cried as he drew her close, as his hard-muscled chest met her breasts and his hands slid down her back, pulling her nearer still. Her breath caught in her throat. "Ormond—no . . . don't . . ." she whispered.

Just as his mouth covered hers.

He inhaled her halfhearted cavil, knew from experience that her breathy protest didn't mean no, and kissing her gently, assuaged her agitation—and his curiosity in the bargain. He'd never kissed a bluestocking; he'd never before been so inclined. But very soon, he decided he might have been wise to experience the sensations sooner. Her lips were soft—softer than others he'd known—and ripe as summer fruit.

That she almost instantly tasted of sweet surrender even as she struggled against his embrace was not unfamiliar and yet different somehow—more arousing, as though the citadel about to be breached was unrivaled. And in contrast to his usual detached approach to foreplay, this time he was curiously impatient—the auburn-haired spinster stimulating some hitherto unknown goad that stirred his blood to instant fever pitch.

Was it because he'd become weary of sameness; had he become tired of pretty blondes and simpering agreement? Was he looking for willfulness and contention with his sex?

Not that introspection mattered at the moment; the lady was beginning to softly moan into his mouth. Nor was undue speculation of import when she made him feel as though he might actually experience the much touted nirvana in her arms. Quickly lifting her onto his lap as though testing the possibilities, he calmed her brief outcry as his rigid erection pressed into her soft bottom, whispering against her mouth, "Hush, hush, no one can see us. You're safe . . ." This wasn't the first time he'd been parked outside some lady's house, playing at love. His driver knew how to deal with interlopers.

The lady's protests almost immediately ceased, replaced by piquant little whimpers that gave him reason to believe she was susceptible to the same passions as he. As she slipped her arms around his neck, laced her fingers through his dark ruffled curls and kissed him back—not like some novice missish girl but like a passionate woman—he knew she'd soon be his. As though in agreement, his cock swelled sizeably.

Even while her voice of reason cried out—RESIST, RESIST—the increasing immensity of his erection sent an intoxicating shiver up her spine.

She chastised herself for yielding to such lurid sensations.

He was taking shocking liberties.

She *shouldn't* permit it; she *shouldn't* be kissing him. She *should not* surrender to the hedonistic rapture inundating her senses.

And yet she felt so alive again, like she once had—loved, desired, indulged, bewitched—tantalized.

The sound of laughter from passersby suddenly rang through the night.

Effectively shattering her halcyon dream.

"Stop!" she whispered. And then louder. "Ormond, NO!" Shamed, filled with guilt, she drew on every reserve of moral strength she possessed and shoved hard against Ormond's chest. "Let me go!"

Had her hips not been gently stirring against his erection, the viscount might have given more credence to her heated protest. Instead of releasing her, he flexed his hips upward so she could feel his hard cock more acutely and was gratified to hear her utter the softest of whimpers. A sound implicit with longing.

A familiar sound.

Understanding that fierce, avaricious desire had effectively curtailed her objections, Ormond rapidly debated his options. A less conspicuous location was required. On the other hand, if he gave his driver new directions—the interruption, however brief, might cause her to rediscover her virtue.

Patience.

Once she reached that wild, fevered point of no return, consummation alone would engage her senses. She wasn't some light skirt intent on accommodating his whims—although Claire's swift and fevered arousal did cause him to reconsider her past. If she was indeed a spinster, she must indulge in solitary vices; for she was not only easily roused, she was panting now and rubbing against his turgid cock as though needing immediate surcease.

Perhaps she was a spinster who entertained lovers with discretion. Certainly a woman who made her own living might gratify her independence in other ways as well—say with the fathers of her students or with a headmaster, if such was the case at her school.

With such lascivious thoughts racing through his brain, issues of patience suddenly became irrelevant. "Come to my apartment," he murmured. "We'll have more privacy." Not to mention comfort, he selfishly thought, leaning forward to signal his driver.

As though the sudden draught of cool air between them once again returned her to stark reality, Claire recoiled at her appalling behavior. She was no better than some harlot or tart who gave away her favors without compunction. Worse, she hadn't been able to withstand Ormond's allure any more than Harriet, whom she'd always considered frivolous and flighty beyond measure. Leaping up, she grasped the door handle.

The viscount pulled her back down, held her firmly on his lap. "Stay. Please." He stopped himself from saying, *I beg of you*, only by sheer will. "I promise complete discretion," he said instead. "No one will ever know. My word on it."

She hesitated when she shouldn't have. When she should have instantly refused.

With practiced skill, he entered that breach of indecision and offered in negotiation, "What if I promise not to court Harriet?"

She swung around to face him. "I wouldn't let you see her anyway."

Her cool, abrupt volte-face surprised him; she was a woman of parts it seemed. Even in the heat of lust, she'd reverted to her role of protector. "You think not?" he murmured, his gaze amused. "Would you be locking up your sister, then?"

"Very funny," she said with a sniff, brushing away his hands.

He obliged her, releasing her when he wouldn't have had to.

But the mood was broken.

There would be other opportunities, he decided. The lady obviously liked sex. It would just be a matter of waiting for the right occasion. "Perhaps we could be friends at least," he pleasantly said, lifting her from his lap and placing her on the seat beside him. He smiled. "You could tutor me in Greek philosophy when you have time." Harriet had spoken of her sister's admiration for the Greeks with mockery. "I confess, Aristotle always put me to sleep."

"I'm sure I couldn't make him any more palatable," Claire said, crisply.

"*I'm* sure you could," he answered with a grin.

"Fortunately, Ormond, that question will remain moot. Although, I thank you for the ride home," she added politely, as if they had just finished tea or ended a waltz.

"And I thank you for the pleasure of your company," he replied in an similar vein. "Perhaps we might meet again under more satisfying circumstances," he suggested.

"I'm sure we won't."

"As you wish." He was all cordial good manners as he opened the carriage door, stepped out and helped her alight. That he wished otherwise, of course, was all that mattered.

As they stood on the pavement, he bowed gracefully and murmured, "Good night, Miss Russell."

Claire nodded like she might to a tradesman or the merest acquaintance. "*Good-bye*, Ormond."

He watched her walk across the pavement, ascend the stairs, and enter the modest house, a faint smile on his handsome face. *Not good-bye, my pet, but au revoir. We shall meet again.*

Very soon.

Chapter Three

"My dear insomniac cousin. Do you ever sleep, James?" Lady Harville inquired as she swept into the breakfast room in a cloud of violet scent.

Ormond looked up from his breakfast. "I sleep when I don't have anything better to do, coz. Sorry to wake you."

Signaling a footman to pour her a cup of tea, Catherine Knightly dropped into a chair beside Ormond. "Dressed like that—"she indicated his evening clothes with a flick of her fingers—"you obviously had a busy night."

He smiled over the rim of his coffee cup. "Don't I always."

"Just toast, Franson—then that will be all." James was here at this ungodly hour of the morning for some pertinent reason, she understood. There was no point in immediately spreading the news throughout London.

The viscount continued with his hearty breakfast, the countess sipped her tea and only after the footman delivered her toast, walked from the room, and shut the door, did Catherine Knightly give her cousin a pointed look. "Now tell me what you want, for obviously you do when this couldn't wait for a more civilized hour."

James glanced at the clock as though to take issue, but grinned instead. "Sorry, Rene, it *is* damned early."

"She must be very beautiful," the countess noted, smiling in return.

"Not in the conventional sense, but yes she is."

"So who is this seductive female? Apparently not one of your actresses or dancers since you want something from me."

Ormond's gaze was amused. "How astute, coz. The thing is, I need a raft of books from your library. Miss Russell runs a school for young ladies and I thought I'd visit her today and bring your donation of books for her school."

"*Your* books won't do?" Ormond had an extensive library.

"Of course not. What will people say if *I* donate books to her?"

"They will say you're trying to seduce the little miss."

"Exactly."

"*What* was I thinking?"

"I have no idea. Perhaps you're still not completely awake."

"Perhaps," she murmured, "since it's *not yet* ten o'clock. However, your high-strung impatience intrigues me."

His look clearly disputed her characterization. "High-strung?"

"Oh, very well," she murmured, knowing Ormond generally didn't care enough about anything to become agitated. "Although you must admit to a degree of impatience at least."

"Lust, I'm afraid."

"Of course—the prime motive in your life."

"We can't all be virtuous. The beau monde would have nothing to gossip about."

"Thankfully, you have been doing your part to generate conversation in that regard."

He smiled faintly. "We do what we can."

"I expect this new woman who pleases you will soon be

in the gossip sheets." Leaning back in her chair, the countess gazed with affection on her favorite cousin. "So tell me why she so engages your attention. Should I have heard of this Miss Russell?"

"No, but I wish you to meet her tonight. To that purpose, I'd like you to invite her to your evening rout. Address your invitation to Mrs. Bellingham, Miss Russell, and Harriet Russell; she lives with an aunt. And if you could pay them some special attention when they arrive, I would be extremely grateful."

"Indeed. Is there anything more you'd like?" she inquired archly.

Ormond grinned. "No."

The countess laughed. "I gather you have not yet taken this miss to bed."

His gaze narrowed faintly. "You don't expect me to answer that, do you?"

"No, darling. You never kiss and tell. I expect that's one of the many reasons the ladies love you so."

"And I them in return," he lightly replied.

The countess gave Ormond a measured looked. "You seem happy." The viscount wasn't an exuberant man.

"I suppose I am."

"Because of her?"

He shrugged. "Who knows."

An ambivalent answer, Catherine decided, but not unexpected. James had been amorously involved with a great many ladies for a decade or more and had never shown any inclination to enter into a permanent arrangement. "I look forward to meeting this astonishing woman. Although you realize, while I may offer her every courtesy tonight, there may be others who will not be so cordial."

"Leave them to me."

She smiled. "I am forewarned." Ormond was famous for his set-downs.

He nodded at the small bell beside her plate. "Be a dear and ring for pen and paper. The sooner I deliver your invitation the better."

"You don't intend to go calling in that condition." She rang for a servant.

"No. I'll detour by way of my apartment first." He blew out a breath. "Then I shall have to offer a plausible excuse for the lateness of your invitation."

"I'm sure you'll think of something."

Suddenly hit with a wave of fatigue, he rose from his chair and moved to the buffet to pour himself another coffee. "She has the same color hair as my mother," he casually remarked.

So that was it, the countess thought. "I always liked that shade of red," she neutrally declared, looking up as Franson reentered the room and quickly giving him instructions.

"Her sister's a blonde," he noted as he returned to the table and sat down once again.

"More your style."

"That's what I thought, too."

"Until?"

"Until I met the older sister."

"She must be fascinating. I've never seen you orchestrate a schedule for any of your lady loves. Rather, they've always been obliged to accommodate you."

"I know." His shoulder lifted in the merest shrug. "I have no explanation."

"You just want what you want."

"Don't we all," he said. "We nobles only labor to amuse ourselves," he cynically observed. Raising the cup to his mouth, he drank it down. "Except for the few like you who have found a love match," he noted, setting aside the cup.

"You, too, might someday find your love match."

He shook his head. "Not likely that. You forget I had the

misfortune to be in contact with my father as a child." His smile was sardonic. "I am deeply scarred."

"Pshaw." Catherine spoke with the surety of a true romantic. "You only need find the right woman to love."

"Perhaps Miss Russell will serve," the viscount drawled. "At least temporarily."

Catherine made a small moue. "You're incorrigible."

"So I've been told on so many occasions I fear it's true."

Beneath his insouciance and mockery she discerned a different Ormond. Was it possible this little schoolmistress had struck some hitherto untouched sensibility? Or was she just not privy to his seductive protocols. Were all his initial pursuits like this? "Ah, here's pen and paper. Tell Franson which books you require and we'll have them delivered to your schoolmistress."

Ormond rose from his chair. "I'll pick them out. Tell Harry I'll replace them, of course. Nor will I select anything from his grandfather's renowned collection. Also, be sure to make your invitation excessively friendly."

"Would you care to compose it? I wouldn't want to take a wrong step."

Ignoring her sarcasm, the viscount cheerfully said, "I trust you, darling. Are you not the most courteous member of our family?"

"Compared to you, I certainly am."

"Exactly. I thank you in advance. Expect us early. I'm not sure their guardian, Mrs. Bellingham, is familiar with the late hours of our set. After you, Franson."

He was whistling as he left the breakfast room, a circumstance that further heightened the countess's curiosity. This woman had to be the consummate paragon of womanhood.

She was very much looking forward to meeting Miss Russell. The countess quickly penned the most gracious and hospitable of invitations, even alluding to a well-known aristocratic bluestocking as though that personage may have been the impetus for her invitation.

Informing Ormond on his return of her reference to Lady Whiteside who was forever holding intellectual soirees no one wished to attend, she added, "If you wish to affix your own explanation to my invitation, please do."

"No, no . . . your attribution is excellent. I couldn't have done better. The books are in my carriage; I thank you again." Taking the note Catherine held out to him, he said with a smile, "I warn you again, we shall arrive unfashionably early tonight."

The countess sat at the table for a few moments after her cousin left and tried to imagine who this woman might be to so enthrall Ormond. He'd said she wasn't conventionally beautiful. Was he drawn to her only because she reminded him somehow of his beloved mother? But his mother had been not only conventionally beautiful, she'd been the reigning beauty of her day.

So it was something more.

She would have dearly loved to share her thoughts with her bosom friend, Betsy, but knew better than to involve her. Any hint that Ormond might actually be susceptible to earnest feelings would race through the *ton* like wild fire. She couldn't be so unfeeling as to offer up his newest inamorata to the rumor mill.

Although, soon enough Miss Russell would be grist for that mill.

The moment Ormond walked into her rout tonight, escorting the three nobodies, everyone would know something was afoot. Not only did Ormond avoid conventional society like the plague, if he deigned to attend some entertainment, he never, *never* arrived with a woman.

And tonight he would have three.

All of inferior status.

A telling display.

She was certain the betting books would have some interesting wagers by morning. The guardian aunt would be dismissed of course, but odds would be given on the other two women.

And depending on where Ormond's attentions were directed that evening, perhaps only one woman would ultimately figure in the wagers.

Chapter Four

After a swift stop at his lodgings to make himself presentable, the viscount hied himself to Mrs. Bellingham's and delivered his invitation.

Harriet squealed with delight; Mrs. Bellingham immediately began planning her ward's wedding and when Ormond explained they would have to forgo their drive in Hyde Park that afternoon, no one offered demur.

"We must take ourselves shopping anyway, Lord Ormond," Mrs. Bellingham replied. "Harriet must look her very best tonight at so grand an affair."

"May I have that rose-colored gown I've been wanting, Auntie?" Harriet pleaded. "I know you said it was too expensive, but for an occasion such as this, surely, Auntie—you could be induced to change your mind."

Ormond winced at her wheedling tone and wondered how he'd ever taken an interest in her. Although her generous bosom couldn't be discounted, he reminded himself, knowing full well how shallow his interests were when it came to bed-partners. Nor could one dispute her blond prettiness. That his focus had shifted was due to unplanned circumstances.

He played the gentleman and visited with the two ladies until such a time as he could tactfully take his leave. A cup of tea and twenty minutes of vapid conversation later, he gave some excuse about a previous engagement and rose. Assuring the two ladies that he would return to convey them to his cousin's rout at half past eight, he left with all due speed.

The moment Ormond exited the room, Harriet leapt from her chair and danced around the parlor all aquiver with excitement. "I shall be a viscountess, I shall be a viscountess, I shall be a viscountess," she sang with glee as she twirled and leapt and capered.

"He is sure to propose now that he is bringing you into the family," her aunt agreed. "There is no other reason for the invitation. And just consider—Lady Harville is the bluest of blue bloods—as is her husband. Lord Harville has connections to the *Royal* family. Imagine, Harriet!" Mrs. Bellingham exclaimed, her eyes flaring wide. "The *Royal* family!"

"I shall—make sure to flirt—with Ormond in the—most beguiling fashion," Harriet observed, dropping panting into a chair. "You know—I am—ever so good at flirting."

"Yes, you are. I was thinking, too—under the circumstances, you might be allowed a slightly lower décolletage tonight. All the fashionable ladies expose half their bosoms. And your bosom is quite exquisite, my dear."

"I know, Auntie. Men always stare."

"You must *not* allow Ormond any liberties, however. You understand?" She waited for Harriet to nod in reply before going on. "Allowing a man liberties is the surest way to compromise your prospects. A man like the viscount only wants what he can't have. Promise me again you will be circumspect in all things."

"Of course, Auntie. I know very well how to keep a man interested. A little flirting, a small kiss from time to time. Anticipation is the greatest goad to a proposal, Auntie. Everyone knows that."

"You have always been the sensible one, my dear. Unlike

your sister who couldn't bring herself to offer the slightest encouragement to George Porter who would have made an excellent husband for her. A vicar with the right patron can command a very comfortable living. Mr. Porter's living may not have been grand like Ormond's, but then Claire does not have the air to attract a man of fashion. I don't blame Mr. Porter in the least for throwing her over. Claire's indifference to him is a lesson for you, my dear. Endearing yourself to a man is all important. Flirtation and flattery is a delicate dance of expectation and hope."

"I know all that. I knew how to make a man breathless with longing when I was still in the schoolroom. Cleery may be more educated than I, but when it comes to attracting men, I have the advantage over her."

"Indeed. And now that you have attracted one of the most eligible men in the kingdom, we must see that he comes up to the mark."

"Don't worry, Auntie. I shall see that he does."

While Harriet and Mrs. Bellingham were busy making plans for the future, Ormond was being driven to Claire's school.

He had plans as well, although his were at variance with the two ladies he'd recently left. Not that he wasn't aware that Harriet and her aunt would take Catherine's invitation amiss. But he had plenty of time to clarify the situation after he engaged Claire's cooperation. If she could be induced to keep him company, he would offer to give Harriet carte blanche entree into society.

A quid pro quo as it were.

Highly eligible suitors for Harriet in exchange for Claire's friendship.

Although how to broach that proposal would require considerable diplomacy.

Shutting his eyes, he leaned back against the padded carriage seat and began planning his speech.

Chapter Five

When the viscount walked into Claire's classroom a short time later, he instantly frowned.

There was Charlie Rutledge conversing with Claire.

What the hell was he doing here?

Charlie hadn't read a book in his life.

Worse, he was an outrageous philanderer, his wife no more than a fixture in his household. Not that Ormond could make any claim to virtue. But then he wasn't married.

Although marriage was hardly a deterrent for any nobleman interested in dalliance.

While fully aware of the social conventions that offered considerable latitude to men—married or not—the viscount, however, wasn't particularly interested in being reasonable right now.

Right *now* he wanted Charlie somewhere-the-hell-else.

Striding to the head of the room, Ormond stopped in front of Claire's desk and shot Rutledge a black look. "What are *you* doing here?" he growled.

"Relax, Jimmy. My daughter is in Miss Russell's class. Since you have no legitimate children though," the earl sardonically observed, "pray tell—why are *you* here?" He didn't relish competition from Ormond who everyone knew could seduce a nun—and had.

"Not that it's any of your business," Ormond gruffly noted, "but my cousin, Catherine, wished me to deliver some books to Miss Russell." The viscount turned to Claire. "She was culling surplus books from her library and thought your classroom might profit from them."

"Thank you. I appreciate it," Claire replied, keeping her voice composed only with effort. With a dozen girls watching—one of them Rutledge's daughter—the last thing she needed was a contretemps in her schoolroom between two men who were bywords for vice. She could not afford scandal. No family would entrust their daughter to a teacher of less than the highest repute. And her students, who were all here to gain some rudimentary scholarship, were considerably more interested in gossip than studies. "If your men will leave the boxes at the back of the room—"she glanced at Ormond's two flunkies standing near the door, each with a box of books in his arms—"I will send a thank you note to Lady—"

"Harville," Ormond smoothly interposed.

"Harville, of course. Now, gentlemen, if you'd excuse me. My students are waiting."

There was nothing for the men to do but take their dismissal with good grace. As they stood outside on the pavement a few moments later, Rutledge noted snidely, "I thought you were enamored of the blond sister with the huge tits and come-hither look."

"And I thought you were enamored of your enceinte opera singer," Ormond smoothly returned. "Isn't she about to whelp any day now?"

"She hardly needs me for that," Rutledge retorted.

"Nor does Miss Russell need your harassment."

"We were just having a friendly conversation."

"I didn't know you actually talked to women."

"I could say the same about you."

"Just don't bother her again," the viscount said, bluntly.

"Are you warning me off?" Rutledge drawled.

"I am."

"Why? I await your reply with bated breath," Rutledge mocked.

"Simply put, neither Harriet nor Mrs. Bellingham would approve of your attentions to Miss Russell." He couldn't express his own interest in Claire without compromising her reputation. "Consider me the Misses Russell's duenna."

The earl smiled silkily. "A new role for you, Ormond."

"Anything to ease the boredom, Charlie. Now be a good chap and find someone else to bed. Miss Russell is off limits."

Rutledge held Ormond's gaze for a moment. "Off limits to everyone or just everyone but you?"

"I brought the books as a favor to Catherine. Unlike you, who were on a less charitable errand. Consider your daughter's position, Charlie. Don't embarrass her in front of her friends."

"How civil and well mannered you are," the earl sneered.

"Maybe I remember my father embarrassing me as a child," the viscount flung back. "Think about it, Rutledge. Sniff out cunt somewhere else—where your daughter doesn't have to watch you. Now get the fuck out of here," the viscount muttered, bitter memory welling up inside him. "Or I'll call you out."

Dueling was outlawed, but not completely curtailed and Ormond's temper had brought him out on the dueling field more than once.

Aware of the viscount's success on those occasions, Rutledge opted for retreat rather than foolish valor. "Suit yourself," he muttered and quickly strode toward his carriage.

"I shall," Ormond murmured, under his breath. Standing motionless, he waited until Rutledge's carriage disappeared from view. Then, entering his own carriage, he had his driver take him to the mews behind the school where he could wait out of sight. Both his carriage and bloodstock were recognizable.

He spent the next few hours dozing, having given his driver orders to wake him when the school day was over. As the students began to depart in the carriages sent for them, he was informed, and as the last vehicle rolled away, he entered the building through a rear door. Quickly racing up the stairs to the main floor, he walked down the corridor to the large schoolroom facing the street. The door was ajar and he paused for a moment, watching Claire seated at her desk.

Her attention was on some papers that she appeared to be grading, her head slightly bent, her mouth pursed in contemplation.

A mundane sight he found captivating for no good reason.

He wondered briefly whether the stark contrast between his usual position, waiting in the wings of the theater for a pretty actress or dancer, and this supremely commonplace event was what he found enticing. Or was he simply spurred by the added difficulty of this particular seduction? Had her rebuff last night intensified his acquisitive instincts? Or was it something—novel and inexplicable?

As he put his hand to the door and shoved it open, however, reflection fell away and he lapsed into familiar, well-honed patterns of behavior.

"I waited for Rutledge to leave. I hope you don't mind," he casually remarked, strolling into the room. "I had an additional message from my cousin," he explained, "and preferred Rutledge not be privy to it. You and your family have been invited to Catherine's rout tonight. I delivered the invitation to your aunt's house prior to coming here."

"Where have you been waiting?" Claire's anxiety was plain, her voice sharp.

"Never fear. No one saw me. My carriage was parked in the mews."

She exhaled softly. "Thank you for your discretion. As you know, I must avoid any taint of gossip."

"I understand. In that regard, perhaps you don't mind that I took the liberty of warning off Rutledge. I told him his presence was sure to embarrass his daughter."

More relieved to be rid of Rutledge's unwanted attentions than vexed by Ormond's interference, she said, frankly, "Thank you again. He has been quite persistent."

"I gathered as much. May I drive you home?" He glanced at the clock on the wall. "I told your sister and aunt I would come to fetch your party at half past eight and I know how women need time to dress."

"Why are we invited to your cousin's soiree?"

No piquancy or excitement about the invitation—only that cool inquiry and cooler gaze. "Could I say I have altruistic motives?" he smoothly parried.

"You could say it, but no one would believe you, least of all me."

"Ah."

"Speak up, Ormond. There's no need for subterfuge. I am not my sister who lives in some dream world."

He blew out a small breath. "You want the truth?"

"I would much prefer it to a lie."

He found himself ill-equipped to deal with such bluntness in a woman. Usually they preferred dissimulation as much as he.

Claire looked at him with her usual directness. "Does the truth confound you?"

"Actually, in this instance, yes."

"Let me make this easier for you," she said in her schoolmistress tone. "You had your cousin invite us to her rout tonight for your own selfish reasons. I'm not sure I appreciate her deceit any more than yours."

"Don't blame Catherine. She's being kind to me, that's all." He smiled. "Since childhood, she's always viewed me as in need of her charity."

"Your explanation makes *her* more attractive at least."

"You would enjoy her immensely. She has no airs."

"Like me, you mean," Claire said in her plainspoken way.

"I meant it as a compliment," Ormond offered. "Women with airs are too common by half."

"And you are looking for the uncommon—is that it? Someone outside your usual sphere, for instance. A diversion, as it were, from the Society belles and actresses."

He could see that she was displeased, but instead of equivocating as he might have in the past, he answered her as plainly. "Nothing about my interest in you was intentional. But when I met you, you immediately intrigued me— perhaps because you *are* different from the women I've known. As for a diversion, I'm not so sure about that interpretation." He smiled. "I'm not introspective. But I agree, this is unusual for me—and that's the truth."

"Harriet will be devastated. She plans to marry you," Claire noted, ignoring his heartfelt admissions.

"You're being facetious, no doubt, Miss Russell—may I call you Claire?"

"No. And I'm not being facetious. She will be heart-broken."

He wished to say—flirts like Harriet didn't have hearts to break, but chose a more tactful response. "Apropos marriage to your sister, Miss Russell, I'm afraid I'm not the marrying kind. Ask anyone—they'll agree."

"You've been leading her on."

"Come, Miss Russell, you know better than that. You spoke differently last night—warning me away from your sister as I recall."

She had the good grace to blush. "It's just so unfair," she said, rankled at the inequities of Society. "If our parents hadn't died, Harriet might have been able to come out. Not in the best circles, but modestly at least and she would have found a suitable husband."

The phrase—unlike you—was left unsaid, although it vibrated in the air like a tuning fork.

"Perhaps, I might be able to help," he said, understanding Lady Luck had practically handed him his prize tied up with a pretty bow. "I would be willing to offer the wherewithal for Harriet to gain her suitable husband if you were inclined to help me in return."

"Do tell." A sound as cool as the winter sea.

"Are you always so off-putting?" he asked with a smile.

"Always," she replied, without a smile.

But she hadn't said no and she was still talking to him, he observed, skilled at recognizing interest in a woman—however minuscule in this instance. He pressed on. "I shan't mince words, then. Here's what I had in mind: If you would be willing to offer me your friendship, I would endeavor to see that Harriet is launched in the *ton*. Not by me personally, which wouldn't do, but Catherine could be induced to serve as her patroness. Now, you know as well as I that Harriet doesn't give a fig whether she marries me or some other wealthy nobleman. Don't feign surprise; it's clear as the nose on her face. Should I go on?" he unnecessarily inquired. Claire was clearly listening.

"Yes."

Miss Russell would make an excellent gambler, he thought. No emotion was evident on her face. "Very well. Once Harriet has entree into society, she will be besieged by any number of suitors, many of whom would be more than willing to marry such a lovely young woman. At the risk of offending you, might I point out that aristocratic men are rarely attuned to a woman's sensibilities, only their beauty. And in that regard, Harriet will outshine her competition. I'll wager you she'll be engaged within the month. So you see, I shan't break her heart and she will have the fine marriage she wants."

"You're very generous."

"I want you to be happy."

"Why?"

He shrugged. "Damned if I know. Ask Catherine. She understands me better than anyone."

"Apropos this friendship of ours. What duration did you have in mind?"

"We'll have to see."

"How soon do you normally get bored with a woman?"

"Does anything ever excite you?" he queried, not sure if he should take umbrage or be grateful for her dispassionate view of his proposal.

"Any number of things excite me. But acquit me, Ormond, of wild excitement over being bought and paid for by a man like you."

"Would some other kind of man elicit wild excitement in you?"

"Perhaps."

"Then I should endeavor to become that man."

"You can't."

"So sure?"

"Very sure."

"If I should be mindful to try anyway, would you allow it?"

"For a month? Why not? You did promise my sister would be engaged within a month, did you not?"

"And she shall be."

"Only to a man of her choice."

"Of course. What did you think?"

"You have enough money to buy someone—that's what I thought."

Like you, he reflected, but kept his tongue. "It must be a man of her choice. My word on it."

"How will I know that you'll keep your word if I agree to this proposal of yours?"

"Catherine will vouch for me. Privately, of course," he added to allay the sudden fear in her eyes.

A heavy silence fell.

He spoke first because he was more impatient—or less apprehensive. "I would not dream of forcing you in any way. I mean it most sincerely. Although," he added with the faintest of smiles, "may I remind you now of the time. If you wish to get ready for tonight, we should leave."

"Very well," she said.

Unsure of her meaning, he inquired, "Very well what?"

"Very well, you may take me to your bed."

"You make it sound like a penance."

"We do not all live in the beau monde, Ormond, where amorous love is a form of entertainment. To people like me, love is love not sex. To simply agree to have sex with you because your bored gaze has fallen on me at the moment is not an easy decision."

"It's not like that."

"Then what is it like?"

"I don't know. I wish I did." Suddenly he was tired of coaxing and cajoling and explaining the unexplainable. "Do you want to or don't you?" he asked, gruffly. "It's up to you."

"No, it's up to you. You hold all the cards, Ormond. And for my sister's sake, I'll play your game."

He almost said, *Forget it. I don't have to beg for sex.* But something stopped him. "Then allow me to escort you home, Miss Russell," he cordially offered.

"Don't you ever get angry, Ormond?"

"Only hope you never see me angry," he softly replied. "Shall we?" He offered her his arm.

A shiver raced up her spine as she placed her hand on his forearm.

Was it fear or something more provocative?

She looked up to find him staring at her.

"I think we'll muddle along just fine, Miss Russell," he murmured, as though he knew something she didn't know. "You please me immeasurably."

Chapter Six

The carriage ride was largely silent, both occupants immersed in their own thoughts. Or in the case of the viscount—in making plans.

He didn't feel he could press Claire now for times and places.

But that didn't curtail him from speculating on appropriate venues.

Nor did it diminish his buoyant good cheer.

First things first, though. He must see that Harriet made an appropriate splash tonight.

Feeling it would be acceptable to at least discuss Harriet's entree into society, he said, "If you'll excuse me tonight, I plan to pay considerable attention to your sister. At the risk of sounding vain, it will add to her consequence."

"I understand."

He could barely hear her reply. "You are distraught. I'm sorry."

"Are you?"

He held her gaze for a moment, understanding what she meant. "Not completely, I'm afraid," he said with a sigh. "Forgive me."

"I would be more apt to forgive you if you were less mercenary."

"If I were truly mercenary, I would accept your sister's overtures and discard her when I was done."

Claire grimaced. "She is truly naive."

"Not entirely," he softly replied. "And I don't mean to impugn your sister's character, but she has a kind of determination that's not uncommon with women who are—" he hesitated.

"Looking to ensnare a husband," she finished with a small sigh. "I understand and I don't mean to be ungrateful, Ormond."

"James, please."

"You must know I am unsettled by all this."

"I'll treat you kindly." He touched her hand. "You have my word."

She looked away before she met his gaze once again. "And Harriet will have her husband."

"I promise."

"Very well," she said as if she were mounting the scaffold. "I shall endeavor to please you."

"You do without trying. Just looking at you makes me smile." The outrageous significance of his remark went unnoticed, so beguiled was he by *her* sudden smile. "There now. That's better. Ah, here we are. Save a dance for me tonight, Miss Russell."

"Claire."

"Thank you." Stepping from the carriage, he turned and offered her his hand.

As she placed her fingers on his palm, she felt a delicious, heated jolt race from her fingertips through her body with such velocity, she gasped.

He heard and engulfed her small hand in his for the briefest of moments. "Until tonight," he murmured, his voice hushed and low, helping her step to the pavement before releasing her hand. "I may need more than one dance," he whispered. "I hope you don't mind."

What she minded was that she couldn't resist his allure. "What if I said I minded?"

His smile was instant. "I wouldn't believe you."

"Damn you," she muttered.

"I have no control either if it helps," he said. "I'm seriously thinking about throwing you back into my carriage and taking you somewhere far away, and damn the consequences."

"Easy for you to say," she pointedly retorted.

"I stand corrected," he said, instantly contrite.

She smiled again, his boyish contrition charming. "I'm not sure I'm going to be able to handle you."

His brows flickered in amusement. "An interesting concept, darling."

"I'm not your darling."

"I rather think you are."

"For the duration, I suppose I am."

He nodded toward the door. "Go," he muttered, "before I don't let you go."

The covetousness in his gaze was so stark, she immediately turned away and hurried toward the house.

"Good idea," he whispered, drawing in a breath of restraint.

How the hell was he going to get through the evening without mounting her? "Damn, damn, damn," he softly swore. He was going to need every shred of self-control he possessed.

Chapter Seven

The level of joy in the Bellingham household was so resounding, Claire couldn't help but be drawn into the excitement.

Harriet had come running the instant she walked in the door, waving the invitation. "Cleery, LOOK, LOOK what Lord Ormond delivered today! You won't believe it, but we've been invited to a grand rout at Lord and Lady Harville's! Auntie bought me the most gorgeous gown in all the world and the most gorgeous silk slippers and the most, *most* beautiful silk stockings with roses on them! We have arrived, Cleery! We have *arrived!*"

"Let me see." Claire took the invitation from her sister and quickly perused it just to make sure Harriet was correct and Ormond was telling the truth. "My goodness," she murmured, astonished at the friendly tone of her ladyship's note.

"Lady Harville says a Lady Whiteside knows of you, Cleery! What do you think of that! Maybe even *you* will find a beau!" Harriet exclaimed with unflattering honesty.

Maybe she already had, Claire thought, although she was not naive enough to consider Ormond precisely a beau. A sexual partner, a lover, a charming companion. And for now, she would be content with that. Since John had died, she'd never thought of marriage again anyway. Ormond was looking for amusement, and maybe she was ready for a diversion as well after so many years. "Show me your new gown, darling," Claire said, smiling at her sister. "I'm sure you'll be the belle of the ball."

"Of course I will," Harriet cheerfully agreed. "I'm always the most beautiful woman in the room."

And so it went in the hours before the viscount arrived. Harriet was in ecstasy, their aunt was dispensing advice at every turn, and Claire was trying to find something in her wardrobe that would suit for an elegant entertainment such as the one tonight.

Perhaps she wished to look her best for other reasons, too.

Not that she openly acknowledged those feelings, but she took special care with her hair and found her mother's pearl ear bobs that she'd put away and even wore a gown that she might have considered too youthful yesterday.

It was a watered-silk in apple green, the style several years old, the fabric worn slightly at the hem, but in a crush such as the one she expected, her hem wouldn't show. She wondered if the scooped décolletage exposed too much bosom and apparently it did, for her aunt sniffed on seeing her.

"Really, Claire," Mrs. Bellingham said, her lips pursed. "Don't you think your gown is a bit daring?"

"It doesn't matter, Auntie," Harriet brightly proclaimed. "You said yourself that Society ladies show almost their entire bosom. Don't worry, Cleery, no one will notice."

Claire understood that Harriet meant no one would notice her when she stood beside her pretty, blond sister. She didn't take affront; Harriet always spoke without thought for other's feelings. And in that regard, Claire hoped Ormond was right and noblemen wouldn't regard anything but Harriet's beauty. To date, that certainly had been the case, although their aunt's social circle was very distant from the rareified world of the *ton*.

When their parents were alive, their entertainments had been generally small house parties to which the gentry in the neighborhood were invited. As a retired colonel and the younger son of a younger son, their father had not had the resources to entertain on a grand scale.

Since Harriet was still in the schoolroom when their parents had died, her experience with country Society had consisted largely of making her curtsy at teatime and answering the usual questions put to children.

Not that she hadn't taken to their aunt's bourgeoise entertainments like the veritable duck to water. She adored being the center of attention. She was a natural flirt. And she confidently viewed the male admiration directed at her as her due.

Claire hoped that Harriet would attract as many gentlemen in the fashionable world.

She was, after all, paying a considerable price toward that end.

The knock at the door came precisely at half past eight and Harriet's squeal of delight resonated throughout the house.

"For heaven's sake, child, hush!" Mrs. Bellingham cautioned. "No man likes a raucous woman."

Harriet instantly put her hand over her mouth and said, "Yes, Auntie," through her gloved fingers.

Claire couldn't help but smile. Harriet was always more than willing to please. And if her girlish aspirations were achieved, Claire didn't doubt that she would make some frivolous young nobleman an accommodating wife.

Ormond was courteous in the extreme as he greeted the ladies, complimenting each of them in turn, paying particular attention to Harriet.

She preened under his regard and winked at Claire as though to say, *You see. I shall soon be his wife.*

Thankfully, her aunt and sister chattered constantly on the drive to the Harvilles, allowing Claire the opportunity to prepare herself for the hours ahead. Not that she expected Ormond to press himself on her tonight. He'd already mentioned that he would concentrate on entertaining Harriet. But still, she was mildly daunted by the prospect of such lofty company and so elegant an affair.

She was in the minority in that regard, however, both her sister and aunt were anticipating the evening's events without a qualm. Mrs. Bellingham's favorite expression parroted her late husband's observation that *Everyone puts their pants on one leg at a time.* And that's a fact, she would firmly declare, secure in her position in the world.

Mr. Bellingham had owned a small brewery, earned a good living, and subscribed to democratic views he'd expressed with great frequency.

His wife was equally forthright.

A point of no small concern for Claire.

She only hoped the guests tonight would be as open to her aunt's proletarian principles.

"Don't worry," the viscount murmured, as he helped her alight from his carriage a short time later. "Relax. I'll take care of everything."

She shot him a quick look.

"You've been frowning since we left your aunt's," he whispered, as though reading her mind. "Come, ladies," he went on in a normal tone. "I'm looking forward to introducing you to my family."

Mrs. Bellingham beamed, Harriet smiled smugly, and Claire forced her mouth into what she hoped was a credible smile. This subterfuge and playacting may be effortless for Ormond, but she wasn't as accomplished at artifice. Nor was her unease lessened when they entered the luxurious townhouse to find several nobles in the entrance hall, divesting themselves of their capes and greeting each other with the casual intimacy of old friends.

Ignoring the raised eyebrows and veiled looks directed at his guests, Ormond guided the ladies through the curious, disposed of their cloaks, and escorted them to the top of the broad staircase where Catherine and Harry were waiting to greet their guests.

The viscount introduced the ladies with a casual politesse and his cousin and her husband welcomed them to their home with equal courtesy. Then, following the few guests who had arrived as early as they—dowagers who were anxious to set about playing cards, young men who had come from their clubs looking for a different location in which to gamble and drink, a smattering of relatives who had been invited to dinner earlier—the viscount's party moved toward the ballroom.

Claire was astonished at her sister's superb aplomb. Harriet was neither nervous nor disquieted by the company or the palatial surroundings. She stood on the edge of the largely empty ballroom floor with a faint smile on her face, waiting to be noticed.

She was—very quickly.

A number of men came in from the gaming rooms in a lemminglike rush, led by Baron Worth who first spied her. They made their bows and asked Ormond for introductions. As the viscount obliged, a becoming blush colored Harriet's cheeks, and she turned an angelic smile on her suitors. Men liked innocence, she'd discovered. Playing her role to perfection, she responded to their flattery and compliments with an artless flutter of her lashes or a demure lowering of the same—exhibiting a chaste, tantalizing purity that clearly appealed to her swains.

The phrase *Lead us not into temptation* would be appropriate to the drama, Ormond cynically thought.

But then was that not the aim.

After having introduced everyone in what turned out to be an ever-increasing throng, Ormond turned to Harriet. "Let me find your sister and aunt a chair and then I'll lead you out in a dance."

"Thank you so much," Harriet purred, lifting her innocent blue gaze to the viscount. "I would dearly love to dance."

But no sooner had the viscount secured chairs in which Claire and Mrs. Bellingham could view the festivities, than he found himself displaced. Harriet and Lord Seego were already on the dance floor, Harriet smiling up at the duke's heir with what could only be termed adoration and young Seego returning her regard with an equally worshipful gaze.

"I'm so sorry, my lord," Mrs. Bellingham apologized, her eyes snapping with displeasure at the sight. "I'm afraid Harriet has forgotten her manners."

"That's quite all right, Mrs. Bellingham. I wish above all for Harriet to enjoy herself tonight."

"How gracious of you," she murmured, thinking that the aristocracy were strange indeed. The viscount didn't display an iota of jealousy. She wasn't quite sure whether that was good or not.

"Perhaps I could induce you to dance, Miss Russell," Ormond smoothly interposed. "It doesn't seem right for you to sit out the dance."

"I shouldn't," Claire demurred, aware of her aunt's frown.

"Nonsense. If you'll excuse us, Mrs. Bellingham," the viscount added, politely, taking Claire's hand and pulling her to her feet. "This song is a favorite of mine."

"My aunt is scowling at us," Claire whispered as he led her away.

"It doesn't matter." The bluntness of the privileged. He nodded toward her sister. "Was I right about Harriet or not?" he queried with a grin, smoothly drawing Claire onto the floor and into a waltz.

"So it seems."

"In spades," he cheerfully observed. "She has a swarm of suitors—not to mention Seego is in the market for a wife. His father wants to see the dukedom further extended before he dies. He's ill, so time is of the essence."

Claire frowned faintly. "How cold that sounds."

"It needn't be. Seego's a pleasant enough fellow."

"But a dukedom. I doubt Harriet can fly so high."

"The present duke married his governess. Don't look at me like that. I'm not disparaging the union, simply stating a fact. The family is open to new blood."

"My goodness." Claire glanced at her sister and her partner with a speculative gaze. "Perhaps Harriet *will* be engaged soon."

"I'm not sure *soon* is in my best interests," the viscount said with a wicked smile, twirling gracefully around two couples. "Perhaps we should have something in writing," he teased.

Suddenly aware that they were the cynosure of burning interest, Claire wondered if her gown had ripped in an embarrassing spot. "Why are those people staring?" she nervously inquired.

"I never dance, that's why. Ignore them."

Only partially relieved, she muttered, "If only I were as dégagé as you, Ormond." He was always the center of attention, she suspected.

"James, if you please or I shall charge you tuppence each time you call me otherwise." His voice was playful.

She couldn't help but smile. "Try to collect."

"Oh, ho . . . what a charming prospect."

"For a man who never dances, you're very good," she said, intent on changing the topic to something less licentious.

"Dancing was one of my mother's great pleasures," he smoothly replied, ever courteous to a lady's sensibilities. "You pass muster rather well yourself."

"We entertained ourselves in our household; my father played the violin, my mother the pianoforte, and we girls danced."

"Definitely an asset for Harriet in her quest for a husband," he murmured. "As for your accomplishments as a dancer, those I intend to keep for myself."

"Am I obliged to yield to those wishes?"

Was that flirtatious or provocation? "Let's just say it would please me if you did," he carefully returned. "I believe I'm jealous," he said with a look of surprise. "It must be your beguiling décolletage inspiring me," he drawled, quick to ascribe his curious feelings to more familiar causes.

"Do you think it's too daring?" Claire nervously queried. "Auntie said it was."

"Hardly," he said. "Most females display their breasts without compunction."

She found herself annoyed at his observation. But she'd no more than acknowledged her resentment, than she chastised herself for a fool. Did she really think a man like Ormond would be anything more than he was? Why wouldn't a rake and libertine notice breasts? Do not forget the kind of man you are dealing with, she warned herself.

But as the music came to an end, Ormond himself prompted her to face the reality of her agreement with him. "Come, we'll see that Harriet is content in the company of her swains, and then I'll show you my cousin's library."

"Meaning?" Did he propose to drag her off without regard for propriety?

"Meaning, I thought you might enjoy seeing the late earl's renowned collection of maps and books on exploration." He smiled faintly. "I have no plans to seduce you this minute if that's what you were thinking. Ah, here comes Catherine. Would you like her to come with us and save your reputation?" he teased.

Lady Harville waved her fan in the direction of the gaming room as she reached them. "I just introduced your aunt to Lady Strand who was looking for a fourth for whist. They are off arm and arm."

"Oh, dear. My aunt is alarmingly serious about whist and a bit outspoken, I'm afraid."

"As is Lady Strand on both counts." Catherine smiled. "Don't worry. All will be well." She glanced at Harriet twirling past in Seego's arms. "I see your sister is being amused."

"Indeed. Thank you for inviting us and thank you too for the wonderful books."

"They were of no use to me and James rather thought you would like them," she replied, not quibbling over the truth when this woman might offer James some happiness—however brief.

"Speaking of books, I was about to show Miss Russell Harry's map collection. Would you care to join us?"

"I would love to if I could get away from my guests. Unfortunately, I see Charlotte over there looking daggers at Anne." She made a small moue. "They are sharing a lover at the moment which makes for bad feelings. Pelham should know better, of course, but he doesn't, insensitive rake that he is. Heavens—they're about to make a scene!"

As she rushed away to intercede, Ormond said with a shrug, "Pelham *should* know better. The man is witless. Come," he added, taking Claire by the elbow and moving toward the doorway. "This is why I never attend these affairs. It's such a graceless assemblage of gossip and over-dressed curiosity-seekers."

Claire shot a quick glance at the dance floor.

"Harriet's fine," Ormond said. "She won't miss you or your aunt."

"I'm afraid you're right," Claire murmured.

"Certainly that's beneficial, is it not?"

"Yes, yes, it is. Only—"

"Only she doesn't need you anymore?" Ormond said with a small smile as they entered the corridor. "You haven't been paying attention, darling."

She shouldn't have responded to the word darling, to the warmth in his voice. And if he hadn't leaned over and lightly kissed her cheek, she would have been better able to resist.

"For heaven's sake, behave." But even as she spoke a rush of pleasure streaked through her body.

"I wish I could. Two days seems like a lifetime." In fact, he'd been remarkably disciplined; two days was a record for him. Women, didn't as a rule, rebuff him.

"Perhaps we should go back to the ballroom." The nervous tremor in her voice was obvious.

"Perhaps we shouldn't," he murmured, kissing her cheek again.

"Don't you dare embarrass me," she whispered, nervously glancing around, grateful to see them alone in the hallway.

"I'll try not to."

"James!"

He took a deep breath. "I'm fine. Everything's fine. Everything will be fine. Although it would have helped if you'd worn a different gown."

"I'm sorry." She shouldn't have given into her vanity.

He smiled. "It's not your fault. I would have found you irresistible in a shift." He grinned. "Probably more irresistible. Here, we've reached the library," he said, opening a door and ushering her in. "Now if you keep your distance, all will be well."

She was partially mollified by his admission. She preferred not admitting that she'd dressed for seduction. That she desired him. That only fear of discovery served to restrain her ardor. "I shall keep my distance," she said, although the lack of conviction in her voice was conspicuous.

His nostrils flared like a wolf on the scent.

Shutting the door behind him, he turned the key in the lock.

Chapter Eight

"Don't," she whispered, backing away from him.

"No one would think of coming into the library." Stripping off his white kid evening gloves, he let them drop.

"Someone might!" Backing into a large chair, flustered, she came to a stop.

"They won't," he said, moving toward her at a circumspect pace. "And even if they did, the door is locked."

"James, I beg of you!"

But the tremor in her voice wasn't fear, her breathing had accelerated, and her nipples were taut beneath the fine silk of her bodice. "Don't worry—you're perfectly safe," he offered soothingly.

"Allow me to disagree." Restive and skittish, she shifted from foot to foot as though about to bolt.

Dare he say to a wavering virgin that he wouldn't come in her—that he never did? Or would such bluntness frighten her more? "I promise you no repercussions of any kind," he said delicately.

"That's not a promise you can fulfill," she said with a small vehemence.

"Forgive me if I'm too direct, but if you fear becoming pregnant, you needn't. I'm very dependable."

"I see." She took a small breath. "That is rather direct."

I'm sorry. I was hoping to allay your fears." He briefly frowned. "This is unusual for us both, I fear."

"Because women normally fall into your arms?"

Under the circumstances, that was not a question he cared to answer. "How can it matter," he said, softly, instead, "whether we make love tonight or tomorrow or the next day?"

"This is not love."

"It all depends on your interpretation." She was right, though, about women falling into his arms. Dealing with a woman who didn't was turning out to be—well . . . time consuming, he facetiously thought, suddenly amused by this curious scuffle.

"Is something humorous?"

"Would you like the truth?"

"I would like to be somewhere else," she pettishly replied, struggling to reconcile her potent desires with the manifold improprieties.

He smiled. "Perhaps in my bed?"

"Very amusing."

"I dare say you'd find it more than amusing."

"Such arrogance, Ormond."

His smile widened. "Now you owe me tuppence."

"How cavalier you are. Do women find your casual impertinence appealing?"

He laughed. "As you noted the other day, women find my fortune the most appealing—your sister included if I may say so without offending you further. Although, if you allow me, I could show you my more admirable qualities." She was too green to hear the truth about what most appealed to his lovers.

"And if I allow that, I shall adore you as well?"

"I didn't say I was adored." He was pleased to see her skittishness displaced by a petulance he knew how to deal with. "Let's just say that the ladies I know are always *appreciative*."

"So I understand. The gossip sheets proclaim you much in demand in the boudoir."

"I admit to a certain popularity," he said, smiling faintly, aware of the most trifling peevishness in her voice, as though she were feeling deprived. "Perhaps I might convince you of what you've been missing if you'd allow."

She made a small moue. "Conceited man."

"I'm good at what I do."

"And why wouldn't you be since vice is the sole focus of your life."

"*Au contraire*. It's the scandal sheets that thrive on sex. I have many interests. When we have more time, I'll tell you about them. As for vice, my sweet little prude, let me change your mind—and your vocabulary apropos pleasure." He dropped his gaze to her taut nipples, then looked up and smiled at her. "I'd wager you're feeling a certain heated palpitation in your—"

"Don't say it," she blurted out.

"I only meant to point out that we have privacy, you and I have agreed to agree and I could assuage your—er—restlessness if you'd like. I guarantee you'll enjoy yourself."

His voice was hushed and low, his provocative offer tempting. And he was right—she'd already agreed to this. "I am not a prude," she whispered. "I just didn't expect this—"she waved her hand slightly, indicating the venue. "In all honesty," she reluctantly added, "I do find myself—"

"Intrigued?"

She sighed. "Yes."

"Then why not think of this as an investment in your sister's future. Would that make it better—easier? Harriet *is* being served up a full array of suitors," he saliently noted. "Which was the point of our arrangement, was it not?"

"I didn't think—that is . . . I wasn't planning on the—well . . . suddenness."

Unlike her, he wasn't indecisive. As for suddenness, he hardly thought waiting two entire days met that criteria.

"The door's locked. The drapes are drawn. Your sister and aunt are intent on their own pleasures." He moved closer; they were only inches apart. "Look," he said, holding out his arms, "You set the pace. I won't touch you. How would that be?"

His deep voice was benign, his offer innocuous. How could it hurt?—the little voice inside her head observed.

"You could start by kissing me," he suggested, not entirely sure a tyro knew what to do. Not sure *he* could wait much longer. Although the heated flush on her cheeks, the agitated rise and fall of her breasts gave him reason to think she might be more ready than she realized.

Would she or would she not give in to her urges?

Could he or could he not continue to play the gentleman with her sexual need so blatant?

Then, fortunately for his peace of mind and aching cock, she moved forward an infinitesimal distance, and clenching his fists he stood immobile—waiting.

Slowly raising her gloved hands, she placed them gingerly on his white satin waistcoat.

And he waited still—breath-held.

The sweet scent of her overwhelmed his senses as she rose on tiptoe and leaned into him. Her soft breasts pressed into his chest, her thighs brushed against his, and then, more pertinently, her lower body came into contact with his hard, pulsing erection.

Only with the utmost restraint did he remain motionless.

Provocatively aware of the rigid length of his penis prodding her stomach, the tantalizing proximity further fanned her already fevered desires and, wild with longing, Claire abruptly jettisoned reason and logic. Overwhelmed by lust, she gave into the more powerful, corrupting force.

Ormond might have told her as much before time.

But perhaps for virgin maidens, experience was the better teacher.

Her last fears and trepidation cast aside, she shut her eyes, gave herself up, and kissed him.

As her lips finally made contact with his, he felt a wild excitement out of all proportion to the simple act. Cynic that he was, he immediately attributed his feelings to the prolonged delay in gaining the lady's favors.

Less cynical, or not cynical at all, further buoyed by a heated rush of incredible pleasure melting through her senses, Claire opened her eyes and kissed Ormond again— gladly and willingly. With the euphoria of having tasted the sweetest of forbidden fruit.

Dropping back on her heels a moment later, newly liberated and giddy with joy, she smiled up at him. "I couldn't resist you. I couldn't no matter what. I expect you hear that often."

"No, of course not," he urbanely replied.

"How polite you are, but never fear—I am content to be added to your list of conquests. The gossip sheets are right; you are irresistible. And now, since the die is cast," she quickly added, as though any deliberation might cause her to falter in her course, "if you'd be so kind as to unbutton me, I won't have to worry about wrinkling my gown." Pulling off her kid gloves, she swung around so her back was to him.

Her swift volte-face from apprehension to this unvarnished candor was unexpected, but never one to reflect overlong when offered sex, Ormond quickly set about doing her bidding.

"You're sure the door is locked?" She could have been speaking to her greengrocer, so prosaic her tone.

"Yes." His fingers flew over the buttons.

"And you promise we'll have no interruptions." She carefully set her gloves on the chair arm.

He laughed, charmed by her engaging frankness. "At the moment, darling, I would quite willingly offer you anything at all."

She flashed him a smile over her shoulder. "I dare say if I were the mercenary type, this would be my opportunity to strike an excellent bargain."

"No doubt about it," he said with a grin, slipping her dress from her shoulders, speaking from experience.

"Although I suppose that window of opportunity is fast closing," she teased, pushing the gown down her hips, and stepping out of it. Feeling suddenly as though she were on French leave from the dull monotony of her life, she turned back to him with the sweetest of smiles.

"I assure you, I will not be ungrateful at any stage," he murmured, winking at her as he stripped off his coat.

As she carefully spread her gown over the back of a chair, he kicked off his shoes and dropped his coat on the floor.

"Now *you're* going to be wrinkled."

"Don't worry about it." He unfastened his waistcoat.

"But I do."

It was her schoolmistress tone—so sensitive to her precarious feelings he readily complied, picking up his coat and placing it on a nearby table. "Better?" he queried, sliding off his waistcoat. "Would you like someone to press our clothes later?" he teased.

"Very funny, I'm sure. While you may not be concerned about—"

Tossing his waistcoat at the table, he picked her up, curtailing any further comments she might be tempted to make by moving forward with all speed. "We'll fix whatever you need fixing afterward," he generously offered, carrying her to a large leather sofa set in the center of the room, sitting down with her on his lap. "If I proceed too fast or too slow, speak up. I am not averse to instructions," he murmured, conscious he had a virgin on his hands.

The prospect gave him pause.

He'd never been with a virgin.

Tonight would be a first for each of them.

"I confess you've been rather constantly on my mind," Claire whispered, intoxicated by his touch, his nearness, his compelling size and beauty.

Ormond touched her cheek lightly. "I have been thoroughly obsessed with you since you first burst into my house. You were a ferocious little tiger—bewitching and bedeviling me. Leading me into temptation."

"And me," she whispered. "Because of you, I am undone."

More aroused by her delicate vulnerability than the most adroit courtesan practicing her craft, he found himself inclined to mount her on the spot. Drawing in a breath, he cautioned himself to restraint. "We are both undone—and I for one am unaccustomed to the feeling."

"You don't mean to—that is . . . you aren't changing your mind?" she said with unseemly panic.

"No, no, indeed not."

"Oh, good. Should I take this off then?" She plucked at her shift. "I don't mean to rush you, but I worry our absence might be remarked upon."

Could he ask for more? "Rush me all you want," he murmured, reaching for the buttons on her shift, gratified that her timidity no longer deterred her.

She didn't wear a corset, although her gown was boned to define the narrow waistline that was fashionable once again. He was thankful for one less garment to remove.

"May I unbutton your shirt?"

The hesitancy in her voice struck some primal nerve, reminding him afresh that there was a world outside the brittle façade of the *ton*. A place where women weren't all experienced at pleasing a man, where innocence wasn't unknown. "Please do," he said, gently, feeling as though he was about to enter uncharted territory.

As she freed the diamond studs on his shirt front, he slipped her shift from her shoulders, taking note of the unadorned cambric fabric much the worse for wear. He would take pleasure in giving her a new wardrobe. She dressed austerely—like a governess—part of her resolve not to be beholden to her aunt, no doubt.

She needn't worry about being beholden to him.

He was generous with his lovers.

And breasts like hers should be covered with the finest silk.

Slipping his palms under her opulent breasts, he gently weighed them in his hands. "You hide these." He smiled. "Now that you're mine, I'm grateful."

"I'm not yours." But her voice was hushed, her fingers arrested on his shirt front.

"Really." He tightened his fingers slightly, leaving an indentation on her soft plump breasts. "I thought we had a bargain."

She shut her eyes against the fevered ecstasy streaking downward from his hands to the throbbing ache between her legs.

"Tell me," he whispered, taking her nipples between his thumb and forefinger, squeezing gently. "Tell me you're mine."

She shuddered as a jolt of desire rippled through her vagina. "Yes, yes."

"Yes, what?" For a man who had always avoided female entanglements, that he required her submission should have been a warning or disquieting at least.

"Yes, yes," she breathed, as he gently massaged her nipples, as her body opened in lustful welcome, as long-suppressed desires overwhelmed all else. "I'm yours. I'm yours . . ."

"Good." A brusque, blunt avowal.

"Would you . . . I mean—could you possibly—"her gaze was fevered, impatient, her breathing unsteady.

"Fuck you?"

She looked away, her bottom lip caught in her teeth.

For a virgin, she was ravenously eager. Although how would he know what a virgin was like? "I'm sorry, that was rude," he whispered, thinking her the picture of unspoiled womanhood, all pink, soft innocence in half undress.

"I shouldn't have asked," she said, turning back, embarrassed, yet impatient, unsure of the degree of wantonness allowed.

"Of course you should have," he murmured. "Ask me anything." And bending down, he kissed her trembling mouth.

She clutched at him and whimpered, offered herself up with a desperate abandon no man with a heartbeat could have refused. Quickly easing her down on the couch, he whispered, "I'll be right with you," and stood to strip off his remaining clothes.

This time, he dropped them on the floor without regard for Miss Russell's sensibilities.

She didn't notice, but he didn't think she would, lying as she was with her eyes closed, shuddering and trembling. Suddenly, her body went rigid, and clenching her fists, she shut her eyes so tightly her eyelids turned white.

An image that gave him serious pause.

It wasn't as though he had a dearth of women wanting to fuck him.

Did he really want this patently reluctant woman?

"I'm not sure I'm looking for a sacrificial virgin," he murmured, although even as he spoke, he was chiding himself for being so magnanimous with his personal pleasure at stake.

"Wrong," she whispered. "Please don't make me wait."

There. That certainly was unequivocal permission.

Not giving himself any more time to question his philanthropic impulses, he quickly lowered himself over her body, smoothly positioned himself between her legs and guided his throbbing cock to her sex. Reminding himself to enter her slowly—losing one's virginity was said to be painful—he carefully eased the crest of his erection into her cleft.

She was succulent and slick, her tissue liquified by lust, but he moved forward delicately, penetrating the merest distance before politely pausing.

To his surprise, she lifted her hips, enticing him deeper.

Grateful for her overture, having never dealt with a woman who had been rigid with fear, he thrust forward marginally and meeting no resistance, drove in deeper yet.

And deeper.

And deeper still.

As he buried his cock up to the hilt in her hot, molten cunt, he suddenly understood that he had misread the implication of her utterance—*wrong*.

Miss Russell was no sacrificial virgin; she was no virgin at all.

Beneath her schoolmistress persona and virtuous pose was a woman of lush voluptuousness and seeming sexual appetites.

He felt enormous relief, profound gratitude, and a seriously explosive ardor. There was no need to tread lightly, as it were. The lady was no novice; in fact from her impassioned response, from her soft sighs and eager moans, her clutching hands on his shoulders and back, her lush, tight, avaricious cunt, he rather thought he'd chanced upon the more sexually liberated of the Russell sisters.

With professionalism and artistry, he set about exploring the silken heat of her willing cunt, moving from side to side, in and out, more fully appreciating her ready response for having thought it absent. As she enthusiastically matched his rhythm, offering variations of her own with a spirited zeal, clinging to him as though he were her sexual salvation, he experienced a new level of erotic sensation.

Overwrought and overstimulated after being celibate so long, Claire drifted in some mindless glow of rapture and ecstasy, a flushing, tingling, all-pervasive mist of ravishment and delight. She felt each spiking impact as he thrust forward, each tactile caress and oscillation, each slow stroke and flutter of withdrawal, and consumed by a red-hot hysteria, she came so quickly the first time, Ormond had to swiftly improvise.

A man of less virtuosity might have failed her.

Fortunately, years of practice came to the fore and swiftly shifting direction, he drove back in, plumbing her depths. Cramming her full, he held himself hard against her womb as she climaxed in a panting, blissful, suffocated scream.

He marveled at her control. Even in extremis, she'd curbed her orgasmic cry. But then Miss Russell was not an impulsive woman. Or under most circumstances she was not, he thought with a smile.

Always a courteous lover, he waited for her fevered sensibilities to cool before slowly resuming his rhythm.

"I am smitten and enraptured," she breathed, her eyes heavy with pleasure. "Although, never fear, I know my place."

"Preferably under me," Ormond murmured, thinking her tactful in the extreme. Women were always quick to stake claim, as though having sex somehow allowed them to intrude into his life. This little schoolmistress wouldn't be demanding it seemed. The perfect woman, he fondly reflected.

"I couldn't agree more." She smiled sweetly and wrapped her legs around his waist.

She recovered quickly, matching his rhythm once again as though she'd not just climaxed. "We need more time," he murmured, thinking a week or so would suit him with a woman of such carnal proclivities.

"I'd like that."

Suddenly they both heard the orchestra for the first time since they'd entered the library as though aware once again of reality. Or perhaps the musicians had been on break and they hadn't noticed.

Regardless, they became conscious of time.

"Once more before we go?" he said with a smile.

"Please, may I?"

His cock increased enormously at the guileless naivete of her response. He almost decided to disregard the possibility of exposure to have his fill of her tonight. Although, that thought died after the briefest of seconds. He was not so rash.

Also, he wanted more than the furtive interval allowed them here.

And while he didn't know exactly why he wanted it, he knew he did.

"You feel glorious around my cock," he whispered, forcing himself deep inside her.

"I adore—him—and you," she whispered back, gasping as he bottomed out, stretching her taut, pulsing tissue.

"Have your fill," he breathed, selfishly hoping it didn't take her too long to come this time, settling into a slow, artful rhythm he'd perfected over the years. It was about feeling, not speed, positioning, not indiscriminating oscillation. It was about watching and listening—about paying attention.

In short order, Claire died away in blissful release once again, uttering his given name in a breathless litany of thanksgiving and joy.

Ormond climaxed a few moments later, although he was less vocal. But he went off the deep end with equal frenzy or in his case with unusual violence to sensibilities he didn't realize he possessed.

Perhaps he had become too jaded.

Sex of late had not been particularly soul-stirring. Which made his reaction to Miss Russell even more surprising. But rather than overintellectualize his feelings, he decided instead to pursue further sensations with Miss Russell and once his breathing returned to normal, he said, "I'll make it better next time. We won't be so rushed."

"You were excellent."

He smiled, feeling as though he'd been graded. "Thank you. I enjoyed your company as well."

She looked up and smiled back. "And thank you too for being—so dependable."

"Selfish motive impels me."

"Nevertheless, your selfishness also benefits me."

He didn't respond other than lift his chin toward the sound of music. "We should rejoin the festivities."

She suddenly felt as though he were aloof, detached. It's over. He's had his fill and he's bored, she thought, feeling a vast unhappiness. He hadn't meant what he'd said when he mentioned not being so rushed next time. It was politesse only, a kind way of taking his leave.

"Just a minute. I'll wipe you off," he said in that same neutral tone as he rose from the sofa. Pulling an embroidered runner from a nearby table, he sat beside her and wiped his semen from her stomach. Shoving the stained cloth under the sofa, he said with a small sigh, "I hate to do this. I'd rather stay. But people might notice."

It was astonishing how a few simple phrases could return joy to her life. "I understand. One must be sensible."

As if on cue, a knock sounded at the door.

Claire instantly went pale. "We are found out," she whispered.

"I expect it's Catherine." If anyone was serious about getting in, they would have put more strength behind their knock. "Let me see." Reaching for his trousers, he stepped into them and strode toward the door. "May I help you?" he asked, in the event it wasn't his cousin.

"Mrs. Bellingham is asking for Miss Russell."

It *was* Catherine. "We'll be there directly." Without waiting for a reply, he returned to the sofa where Claire had already pulled on her shift and was sliding on her slippers.

She should have new slippers he thought, taking in the state of the worn leather. "It *was* Catherine," he said instead. "Your aunt is looking for you. Don't look so worried. We can exit the library and enter the ballroom through the refreshment room next door." He nodded toward a narrow doorway set between bookshelves. "It's a private entrance."

"How convenient."

"You needn't speak in that tone. I have never made use of either the library or that door. Harry uses it. It allows him access to a concealed stairway leading to his bedchamber upstairs."

"Oh," Claire said in a very small voice.

He grinned. "I accept your apology. Now, do you need help?"

"With the buttons, if you please." She pulled her gown from the back of the chair and lifted it over her head.

The buttons were quickly fastened and while Claire stood before a gilt-framed mirror pinning up her hair, Ormond dressed with the speed he'd acquired escaping women's boudoirs.

"How do I look?" Claire nervously asked a few moments later, adjusting her décolletage before smoothing her palms over her skirt.

Ormond glanced up from buttoning his waistcoat. "You look perfect. Not a wrinkle in sight."

"Now, you're sure we can return undetected?"

"Positive." He slipped on his coat, snapped his cuffs into place, and surveyed the immediate area for any missed items.

"How can you be so cool and collected?"

"Darling, no one will dare say a word to me."

"They will still stare at me."

"You worry too much. This is my cousin's house. I visit often. Even if someone were to see us come out, I can show anyone I please the library. You're a schoolmistress, after all. Why wouldn't you enjoy seeing Harry's collections?"

"Sometime I actually might."

"Anytime, darling. Just say the word."

He made her feel as though he could deal with any conceivable situation, that she was safe, that the world was his to command. "Thank you for your calm. I confess, this entire evening is intimidating."

"You seemed relaxed a few moments ago."

She blushed. "Thank you for that as well."

"*Au contraire.* Thank *you* for making this miserable rout altogether enchanting. Ready?" He nodded toward the small doorway.

She nodded.

"Give me a second to unlock the main door." He quickly did so, picking up his gloves in the bargain and slipping them on. Returning to her side, he said, "Plan on seeing me tomorrow after school."

Yes, yes, yes, she wanted to say. Faced with reality, she said instead, "I usually go home soon after the school day is over."

His brows rose.

"I'll make some excuse."

"Thank you," he crisply said. Then he leaned over and kissed her as though in apology. "Forgive me. I'm impatient."

"I could say I'm grading papers—but I can't stay long. My normal routine is quite fixed."

"I'll have to make it worth our while, then," he said with a grin. "Although, I warn you, I won't be content with these rushed occasions for long. So begin making plans," he said with the casual prerogative of his titled position. "Now here we go, darling," he went on as though the matter was settled. He opened the door. "We're on stage.

Chapter Nine

They stepped into the refreshment room where tables were arranged with ices and cold cuts, with champagne and sweets, with two chefs presiding over gargantuan sides of beef and warm collations for those guests wanting heartier fare.

Threading their way through an array of small tables set up for dining, Ormond made for the entrance to the ballroom while Claire nervously scanned the crowds that now filled both rooms.

"Courage, darling," Ormond murmured as they approached the ballroom, patting her hand that rested on his arm. "We are about to run the gauntlet unscathed."

Conscious of numerous examining looks directed at them, Claire said, "I see that. Apparently you *are* intimidating."

He glanced at her sideways. "You didn't believe me?"

"I certainly do now."

He smiled. "Then consider how well protected you are with me."

"*Protected?*" It was not a public role she cared to assume. Not if she wished to continue attracting students to her school.

"How safe you are," he quickly amended as they entered

the ballroom. "Don't look now, but Harriet is being dragged off the dance floor by your aunt." He smiled. "I wonder if she's being snatched from the arms of a man considered less suitable than—"

"You?" Claire chuckled. "You understand, don't you, that you are the central figure in Auntie's marriage strategy."

"In that case, I shall speak to Seego posthaste."

"That seems rather callous."

"And your aunt isn't?"

Claire grimaced. "This is all becoming much too complicated."

"Leave it to me, dear."

At the moment, she was inclined to do just that. She didn't relish a fight with her aunt whose plan to add Ormond to their family would not be easily derailed. "Just remember, Harriet must be happy," she said, taking the path of least resistance in what was turning out to be a French bedroom farce.

"Yes, dear."

She shot him a look. "I mean it." His tone had been much too suave.

"She will be happy, I assure you." This time he took care to speak with unequivocal sincerity.

She frowned faintly. "How can you be sure?"

He dipped his head and smiled. "You don't know how focused I can be."

"Perhaps I do," she said, offering him a fleeting grin.

His dark brows flickered in teasing reply. "As you say. So consider me Harriet's new, highly motivated matchmaker. I guarantee everyone will be happy soon. You, me, your aunt, and the potential bride. Ah, do I detect more than a modicum of trouble?" he murmured as they approached Claire's glowering relatives.

Harriet was sitting rigidly in her chair, visibly displeased: her bottom lip stuck out in a pout; her jaw set; her sky blue eyes rife with storm clouds. Mrs. Bellingham was in equal high dudgeon, having been forced to abandon her winning hand of cards twice because of Harriet's behavior, the last time on spying her niece in the arms of an old roue who everyone knew didn't have two guineas to his name.

She'd said as much to Harriet in no uncertain terms as she'd hauled her away, ordering her for the second time that evening to save her flirtations for Ormond. He had more money than God and was so near to proposing, they could practically send out wedding invitations.

She had ordered Claire to be fetched after she'd warned off Lord Halston. And now she had had to do it again with Buccleuch. When one was winning a goodly sum at whist, one did not have time constantly to monitor a niece. A point Mrs. Bellingham made clear the moment Ormond and Claire reached her.

"You cannot go off and leave your sister unattended," she snapped. "I was required to forsake Lady Strand in order to rescue Harriet from men old enough to be her grandfather. In future, Claire, kindly do your duty."

"I fear I was to blame, Mrs. Bellingham," Ormond smoothly interposed, his voice mild even as he took issue with Mrs. Bellingham's rudeness to Claire. "I wished to show Miss Russell Harville's extraordinary collection of maps."

"Forgive me, Lord Ormond," Mrs. Bellingham replied, conscious of the viscount's cool gaze. "I fear I'm overwrought. A young girl's reputation is so important and Lords Halston and Buccleuch, well—" she shook her head in disgust. "Everyone knows what they are like. In any event," she went on, patting Harriet's hand as it lay on the chair arm beside her, "dear Harriet understands the importance of an unsullied reputation now—don't you, dear." She glanced at her niece.

"I was just dancing," Harriet muttered, mutinously.

"Just dancing!" Mrs. Bellingham rolled her eyes. "Claire, you must stay by your sister's side—do you understand?

And I do hope, Lord Ormond, that you will overlook Harriet's youthful naivete. The firm hand of a husband will do her a world of good, I don't doubt," she said without subtlety. Rising from her chair, she shook out the Brussels lace ruffles on her skirt before turning an irritable gaze on Claire. "Sit," she ordered, pointing to the chair she'd just vacated. "And do not desert your sister again. I shall be at cards for some time."

"Very well," Claire replied, in measured tones, restraining her temper with effort.

"We shall both see that Harriet is enjoying herself, Mrs. Bellingham," Ormond offered, when he would have preferred giving Mrs. Bellingham the set-down she so richly deserved. Claire merited better treatment than that of a servant. That he felt impelled to care for her was an unprecedented response.

As Mrs. Bellingham rushed off to her card game, Harriet said, "Sorry, Cleery, to take you away from your maps. There was no crisis as you well know. Both Halston and Buccleuch are old and harmless."

Ormond repressed a smile, Harriet's assessment eminently accurate.

"And I don't suppose you want to dance with me anyway," Harriet went on, looking at Ormond. "Everyone but Auntie knows you detest dancing."

"I fear you're right. But perhaps we could find you a suitable partner. There's no reason you should not dance when any number of men would appreciate your company."

Harriet's expression brightened. "My thoughts exactly. I love to dance above all things. Cleery, you keep Ormond company while I have fun."

She spoke with such artlessness, Claire shot a look at Ormond to see if he took affront.

He gave her a quick wink before turning back to Harriet.

"Allow me to find you a partner. Then your sister and I shall discuss maps while you dance."

"You are ever so pleasant, Ormond. Did I not say as much, Cleery?"

"Yes, indeed you did. We both appreciate your gallantry, my lord," Claire said, smiling up at him.

With heated memory still vivid in his mind, it took a certain degree of self-control to keep from spiriting away the lovely Claire on the spot, gossip be damned. Not that he could actually be so selfish and ruin her reputation. "Allow me to cultivate your good wishes further, ladies," he said with gentlemanly good grace and, lifting his hand casually, he waved Seego forward. The young marquis had been hovering nearby—as had several other of Harriet's suitors. "Miss Harriet desires to dance," the viscount noted. "Kindly do us all a favor and oblige her."

The young marquis glanced at Harriet, then at Ormond, his hesitation obvious. One did not cross the viscount with impunity.

"Come, Seego, she likes you. I can tell," Ormond kindly remarked.

"I would be honored, sir, Miss Harriet," Lord Seego murmured, glancing from one to the other, tardily remembering his manners and turning to Claire with a bow and a polite, "Miss Russell."

"Perfect—everyone is of one mind, then," Ormond said with avuncular good cheer. "Off you go, children. Enjoy yourselves."

As the young couple walked away, Ormond handed Claire into a chair. "Did I do well?" he asked, sitting down beside her.

"You are feared and obeyed, my lord," she quipped. There had been no mistaking Seego's deference.

Sliding down on his spine, he smiled at her from under half-lowered lashes. "Now if only you would follow suit."

"I suspect you would soon grow bored if I did."

"No doubt."

"Like now."

"Sorry." He sat up straight in his chair and surveyed the crowded room with a jaundiced gaze. "Don't you find these affairs tedious?"

"You are excused, Ormond. Take yourself off to the card room with my blessings."

"There's no serious play here."

"Then leave." She smiled. "You need not be chivalrous on my account."

His expression brightened. "My God, you're a sensible woman."

"Yes, I am."

He grinned. "You're vastly charming in other ways as well."

"Go. I'm not a flirt like Harriet. I don't require flattery."

"You're sure?" He was being given his freedom, the offer so novel in a postcoital situation, he required further confirmation.

"I'm absolutely sure."

That one could love a woman like this came suddenly unbidden to his mind, the rash thought as quickly dismissed. Rising to his feet, he took advantage of the opportunity given him. "I shall leave my carriage for you and your family."

"Thank you."

"And I shall see you tomorrow afternoon."

He spoke in such an ordinary way, he might have been talking about the weather. "Yes," she said, curtailing her reply since she was not so blasé. The thought of seeing him tomorrow stirred up a feverish tumult throughout her body.

He bowed. "Au revoir, Miss Russell."

She only nodded, his parting smile sending a jolt of desire racing through her senses. Clenching her hands in her lap to keep them from shaking, she watched him walk away, the crowd parting for him as though he were royalty. And like royalty, he accepted their deference as his due.

Had she known, his indifference to the crowd was the result of a preoccupation with other matters. He needed to talk to Seego. The boy normally appeared at Brooks later in the evening, as did most noblemen if not busy with their inamoratas. Still too wet behind the ears to have a mistress, Seego was a regular at Brooks in the wee hours. Although, from what Ormond heard, the boy was more apt to fall in love than set up a mistress.

The result, no doubt, of Seego's parents' unconventional love match.

Unlike *his* parents' marriage of convenience that had turned out to be exceedingly inconvenient for everyone concerned.

If all went as planned Ormond was hoping to persuade young Seego to pay court to Harriet. The boy was the most acceptable of her suitors—and he knew of what he spoke.

Not that he expected the marquis would be difficult to persuade.

Although it never hurt to offer an inducement of one kind or another. He was thinking young Alastair might like one of his racehorses as a preengagement gift. Or some bauble for Harriet that would encourage her interest. As for baubles, he needed some of his own. Claire had little jewelry from what he could tell and what she had was inexpensive. A situation he was eminently qualified to correct; he had an open account at Grey's. And then there was the matter of her wardrobe. If she didn't wish to be beholden to her aunt, perhaps he could persuade her to let him refurbish it.

By the time he exited Catherine's, Ormond was in extremely high spirits. Striding down the pavement, he began organizing his morning schedule. He would require the presence of his secretary, solicitor, Catherine's decorator, his housekeeper, and a modiste in order to orchestrate the events required to bring his plans to fruition.

He actually considered going to bed before morning for the first time in years. He didn't wish to be fatigued for his rendezvous with Claire.

He might even shock his chef and have him prepare breakfast for him.

Chapter Ten

Mrs. Bellingham fretted on the drive home, grumbling about noblemen's manners with regard to Ormond leaving early. Although, she grudgingly had to admit that, overall, the evening had been a great success.

"And Ormond will call tomorrow, mark my words," Mrs. Bellingham said with the absolutism that was a hallmark of her personality. "Lady Strand said his fortune is so vast, it defies speculation. His mother was an heiress and he was her sole heir. That is the way of the aristocracy, you know," she went on in her same doctrinaire way. "Wealthy families make certain their money doesn't go astray."

"I understand Ormond's father has considerable wealth as well," Claire pointed out.

"That may be, but nothing like his mother's. Lady Strand said when Annabella FitzClarence made her bow, she was not only the most beautiful girl of the season, but the richest."

"It doesn't matter whether the man you love is the richest or not," Harriet said with a little sniff. "Everyone knows, money doesn't buy happiness."

Harriet's comments were so shockingly contradictory to her previous views on the merits of love and money, that

Claire and her aunt stared at her as if she'd sprouted another head.

"I'm sure you're right," Claire said, finding her tongue first. "There are any number of wealthy marriages that are unhappy I'm sure." Ormond's family came to mind.

"Ormond's mother ran away from her husband. And they were both rich. So you see," Harriet declared as if she'd not only read Claire's mind, but delivered irrefutable evidence that marriage without love was oppressive.

"My dear late husband always used to say that you can love a rich man as well as a poor one. He was quite right," Mrs. Bellingham declared, undeterred by Harriet's assertion. "And since Ormond is interested in you, my dear, the question of wealth is irrelevant, is it not?"

"I may find that I prefer another man," Harriet muttered.

"Nonsense, you don't know any other men," Mrs. Bellingham returned, sharply.

Claire gave her sister a warning look.

Harriet wrinkled her nose, but judiciously curtailed the remark she was about to make. Then with a toss of her blond curls, she slumped down in her seat and sulked for the remainder of the drive.

Once they were home, Claire intended to speak with Harriet in private. But her aunt insisted Claire help her undress and ready herself for bed, rather than wake her maid. By the time Claire had completed her duties, Harriet was fast asleep.

She'd have to speak with her sister tomorrow. There was something about Harriet's objection to their aunt's sponsorship of Ormond that was perplexing. Prior to the rout tonight, Harriet had been unshakable in her resolve to become the next Viscountess Ormond.

And now?

What had changed?

* * *

As for the man intent on making that change, he was in the reading room at Brooks putting pen to paper, enumerating various tasks to be accomplished tomorrow—a bottle of cognac at hand to facilitate his labors.

He'd left orders to be notified when Seego arrived and he'd look up from time to time, as though impatient. When, at last, he saw the boy walk in, he immediately waved him over.

"I have been looking for you, sir," the marquis said with a mannered bow on reaching Ormond's side. "You were not at your usual locales."

"We have been at cross-purposes, then. I have been here waiting for you. Sit down," Ormond offered, indicating a chair opposite him with a nod of his head, pleased that they were apparently of one mind. "Cognac or something else?"

"Actually, I don't drink much," Alastair said, sitting down across from Ormond.

"Coffee? Tea?" He should have known. The youngster was so fresh-faced and unspoiled. "A lemon punch perhaps?"

"No, nothing. The thing is," Seego said, nervously running his fingers through his pale hair, "I've come to ask something of you."

Ormond pushed away his pen and paper and sat back in his chair. "Ask away."

"I understand you have been calling on Miss Harriet Russell."

"I have."

"Then my question is—" the marquis swallowed hard— "exactly what might your intentions be with regard to Miss Harriet? If I might be so bold as to ask," he quickly added, turning bright red under Ormond's studied gaze.

"Rest easy, my boy. I have no intentions at all. As you know, I am accused of inconstancy in my relationships with women and that is an accurate assessment."

"Sir, how dare you use Miss Harriet in such a cavalier fashion!"

The youth had gone from unease to indignation with such lightning speed, that Ormond spoke in his most soothing voice—wishing above all things to avoid being called out by the silly boy. "You misunderstand. My friendship with Miss Harriet was of the most casual nature. What I meant to say is that I have no claim on her affections."

An instant smile reversed Seego's former frenzy. "That's exactly what *she* said," the boy blurted out. "Her damned crotchety old aunt's interference notwithstanding. Not that Miss Harriet spoke in such strong terms, sir," he quickly amended.

"Naturally. I understand. Do I detect a certain interest on your part in Miss Harriet?" Ormond inquired, blandly.

"Indeed. I love her with all my heart," Seego pronounced with sweeping conviction.

"On such short acquaintance? What might your parents say of such a sudden attachment?" Ormond debated bringing up the subject, but if obstacles were at hand, it was better to be forewarned.

"Oh, they, too, will love her instantly," the marquis enthused. "She is the most *beautiful* woman in all the world," he added with an adoring sigh. "And ever so sweet as well. We talked and talked tonight and discovered that in all things we agree."

"Admirable," Ormond murmured. He didn't realize Harriet could actually carry on a conversation, having experienced only her tiresome banter. But then, his interest in Harriet had not been of a conversational nature. "I wish you all the best, Seego. If I may be of any assistance in your courtship, you need but ask."

"Actually," the marquis replied, leaning forward as he spoke, "if you don't mind, I do have a question or two. In contrast to you, I am relatively inexperienced with women so I was wondering . . ."

For a lengthy interval, the men discussed a number of issues having to do with women—what they liked and didn't like, how best to please them, what gifts were most likely to gain their affection, in particular what a young woman like Harriet would find attractive in a man.

When at last, the marquis rose from his chair, he said with a great deal of feeling, "You have been exceedingly gracious, Ormond. Thank you for your advice."

"I'm pleased to be of help, my boy. How old are you?" Ormond asked on the spur of the moment.

"Twenty-two, sir."

Good God, he felt old. Had he ever been as innocent as Seego? The sad truth was—no. And now, at thirty, it seemed as if he'd already lived a dozen lifetimes. "I wish you happiness," Ormond said, envying the boy his artless joy in living.

"And you too, sir," Seego replied as he took his leave.

Not likely that, Ormond thought, as he watched the boy jauntily stride away. Too much had transpired in his life for him to ever recapture that same youthful zest for living. Or perhaps it was only that he was too familiar with melancholy to begin again, his demons too numerous to defeat.

Oppressive memory was a constant in his life. It kept him awake at night, gave rise to his excesses, made him the man he was.

Reaching for the cognac bottle, he poured his glass full once again in an effort to numb his afflictions. As he lifted the glass to his mouth, he suddenly saw Claire's smiling face in his mind's eye and he couldn't help but smile back. With what ease her image cured his black mood. How simple it was to forget when she reminded him of more pleasant pastimes. How intriguing it was to think about seeing her tomorrow.

Setting the glass down untouched, he picked up his pen and returned to his list-making.

Before long he was humming under his breath.

Chapter Eleven

Neither Harriet nor Mrs. Bellingham had wakened by the time Claire departed for work in the morning. Her conversation with her sister would have to wait. Not that it was particularly pressing. There would be time enough later.

And in all honesty, her thoughts were rather obsessively devoted to Ormond anyway. Fond memories of last night occupied her thoughts, causing her to smile a good deal as she readied herself for work. There was no doubt why the viscount was in such demand with the ladies. He offered incredible pleasure with the most delightfully casual charm. As though carnal passions were perfectly natural—*perfect* the operative word.

In anticipation of perhaps feeling *perfect* again today, Claire took particular care with her toilette. Passing over her serviceable gray and navy bombazine gowns that had become her uniforms of late, she chose a tartan silk skirt that had once been her mother's and a muslin blouse she'd not worn in years. She was being silly, perhaps, she thought a few moments later, tying the bow on the collar of her pelisse. There was a very good chance Ormond wouldn't remember their plans to meet after school.

She wasn't entirely sure a man of his immoderate nature would recall what he had promised the evening past. Or care if he did. He'd left any number of women in the lurch, she suspected.

It might be wise to steel herself against disappointment. A not uncommon state since the death of her parents, she reflected, setting her bonnet on her head and tucking her curls under the brim. Silver linings seemed to have disappeared from her world.

As though in contradiction to her sober mood, the morning was sunny and bright as she walked the several blocks to work. The air was fresh and clear, not always the case in the city. Even the birds in the trees seemed intent on joyfully greeting the new day.

How could one not succumb to the glorious morning?

Having moved through the streets with all the other workers on their way to their labors, Claire reached the building housing her schoolroom and found even more bustle and activity. Dray wagons lined the entire block, waiting their turn to unload, while scores of workmen were busy carrying items of every ilk into the building.

The extent of the operation piqued her curiosity. Obviously a new tenant was moving in, but to what purpose in this neighborhood of small businesses and shopkeepers? Walking up to a man stationed at the front door with a notebook and pencil who was busy ticking off each piece of furniture or parcel as it passed by, Claire politely inquired, "Pray tell, what is going on, sir?"

"You ken ask, ma'am, but I know naught. Me orders is to see that everything delivered is carried upstairs. To the third floor, ma'am, if'n that's any help. A new tenant, I surmise, but no one tol' me and that's a fact."

Thanking him, Claire moved up the stairs with the laborers, going her separate way on the second floor to unlock her schoolroom. She set about preparing her lessons for the coming day and when her students arrived at eleven, all was in readiness.

But the girls were not prepared to learn anything with the exciting display of objects being trundled into the building and up the stairs. Despite her remonstrances, her students kept running to the windows to monitor the activity, delivering pronouncements on each and every item as if they were participants at a Christies auction.

"This is no concern of ours. Come back to your seats, ladies," Claire would decree to what turned out to be an increasingly unresponsive group. Very soon, she felt as if she were trying to herd cats.

Claire attempted to discuss their reading assignment with her students, but they would have no part of Julius Caesar. While it was never easy teaching young ladies of wealth and privilege who rightly assumed they could do as they pleased, it turned out to be impossible on this particular day.

Finally, Claire gave up, dismissed class and allowed the girls to ogle and stare without restraint. Speculative gossip was rife, the vast amount of furniture and the equally large number of workmen on site suggesting countless possibilities for fertile young minds. In this case, young minds much too familiar with gossip as the sine qua non of life.

The scraping of furniture being put into place was audible overhead, as was the sound of someone playing the pianoforte that had been hoisted in through a window. Perhaps a music conservatory was about to open for business or an opera star was moving in the girls surmised. But when a host of female servants began carrying up a large amount of women's clothing, the girl's began to giggle and speculate along entirely unsuitable lines.

"That will be quite enough," Claire sternly declared, nipping such inappropriate comments in the bud. "I'm sure there's some perfectly reasonable explanation." She wished to point out that the furniture passing by was too splendid for a brothel, but she didn't care to explain why she would possess such knowledge. Nor did she have personal experience in that area. But she strongly suspected that however elegant a brothel might be, it would hardly be furnished with pieces of such superior quality.

When at last the girls' carriages began arriving, she felt profound relief.

Or was it giddy anticipation?

It was relief, she silently insisted as the last silly schoolgirl exited her schoolroom.

At times like this, she found the need to earn her own living more onerous than usual. An entire day of foolish chatter had been wearing on her nerves, while her students' indifference to learning was exhausting both in terms of her patience and goodwill.

Or was it the sight of all the luxurious items passing by for hours that had brought her spirits low? She rarely allowed herself to dwell on the straitened circumstances of her life, but occasionally—as today—she was vividly reminded of the vast discrepancy between her past and present life.

Between her current poverty and her previous comfort.

Between what might have been and what had transpired.

At least Harriet would have a comfortable life, she thought, pleased her sister would not be obliged to earn her way in the world. It was only a matter of Harriet choosing which of her suitors best suited *her*. Tonight, perhaps, Harriet would tell her who that person might be.

Feeling slightly mollified by her sister's prospects, Claire began tidying up the schoolroom—stacking the books on the shelves, putting the chairs back in order, picking up the papers scattered about.

Waiting.

Above all—waiting.

She glanced at the clock once, twice, three times before she stopped herself and cautioned prudence. There was a very good possibility that Ormond had forgotten their appointment.

In all likelihood he had already dismissed her from his mind.

She would wait until half past four and not a minute longer.

Seated at her desk, trying to concentrate on tomorrow's assigned reading, she found herself stalled on a single sentence. Julius Caesar's history of his campaigns in Gaul had always been one of her favorite books and she'd hoped to instill that same love in her students. But, today, like her students who rarely read their assignments, she found herself equally distracted.

She heard the sounds from the street outside as though magnified; the tick of the clock was thunderous in her ears. Even birdsong insinuated itself into her schoolroom despite the windows being closed. Until suddenly, she realized the entire building was silent. Walking to the windows, she looked down on a street empty of dray wagons and workmen. Returning to her desk, she sat down and attempted to read.

But her senses were on high alert.

High, *quivering* alert.

She jumped at the approaching sound of boot heels in the corridor outside.

As the measured footsteps halted at her door, she went rigid.

When the door opened and Ormond walked in, it seemed as if her heart had stopped.

"I'm early," he said, his smile inexpressibly beautiful as he moved toward her. "I hope you don't mind. I confess to a novel impatience."

She thought he'd said four, but perhaps he hadn't. "No, I don't mind at all," she said, smiling back, pleased by his confession.

He stopped before her desk, darkly handsome and superbly dressed in black trousers, a soft white linen shirt and silk waistcoat, dark cravat and bottle green frock coat. "So then, do we have a few hours in which to amuse ourselves?"

A blush rose on her cheeks.

"You decide on the amusement, of course," he graciously said. "We could have tea and talk if you like."

"I must be home by six. I left a note," she explained, nervously, not at all sure she was dégagé enough to decide on anything having to do with Ormond.

"Excellent." Time enough to explain that he too had sent a note to Mrs. Bellingham's. In his experience, a lady was rather more amenable to a change in her schedule once she'd climaxed a few times. "Shall we?" Moving around her desk, he held out his hand.

He was so splendidly attired, she felt like a church mouse even though she'd worn her pretty tartan skirt. But as she rose from her chair and took his hand, his smile mitigated her unease, lush pleasure warmed her senses, and their mismatched lives suddenly were inconsequential.

As they exited the schoolroom, the viscount casually inquired, "Did you have a pleasant day?"

She glanced up, misgiving in her eyes. Was she no more than another in a long line of women who entertained him?

"Forgive me. I was trying to put you at your ease and obviously failed."

"I've never done this before."

"I understand." He smiled ruefully. "One falls into certain patterns. My apologies again. In truth, I have never done precisely this before either."

"My life is not like yours. I cannot afford a mistake."

His life had been a continuous series of mistakes—most commonly waking up where he didn't wish to be. "Then we shall see that no mistakes befall you," he said with a gravity she'd not heard before. Ormond was not a somber man.

"I am somewhat relieved," she said, mollified by his understanding.

"And I in turn will endeavor to see that you are further relieved of your concerns." He lifted his chin as they reached the stairway to the third floor. "I believe tea is awaiting us upstairs."

Her gaze narrowed. "You were behind all this activity today? The wagons and workmen and throngs of domestics?"

"I thought this locale would be more convenient for you."

"Or you."

He shrugged. "Very well. For us both. Come, don't scowl at me before you see what I have wrought."

A certain apprehension filled her mind as they ascended the stairs and walked down the hall. As Ormond stopped before a door directly above that of her schoolroom, he offered her a boyish smile. "I hope you like it." Opening the door, he ushered her in.

"I am awestruck," she whispered, standing just inside the threshold, gazing at a drawing room of impeccable style and beauty. The furniture was scaled to a woman's size, many of the pieces spectacular in their ornament—although of a sumptuous rather than a grandiose nature. She had an uneasy feeling several of the items might have once resided at Versailles.

"Catherine's decorator will be pleased you like it. Come, sit down." He waved her forward. "Our tea is ready."

If she had momentarily overlooked the discrepancies in their lives downstairs, those distinctions returned with a vengeance. She wore a hand-me-down skirt and shabby slippers while Ormond casually assembled a luxurious apartment on a whim. "I don't know . . . this is all rather overwhelming."

"The tea is quite ordinary, I assure you." Taking her hand, he drew her toward a small table set for tea. "Sit, relax, tell me of your day." He pulled out a chair for her. "I watched all your twittering students depart. How do you deal with their babbling silliness and stay sane?"

It was as if he not only understood how unmanageable her students were but fully sympathized with her plight. "I *could* use a few moments to relax," she murmured, experiencing a sudden wave of self-pity that effectively forestalled issues of unequal status. "Trying to impart anything remotely educational to my young ladies is indeed an exercise in futility."

"I expect I was the despair of my tutors as well," he said, sitting down in a large chair apparently selected for him. After pouring her tea, he looked up to see if she wanted cream.

"Yes, please." How pleasant it was to be waited on. Especially on a day like today when her schoolroom had been continuously at sixes and sevens.

Pouring cream into her tea, Ormond added sugar without asking, as though he knew women always took sugar. "When I grew into maturity, I read a great deal, but as a youth—" he shrugged—"I was completely indifferent." He lifted a liquor decanter. "Do you mind?"

"No, of course not."

"Would you like some? It's a very fine cognac."

"Perhaps just a little." She smiled. "I had a very trying day."

Pouring them both a glass, he set hers down beside her teacup, leaned back in his chair, and resting his goblet on his chair arm, said very softly, "You wouldn't have to work."

"Pray, say no more." She held his gaze. "What I have agreed to is temporary."

He gazed at her over the rim of his glass. "I dislike seeing you in such reduced straits. It seems unfair."

"In case you haven't noticed, the world is unfair." She smiled tightly. "Although, perhaps in your privileged case, that fact has escaped you."

"*Au contraire,* darling. I have drunk away a good many years because the world has been unfair." As though in illustration, he lifted his glass to his mouth and drained it.

"Then we need not argue."

His smile was instant and above all amiable. "I agree." Refilling his glass, he indicated her teacup with a dip of his head. "Drink your tea, try some of those pink frosted cakes, and we will speak of more pleasant things. Did your sister enjoy herself at Catherine's rout?"

"She did. And I think she's found a new beau. I hope you're not offended."

He laughed. "Not likely."

"I'm not certain who it is. My aunt, of course, wouldn't hear of anyone but you as a suitor, so Harriet dropped the subject." Taking a sip of tea, she found the tension in her shoulders and neck noticeably lessen.

"I'd say it's Seego."

"He did look rather enamored last night. Might he be serious? I shouldn't like Harriet hurt. By the way, these cakes are delicious."

She had a delicate pink frosting residue on her lips that was tantalizing as hell. "I'll let my chef know you liked them," he said, restraining an impulse to kiss away the frosting. "As for Seego, he is *most* serious. He sought me out last night at Brooks. His concern was that I had some prior arrangement with your sister. I assured him that he was quite wrong in that regard." Ormond grinned. "I have found the elder Miss Russell more to my liking."

"If only you didn't find *every* woman to your liking," Claire sardonically noted, "your flattery would be more gratifying." She smiled. "But thank you nonetheless. I find you extremely likable as well. As for Harriet's prospects— Seego is a highly eligible party. We must hope that he is the man who Harriet found favor with last night." She made a small moue. "Not that Harriet couldn't be influenced by a future dukedom."

"You may rest easy. It rather sounded as though the two youngsters were mutually enamored. I believe Seego used

the romantic designation of—" the viscount's brows rose—
"*soul mates.*"

"No!"

"Oh yes." Ormond's eyes gleamed with amusement.
"The young boy was quite positive."

Claire sank back in her chair and softly exhaled. "I must
say, I am greatly comforted by your news. If indeed, the two
young people have an attachment, I am pleased. He is so
much more suited to Harriet than—" she abruptly paused,
realizing she'd almost been uncivil.

"You needn't be tactful. I quite agree. And at the risk of
offending you, I'm not likely to change."

"I understand." Ormond's statement had been blunt in
the extreme. "But then I am not an innocent like Harriet,"
she calmly noted.

"So I discovered." He peered at her with a searching gaze.
A small silence ensued.

"I needn't explain to you," she finally said.

"I just hope it wasn't Charlie Rutledge."

"No! My God, what do you take me for?" she cried, her
face turning cherry red.

He was surprised at the degree of relief he felt. He was
more surprised that he wished to be apprised of the men in
her life when his philosophy had always been a cavalier live
and let live. "If not Charlie—who then?"

Picking up her cognac, she held his gaze. "You don't see
me asking that of you, do you?"

He shrugged. "I wouldn't care if you did. Tell me."

"No." She took a sip of cognac. "It has nothing to do
with you."

"Obviously," he drawled.

"Should I leave?" Purse-lipped, she set her glass down.

"No." He could have said we have an agreement and
I've already settled things with Seego, but he didn't. Then
perhaps because he had been selfish so long, and he was

here today for his own pleasure, he sensibly shifted his stance. "It was wrong of me to press you," he said with a conciliatory smile. "I apologize. Am I forgiven?"

How many times had he spoken thusly with that disarming smile and imploring gaze? How many times had women like her, forgiven him? "There's no need to apologize," she said, perhaps as selfish as he. "I just prefer not laying bare my life. I hope you understand."

"Of course."

"Thank you," she murmured.

Neither could be faulted for their deft volte-face.

"Are you finished?" He nodded at her tea.

There was an authority in his voice that demanded compliance or was it the seductive allure in his dark gaze that made her answer, "Yes."

He stood instantly, as though he'd been impatiently biding his time, and walking around the table, he pulled out her chair.

She took note of the small tick over his cheekbone as he helped her rise and the hard, firm line of his jaw. "You're still angry."

"Not in the least," he smoothly replied.

"Nevertheless, I'm uncomfortable with you looking at me like that." Was this situation turning out to be more perilous than she'd foreseen?

Quickly composing his features, he offered her his most charming smile. "Better? And if you need further verification of my good intentions," he said, waving her toward an inner doorway, "very shortly, I pledge to make you *exceedingly* comfortable."

He was being gracious. She would be foolish to relinquish the pleasure he offered since she'd thought of little else the hours past. "I gather you don't like to be thwarted," she murmured, moving past him.

"Generally not." He smiled, in better humor now that he

was moments away from doing what he'd come here to do. "But I'll make an exception for you."

"As I will for you. We agree then."

She was a stubborn little minx, but then she was a hot-blooded little vixen as well and the latter easily trumped the former. "I gathered as much last night—that we agreed . . . in any number of ways." In the grip of a novel possessive impulse, he heard himself say, "In fact, I may decide to lock the doors and keep you here for myself alone."

She smiled at his absurdity. "Even you would not be so rash as to draw my aunt's wrath upon your head."

His surprise overcome, he answered with the lordly presumption of his class. "I would without question."

"Then I must find some other deterrent to your threat," she offered, sportively, thinking surely he couldn't mean it.

"Good luck."

His curtness stopped her in her tracks. She shot him a look. "Have I mentioned how much I detest authoritarian men?"

"Do you know many?"

She understood from his tone that she'd broached a contentious subject, but she refused to be intimidated. "No, I do not. Satisfied?"

He wasn't, nor would he be until he knew the extent of her amorous amusements. But he replied, "Yes," because he neither cared to acknowledge why her amusements mattered to him nor—more important—did he wish to delay further having sex with her. Taking her by the arm, he propelled her forward into the bedchamber. "Perhaps we can concentrate on satisfying ourselves in other ways, right now. We can discuss your dislike of authoritarian men," he added, crisply, kicking the door shut behind him, "after you and I both come."

"I may not want to come." Her tone was as crisp as his, her spine rigid with affront.

"Let me be the judge of that," he murmured, astonished

even as he spoke that his words had such an arbitrary ring. "As for what you may or may not want, need I remind you that you have already agreed to please me."

A taut hush fell.

"Would you like to withdraw from our agreement?" he inquired, breaking the silence. "If so, I could tell Seego that my partiality for Harriet terminated once I had my way with her."

"Knave!" Claire spat, her eyes hot with temper. "You would ruin my sister so callously?"

"That and more I assure you," he calmly replied. "You know as well as I that I am a rogue. So what will it be? You decide." That he was experiencing the pangs of jealousy, he would not affirm. That he wanted what he wanted was more easily acknowledged.

"I seem to have no choice," she said with icy disdain.

"Virtue is it's own reward, is it not?" he noted with excessive sarcasm. "I'm sure your sister will profit by your sacrifice." He nodded curtly toward the bed. "Take off your clothes and wait for me there."

She should summarily refuse. And had Ormond not threatened cruelly to wreak havoc on Harriet's prospects, she might have, she thought, moving toward the bed. Although the harsh truth was that it was not Harriet's happiness alone that caused her to stay—but hers as well . . . however fleeting it may be.

At the sound of a key turning in a lock, she spun around.

"I'm not in the mood for interruptions," he said, tossing the key on a table.

"You're expecting company?" A hot, resentful query.

He didn't answer for a moment, then he softly sighed. "I'm in a brutish mood. I apologize. Perhaps I'm too sober. I'm rarely sober at times like this."

"My misfortune."

He stared at her with a jaundiced gaze. "You're a prickly little bitch. I should throw you out."

"If the door wasn't locked, you wouldn't have to throw me out—I'd leave!"

Taking a step toward the table on which the key rested, he picked it up and without explanation, slipped it in his coat pocket. "I need a drink. Sit down," he said, nodding at two chairs flanking the fireplace. "Relax. I'm not going to attack you."

Much preferring his last suggestion to his previous order, Claire quickly complied, sitting down on an elegant green brocade fauteuil. She watched him pour himself a drink from a decanter set on a small pietra dura table. She watched him drink it down, refill his glass and do the same once again with a kind of strange acceptance, as though his moodiness matched hers.

She knew very well that she shouldn't give into her passions, that making a pact with the devil for Harriet's sake was unwise. Any sensible woman knew that when all was said and done, Ormond would bring her misery. But as Dryden said, "We loathe our manna, and we long for quails." And dear God, the wild, heady passion Ormond offered—however transient—was the undoing of every woman who came within his scope.

She was no different.

And perhaps therein lay the rub.

In fact, just the sight of him approaching her now, sent a shiver of anticipation through her senses. She sat up straighter as though uncompromising deportment might fortify her against temptation.

Taking the seat opposite her, Ormond set the decanter he'd carried over on the floor beside his chair, and slid into a lounging pose. "Why don't you just tell me about the men in your life," he murmured, appraising her with a moody gaze, "and I'll become normal again."

"Normal? I doubt it." She'd heard all the stories. Who hadn't?

"Normal for me, then. It's not as if I'd ever slept with a virgin or even wanted to—until you." He smiled tightly. "Although, my luck held out. You weren't."

"How fortunate for you," she replied, huffily, loathe to be categorized with the throngs of women in his past.

He ignored her huffiness; a few stiff drinks perhaps blurred the nuances. "I am mystified by my need to know," he said, his singular focus undiminished. "But there it is. So humor me. Consider how gratified Harriet will be if Seego comes up to scratch."

"Are we haggling here?"

"Call it what you like." Picking up the decanter, he pulled out the stopper, lifted the cut-glass bottle to his mouth, and poured a large draught of liquor down his throat.

Concerned that he might become even more unmanageable should he empty the decanter, Claire weighed her options—along with her rather potent amorous desires—and came to a decision. A foregone conclusion any objective observer might have pointed out. "If I tell you what you want to know, will this conversation be at an end?"

"Yes." Immediately setting down the decanter, Ormond gave her his full attention, an anomaly in situations like this. His normal pattern with women was to be attentive only to the degree tact and courtesy was required to attain his sexual goal.

Claire didn't speak for some moments, finding it difficult to exhume feelings long buried. She had never before divulged her relationship with John Darton. But with Harriet's future at stake, she steeled herself against painful memory. "I was once secretly engaged," she began, speaking briskly as though once having made her decision, she wished the conversation quickly done. "My fiancé did not have the means to offer marriage at the time and we were content to wait. A wealthy uncle of John's consented to purchase a captain's commission for him and John sailed for India with the Light Dragoons. He hoped to prosper there and we would marry on his return. He died of fever in Calcutta instead," she finished, holding Ormond's gaze for a moment as though to say—Are you satisfied now?

"Your family didn't know?"

She shook her head. "There was no point. Our marriage was impossible at the time. My father was retired on a colonel's half pay; there was no money for my dowry and John's family was in equal straits."

"And there has been no one else?"

"Dear God, have you no heart?" she peevishly exclaimed. "I offer up bitter memories and that is all you can say?"

He shrugged. "I have no heart of late, it seems. My apologies."

"Why does it matter anyway—whom I have known?" she asked with asperity. "You and I are nothing more than partners in lust."

"It matters. Don't ask me why. I couldn't tell you."

His stark statement had none of his mannered nonchalance. It was blunt and grudging. "There has been no one else," she shot back, speaking with equal bad grace.

He had been reaching for the decanter and stopped. His dark gaze held hers for a telling moment before he pulled himself upright in his chair. "I'm sorry for your loss." His voice was gentle, the moodiness gone from his eyes. "Having traveled that mournful path myself, I offer you my condolences."

Disarmed by both his humanity and his recognition of their shared afflictions, she answered him more kindly. "Time heals I've found—at least to a degree."

He smiled ruefully. "So I've been told."

Experiencing a compassion she had not felt short moments ago, she wondered whether his sulky discontent only added to his allure, whether other women, too, felt the need to console him. "Let us not be blue-deviled today," she murmured, "when we have reason instead to relish life."

He smiled faintly. "Indeed—we should gather our rosebuds while we may." He ran a hand through his ruffled curls. "I am grateful for your company, even though," he added with a small grin, "I have done my best to disabuse you of that notion. Forgive my boorishness."

She waved away his apology. "We both have our demons." Perhaps now was the time to stop grieving over what might have been, she precipitously thought, her sudden postulate making her feel as though a huge burden had been lifted from her shoulders. "Let us dwell on pleasure today."

"Agreed. May I offer you a drink? I find the world is always more tolerable after a drink or two." She might need time to deal with her confession, he reflected, while he, in turn, needed time to digest her disclosure. Another layer had been added to the intriguing Miss Russell.

She smiled. "Perhaps one."

Ormond lit the fire that had been laid and with their drinks in hand, they watched the dancing flames in an atmosphere of harmony and calm.

"You color my world most pleasantly," Ormond said after a time, smiling across the small distance separating them.

"You offer me a degree of pleasure I find impossible to resist."

"How is it," he murmured contemplatively, "that we found each other in this vast and brittle world?"

"I believe you were trying to seduce my sister."

He laughed. "Fortune, it seems, was on my side. I found you instead."

"Or fortune was on mine," she flirtatiously replied.

"Speaking of mutual desires," he softly drawled, "might I interest you in trying that rather flamboyant bed over there? I'm told it was once in the Trianon."

"I rather thought it had the look of France. And yes, you could indeed interest me in your bed."

"Your bed."

"We'll see."

He didn't argue, but set down his glass instead, stood and offered her his hand.

He undressed her slowly, slowly, as though wanting to remember this occasion, as though these moments were auspicious.

She did the same for him with a kind of fastidiousness he found charming—with a kind of breathless awe that was particularly provocative. Regardless of her engagement, she was still relatively uninitiated in the world of amour and for a man who had always preferred experienced women, he found her naivete wildly arousing.

When she at last stripped away his linen small clothes, her eyes opened wide at the sight of his upthrust erection. "My goodness," she breathed, glancing up at him. "Did all of that fit inside me?"

He smiled faintly. "To perfection as I recall."

"May I touch it?"

She was already about to do so, her fingertips poised a hairsbreadth away. Not that he would have said no in any case. "By all means. We would like that immensely."

She glanced up at the amusement in his tone. "I suppose every woman asks you the same."

"Some do," he lied. His partners were not so virtuous as to be astonished at a cock in full rut. That they touched him, he couldn't deny, but for reasons other than Miss Russell's guileless sense of discovery.

She tentatively brushed the engorged head of his penis with her fingertips and watched amazed as his erection increased, stretching upward, each pulse beat fueling its expansion visible in the corded veins of his penis.

He took a small sustaining breath, his self-discipline legendary in the boudoir. Along with his stamina.

"I know now why you are so much in demand," she whispered, slipping her cupped fingers under his heavy testicles. "Everything about you is—gigantic."

"As long as you are tempted, I am content."

She looked up again, his testis warm on her palm. "Everything about you tempts me. As you no doubt can tell." No woman could resist him, she thought, gazing up his hard, muscled form, wondering if his amorous activities alone accounted for his strength and virility.

"And you me as you can see," he murmured. "If you do this—" he took her hand in his, curled her fingers around his rigid length and eased her hand downward—"see what it does?"

"Oh," she squeaked. She shot him a quick smile. "How exciting. May I do it again?"

She was an eager student and he in turn was highly appreciative, but there came a time when a man could only take so much. "Why don't we see if you're as ready as I? Come," he said, easing away her grip on his penis. "Lay with me." Without waiting for an answer—he had no intention of climaxing before exploring her luscious cunt—he drew her to the bed. Throwing back the coverlet, he lifted her onto the bed and joined her.

"Unlike last night, we don't have to rush," he whispered, lying beside her, leaning over and kissing her mouth and eyes, her fine straight nose and rosy cheeks, taking a novel pleasure in his artless spinster. He'd always avoided women of moral piety and yet his libertine soul liked the taste and feel of the naive Miss Russell.

Warmed by his kisses, by his hard, taut body lightly touching hers, by the delicious possibility of lying with him in this gorgeous bed—like ordinary people might in love and friendship—provoked such wistful longing Claire had to remind herself that Ormond had gone to these great lengths today for sex not love. That he had manipulated scores of people for sexual gratification alone.

Not that her lustful desires were not in full, impetuous accord, nor was she averse to orgasmic pleasure. In fact, the intensity of her passion was perhaps more fierce than his. A master of this game, he was a man jaded by sensation— when she was not. While in terms of sexual restraint, she was clearly inept. He wasn't even breathing hard, while her breathing was becoming erratic. "Are we going to kiss much longer?" she blurted out, hot desire spreading like wildfire through her blood.

"We don't have to." He pulled away enough to smile at her. "Would you rather move on?" he murmured, soft suggestion in his tone.

"That would be ever so nice. I don't mean to—er—pressure you . . . but—that is, I am absolutely famished for you."

He softly chuckled, his gaze amused. "So I needn't be polite?"

"Please no. I suppose I seem incredibly unsophisticated, but you felt so wondrous last night and made me feel more glorious than I've ever felt before and the thing is—" she shuddered as a jolt of desire rippled through her vagina—"I don't think—I—can wait," she gasped.

"Nor should you have to," he gently said, smoothly rolling over her, more than willing to cut to the chase. How unlike she was from the usual ladies in his life who preferred flirtatious coyness to honesty.

"I've been wanting to feel you inside me all day and all of last night and ever since I first saw you at the masquerade," she whispered, spreading her legs wide and clutching his arms as though he were her salvation.

He smiled faintly at her candor. She was soft and warm and sweetly willing, too—everything he wanted in a woman.

She was also, he decided, as he obliged her and slid inside her honeyed warmth, a woman who incited a degree of pleasure quite separate from the sensational, slippery friction of cock against cunt, of raw nerve endings vibrating in fervent unison. She was a woman he felt an unquenchable need to fuck—when in the past sexual glut and swift boredom were always the norm.

In some undefined and inexplicable way, she inspired previously untouched emotions. Or was it simply her highstrung, frantic neediness and the wild oscillation of her hips beneath him? "You're going to have to stop me when you've had enough," he murmured, feeling a kind of reckless indiscretion foreign to his persona. "I'm not in a particularly reasonable mood."

"I know what you mean; don't worry," she breathed, raising her hips high into his downstroke, shutting her eyes at the fierce, flame-hot spasm shocking her senses.

He wasn't worried for himself—his penis was calloused from hard use. Her vaginal tissue on the other hand might be more fragile. But a second later, he dismissed speculation in favor of raw sensation for she'd wrapped her legs around his hips and was drawing him in with some amazing, vaginal muscles.

In very short order she was frenzied and frantic like he remembered. She was dripping wet and flame-hot simultaneously—a combination that offered him the sleekest plunging descent and the most silken of withdrawals. She was deliciously tight—really, a-gift-from-heaven tight—their ensuing flesh to flesh contact jolting through his brain with such wild delirium he literally gasped on each downstroke.

She didn't notice, her own feverish respiration claiming her attention, the deafening echo of her heartbeat in her ears further adding to the tumult in her brain. A manic litany—in and out, up and down, harder, deeper, more, more, more—overwhelmed her senses and insensible to all but her selfish, volatile, all-consuming passions, she exchanged reality for a phantasm of overwrought bliss.

Until she abruptly cried out—a small suppressed sound.

"No one can hear," he breathed, recognizing her preorgasmic utterance no matter how restrained. Immediately sliding his hands under her hips for better traction, he said, "Scream all you want." Then, lifting her into his downstroke, he crammed her full, wanting her to feel every possible taut, shimmering sensation, each deep, forceful downthrust—a not entirely unselfish intent. "Am I in far enough?" he murmured, swinging his lower body forward, driving in deeper. "Can you feel me?"

She promptly screamed—and screamed some more, her high-pitched cries echoing her orgasmic tremors, initiating the Trianon bed in its new London location, bringing a satisfied smile to the viscount's face—in due time leaving the lady prostrate and in thrall to Lord Ormond's sexual expertise and phallic perfection.

After a time, she opened her eyes very, very slowly and gazed up at the viscount with a balmy, sybaritic smile. "If you could do that again I would be ever so grateful," she breathed. "Or do I have to wait?"

He smiled at her beguiling query. "You don't have to wait." His capacity for dalliance was honed to perfection; self-control was rarely an issue. "You tell me when you're ready."

"Would you think me too greedy if I said, now?"

"Not in the least." Holding her impaled on his cock, he rolled over on his back.

"How strong you are—*everywhere*," she whispered, easing upright astride his hips, shifting her bottom in a little voluptuous wiggle that made his erection surge higher.

"How pink and plump these are." His fingers slid over the high rounded curves of her breasts, down the deep Vee of her cleavage. "And your nipples—" he squeezed the taut buds lightly. "I'd say they're ready for sucking."

She softly moaned, awash in blissful sensation—his erection buried deep inside her, his fingers delicately stroking her nipples, her vagina bathed in a fresh rush of slick arousal.

"I can't reach you," he whispered, tugging on her breasts to bring her closer, half rising himself in a ripple of stomach muscles until her nipples were within reach.

As his mouth closed over one taut peak, she gasped at the flame-hot rapture streaking downward to meet the seething pool of frenzied nerve endings in her vagina and clit. Obsessed, ravenous with desire, she ground her bottom against his crotch in a frantic gyration of her hips, greedy to feel every virile flesh and blood contour of his huge, rigid erection.

He watched her through his lashes with an inexplicable pride, as though he was the means and instrument of her delight, as though he had discovered this unravished beauty who wished now to be ravished by him.

How was it that her innocence stirred him so profoundly? Why did her dewy-eyed sensuality disarm him so completely? More shocking—why did Miss Russell and the thought of permanence suddenly leap into his mind? Never one to allow an injudicious thought to endure, however, he quickly turned his attention to more pleasant conceits.

She came twice more before he decided to take his turn. It was either that or come in her—a consideration so beyond the pale he instantly dismissed it. Although she said afterward, "It wouldn't really matter if you came in me once would it?"

He stopped breathing for a second, her words the equivalent of a trap about to spring. "It probably wouldn't be a good idea," he replied in an excessively courteous tone. "For your sake, of course," he added, quickly easing away from her. "Let me get a towel."

What had come over her to even voice such a question? Claire restively thought, alarmed at how close she had come to disaster. It just went to show, how passion could overrun reason. How the gratifying pleasures of sex with a gorgeous, superbly endowed man like Ormond could affect one's better judgment. How infatuation could turn too quickly to fondness or more when in Ormond's embrace. It would not happen again, she silently affirmed.

When the viscount returned to the bed, he brought two items of jewelry as a means of diverting the lady from further thoughts of his coming in her. Jewelry, he'd found, generally soothed over any and all awkwardnesses.

As he placed the two items in her palm, Claire murmured, "You shouldn't."

"Take them, they're small." Sitting next to her, he added, "Try them on."

They weren't small, of course, the necklace and earrings of large pearls an extravagant gift. "Are you sure?"

"I couldn't be more sure."

Indecisive, she looked at the pearls, then at him.

"Come, darling." He held out his hand. "Pearls are a innocuous gift. Let me help you put them on."

She had never had so grand a gift. "I don't know . . ."

"Leave them here to wear if you'd rather," he offered, suspecting her reservations had to do with propriety. "No one need know."

Her misgivings eased by Ormond's discrete alternative, she gave into wistful desires. "I thank you then, most kindly. They're very beautiful."

Her delight pleased him more than he would have thought possible. After helping her put on the baroque pearl earrings and necklace, he watched her flushed smile as she gazed at herself in the hand mirror he'd brought over. How fortunate he was to have invited Miss Harriet to his masquerade, he reflected. If not for that calculated lure, he would not have met this little auburn-haired tigress with her lush body and greedy cunt. And he would not now be trying to decide how long he wished to keep her.

Which thought prompted him to rise from the bed, walk to the armoire and take out one of the new gowns he'd commissioned. He, better than most, understood how a new wardrobe could influence a lady's decisions.

"No, no, I can't possible take it!" Claire exclaimed as he carried over a sumptuous yellow tulle gown embellished with diamont sparkles that shimmered like sunbeams.

"I thought this color would go well with your coloring," he said, ignoring her protest and dropping the frothy cloud of tulle on her lap.

"Oh, my goodness," she whispered.

"You could wear it to Catherine's next entertainment," he said, knowing that Madame Leonie's creation had accomplished its mission.

"How did you know the size?" Claire inquired a few minutes later, twirling before the cheval glass, wide-eyed in awe.

"I guessed." He was standing nearby after having hooked up the back of the gown, admiring her mounded breasts spilling over the low décolletage.

She stopped twirling. "Because you do this often."

"Never," he lied. "Don't look at me like that. I was fortunate. I guessed right, that's all. Now come here so I can take it off. I'm going through withdrawal already."

"What if I say no?" Whether she was half teasing or dead serious, she wasn't quite sure. Her obsession with him was unnerving; everything about this luxurious apartment he'd forged in a day for his sexual pleasure was disquieting.

"I'd say don't waste your time." He crooked his finger. "Come here."

"I don't have to do everything you say." Could she resist or couldn't she? Did she even want to when he offered a degree of pleasure beyond her wildest imagination?

"Of course you don't," he murmured, advancing toward her.

"James, don't you dare!" She ran behind a chair, her feelings volatile and capricious. Her body on the other hand, already liquid with longing.

He stopped in his tracks, gauging her response, assured after surveying her flushed cheeks and heaving breasts that what she said and what she meant were at odds. "That chair's not going to save you, darling."

"If you must know, I'm fighting my obsession with you. There, I have confessed. You may add me to your adoring ranks of females."

"We are both obsessed, darling. I'm obsessed with everything about you," he said, surprising himself with his honesty. "And to be perfectly frank—" he paused for a moment, debating whether to voice his surprising thought—"I've never felt this way before." There, that was truthful and ambiguous at the same time; he relaxed.

"Oh, that is excellent above all things," Claire said with relief, "because I'm not sure I can actually do without—well—" she paused, her gaze on his upthrust erection lying flat against his stomach.

"This?" Back on familiar ground, he smiled. "It's all yours," he added, running his fingertips up his turgid cock.

She took a small breath as his erection soared higher. "I don't know what I'm going to do," she whispered, passion and reason at loggerheads. ·

"I do," he said, very, very softly, moving forward, lifting the chair aside. "You and I are going to make love," he murmured, taking her in his arms. "And afterward I'm going to hold you close and tell you how wonderful you make me feel."

"This is very strange," she breathed, gazing up at him.

"It's good strange, darling."

She nodded and smiled and gave herself up to the pleasure he so casually dispensed.

Her gown was removed with dispatch. Ormond's facility for undressing women was second to none. In the course of the afternoon, they made love in infinite, passionate variety. She had a tyro's enthusiasm that could awaken the most jaded appetites, while his expertise was put to the test by the lady's insatiable desires.

At last, recognizing she was becoming weak from pleasure—her last climax ending in a voiceless sigh—he paused for an intermission.

Not that he wasn't still in hot pursuit.

But for the interim, he was hugely and unconditionally gratified.

Chapter Twelve

Turning his head on the pillow a few moments later, Ormond gazed at Claire lying beside him. "You make me happy," he murmured, a contentment he'd thought forever lost, recaptured. A slow smile lifted the corners of his mouth. "What conjuring spell have you placed on me?"

Sluggishly coming to her senses, the deep timbre of his voice triggering every pleasure receptor in her body, Claire whispered, eyes shut, "*Au contraire*—I am bewitched by *you.*"

"Then stay. Don't go. Stay now and tomorrow and—"

His allusion to time burst her blissful bubble. Springing up into a sitting position, Claire shot a look at the clock. "It's almost six!" she cried, scrambling to reach the edge of the bed.

Quickly grabbing her, Ormond pulled her back down. "Hush—everything's fine. Your family is having dinner at Catherine's tonight. I forgot to tell you."

"While I forget the world is yours to command," she muttered pettishly, reminded once again with what ease he used his authority.

"I only did it because of you. I am caught in your enchanted web." Rolling on his side, he dipped his head and kissed her gently. "And strangely, I don't care."

She wrinkled her nose at him. "You will soon enough." Her life did not allow for prolonged flights of fancy.

Propped on one elbow, he gazed at her with amusement. "Since my feelings are my own, my mulish little darling, allow me to disagree. I don't suppose you could close down your school for a time?" he went on with the restraint of a Quaker. "I'd like you to see my country home."

"You know I can't." Wincing at the sourness in her words, she added, "I have enjoyed myself immensely, you know that. It's just that I have obligations."

"Think about it at least."

"Very well." She chose not to argue with Ormond; as she'd discovered recently, he had a most delicious way of challenging defiance. Not that she was complaining with her body still basking in the glow of numerous orgasms.

"Perfect." He kissed her again, for a more lengthy interval this time.

For such a gratifying and beguiling interval that Claire began to waver on the prospect of a country holiday.

"I could find you a substitute teacher," he whispered against her mouth, as if he knew, as if her heated little whimpers were a precursor to a more tractable position on the subject of visits to country homes. "You could tell your aunt you've been hired for—"

A knock echoed from the drawing room.

Claire instantly recoiled, her wide-eyed gaze filled with alarm. "You have servants here?" Servants' gossip being what it was, her name would be linked with Ormond's by morning.

"I thought you might need something," he said with his usual disregard for the world at large and servants in particular.

"Good God, James!" she whispered, nervously pulling the covers up. "What could I possibly want from your servants?"

"I don't know—food or a bath," Ormond calmly replied,

rolling out of bed. "Or someone to help you with your hair," he nonchalantly added, striding naked toward the drawing room. "There's nothing to worry about."

Or so it was in *his* world, she noted, horror-stricken that he hadn't shut the bedroom door behind him.

As Claire lay in the princely bed fearful that she would be discovered, that her career would be in ruins—that *she* would be ruined, the viscount opened the outside door without regard for his nudity. Taking the envelope offered him by his valet, he nodded in dismissal, shut the door, unfolded the sheet of paper and read the note as he walked back to the bedroom. He was smiling broadly as he handed the paper to Claire. "This was delivered to your schoolroom. Forgive me for opening it, but I saw it was from your aunt and I thought she might alarm you in some way. Actually she has excellent news—her scurrilous comments aside."

Sitting up, Claire rapidly scanned the sheet with her aunt's large, bold handwriting. A moment later, she looked up, wide-eyed at Ormond. "Eloped?" she whispered.

"The deed is done and unless I miss my guess, Seego's parents had a hand in it. Seego would need a special license, not easily acquired, and of course a charitable curate—his father's no doubt. We must send congratulations to the happy couple."

"My aunt is raging."

"Very foolishly I would say. Harriet has made an excellent match."

"Are you sure?"

He smiled at her from the foot of the bed, thinking she belonged in his bed wherever it may be. "Why don't I find out the particulars," he pleasantly offered. "Will that assuage your doubts?"

"Certainly it would help. You don't seem surprised." Her gaze narrowed. "Did you have a hand in this?"

"I *may* have mentioned the word elopement, last night at Brooks," he said with a flash of a grin. "And don't say you're angry with me when your sister has come off so well."

"I'm not angry, if it's true," she answered, a modicum of doubt evident in her voice.

"Never fear. It's true. If you had talked to Seego last night, you would know. But let me send off a messenger." Turning away, he walked into the drawing room and shouted for his valet.

A small, wiry, middle-aged man appeared on the run, the men exchanged a few brief words, and Ormond returned to the bedroom.

"Who was that?" Claire whispered, huddled under the covers, knowing she could never be so dégagé as to stand naked before a servant.

"Lamont, my valet. He's completely trustworthy. Have no fear. I took the liberty of sending your aunt a message as well. I told her you were invited to dinner at Lord and Lady Arnoudt's. She is not to worry."

"It seems your world is always smooth water and fair winds." She tried to keep the petulance out of her voice and failed.

"Allow me the pleasure of easing your life as well," he gently said, understanding the reasons for her peevishness.

"I should become spoiled. Then how would I feel when you grew bored with me?"

"I won't." He was unprepared for the intense pleasure he felt at his reply. "Furthermore," he added, her mention of boredom bringing to mind the reason he'd needed his solicitor that morning, "I have a guarantee that you will enjoy independence in all respects—although hopefully not from me."

Moving to a small bonheur du jour in the corner of the bedroom, he extracted a sheaf of papers from the drawer. "You are the new owner of this building," he said, returning to the bed and handing her the papers. "So you will no longer be beholden to your aunt, your school will not be in jeopardy, and I will continue as your tenant as long as you want *me*." Dropping onto the bed, he stretched out in a lazy sprawl. "You see," he said very softly, "you hold my happiness in your hands."

Pushing up on the pillows, she quickly scanned the document. "I can't take so generous a gift," she said, dropping the papers on Ormond's chest.

"Too late." He tossed the pages on the carpet. "Your name's on the deed. Sell it if you don't want it."

"It's too much," she explained. "It's outrageously extravagant."

How to reply without belittling her worth when the purchase price was a mere bagatelle for him. "You deserve much more, darling," he replied. Tracing the curve of her arm with his fingertip, he knew he didn't wish to let her go, not now, not ever. Whether it was primal male prerogative or the more admirable emotion called love he knew not. But he didn't want her to leave him. "What would you say to the proposition that we take a page out of Seego's book and elope?" A gambler by instinct and choice, he went for broke.

It took her a moment to reply. Unlike Ormond, she was no gambler. "You'd be sorry within the week. You would soon find me no different from all your other women. Admit it—you are even now wondering why you said what you said."

"I beg to differ with you. As for me not knowing the difference between one woman and another—" his brows rose—"I am an authority on the subject."

"Kindly don't remind me," she said, half pettishly, half teasing because he was lying beside her in all his godlike splendor with his lazy, sardonic smile directed at her. "I would much prefer you were a virgin."

He laughed. "Surely, you jest. You like to play—admit it."

"Perhaps . . . just a little."

"More than a little." He grinned. "I have had to utilize all my—if I do say so myself—considerable resources to keep you happy."

"And I thank you from the bottom of my heart."

He smiled. "The feeling's mutual, believe me. In fact, I'm feeling all warm and cozy when I'm usually looking for the nearest exit. It must be a sign. So what do you say?" He'd spent his life taking risks. "Come darling, Fortune sides with him who dares. And what do you have to lose? Life with your aunt?"

She sat up as though if she were upright, she would be more rational. "You wish me to elope with you on a dare?"

"You were cautious once—and lost," he gently noted. "Think of that."

She had been; he was right. And the years since then had offered her little. "So I should throw caution to the winds?" she whispered.

He smiled. "The scandal sheets would be pleased if you did."

"Because I have brought the infamous Ormond to heel?"

He grinned. "I couldn't have said it better. We will save the editions for our grandchildren to see."

"Grandchildren?"

"Believe me, I'm as surprised as you. I've never wanted children; I've been scrupulously cautious as you know. And suddenly the notion of your children—our children—" he smiled—"pleases me. Say yes and I will see that we are married."

"Just like that?"

"Say, yes."

"I don't know—"

Reaching up, he stopped her protest with a finger to her mouth. "Yes—say it."

She saw something in his eyes that she'd never seen even

with John whose memory she'd cherished for so long. It was a wild and heady consciousness that life was for living and Ormond was offering himself to her in all his prodigal beauty and entanglements.

If she but had the nerve.

"You are rash," she whispered.

"Yes."

"And headstrong."

He nodded.

"Bold and audacious, too," she murmured, uncertainty in her voice and eyes.

"But I will make you happy." He was not a man who harbored doubts. "Now, say it," he whispered, drawing her into his arms so his scent filled her nostrils, so his breathtaking beauty overwhelmed her—so she could no longer pretend she didn't want what he wanted.

"Yes."

It was the smallest, most trifling of sounds, but he heard it with the clarity of thunderous artillery. "Don't move," he muttered, quickly kissing her before leaping out of bed and bellowing for his valet.

They were married in the drawing room three hours later, the bride attired in a sumptuous gown of gold-embroidered lace, the groom *point-de-vice* in somber black. The minister had been dragooned from the king's own household, the witnesses Ormond's servants, the special license signed by the bishop of London.

It was a quiet affair, but joyous in every respect for the bride and groom knew better than most that happiness was exceedingly rare in the world.

They were grateful beyond measure.

The scandal sheets were even more grateful.

Every detail of Ormond's life was hashed and rehashed in the following fortnight, while his new bride was portrayed as a sorceress of mesmerizing charms to have bewitched the most eligible bachelor in the kingdom.

Not that the Viscount or Viscountess Ormond paid any mind to the tittle and tattle that passed for amusement in the *ton*.

They were at the viscount's country house, busy making babies.

Mischief and the Marquess

Sylvia Day

*To Kate Duffy, who saw that I was lost
and showed me the way.
Thank you, Kate.*

Acknowledgments

Thank you to my critique partner, Annette McCleave (www.AnnetteMcCleave.com), for her help, and to my friend Renee Luke for the much appreciated support.

Chapter One

Northamptonshire, 1817

For most men, spinsters were a breed of female to be avoided at all costs, and under any other circumstances the Marquess of Fontaine would be in hearty agreement with that sentiment. But not in this circumstance. And not in regard to this particular spinster.

"The years have been kind to her," the Dowager Lady Fontaine said, peering out the window beside him. "She is more beautiful than before, despite all that she has suffered."

"It pleases me to hear that," he murmured, his gaze locked on the willowy figure strolling through his rear garden.

He wished he could see her face, but it was shielded from the sun by a wide brim hat and the distance from the second floor window to where she stood made the cataloging of finer details impossible. Lady Sophie Milton-Riley had been barely a woman the last time they met, soft and sweet with a penchant for mischief that had once goaded him to say, *"Why can you never be serious?"* To which she had replied, *"Why can you never relax?"*

She seemed too serious now. She once traversed rooms

with an elegant glide that forced him to stare and covet, but her present stride appeared to be confident, sure, and firmly grounded.

"How long will they be visiting?" he asked.

"Presently, a fortnight. But this is the first occasion Lady Sophie has ventured away from home since the scandal. I cannot be certain they will stay the duration."

Sophie had come with her grandmother, who was in collusion with his mother in this poorly veiled matchmaking scheme. The two women had been the best of friends for as long as he could remember. He was certain that in their minds the joining of their progeny in marriage was absolute perfection. Once, he had thought so, too. Back when he was a young lad hopelessly infatuated with the vivacious Sophie. Her feelings for him had been nowhere near as amorous, however, and when she had come of age, it was Lord Langley who had won her favor and her promise to wed.

"If you had not been so rude as to avoid their arrival," his mother said with undisguised chastisement, "you might have made her feel more welcome."

"You told me of their arrival only moments before the fact. It would have been far more appalling for me to greet them when I was mud-stained."

His mother could say nothing to that without admitting more than she wished to. The truth was, she had feared his refusal and so had hidden her actions. He understood why she had resorted to subterfuge, but the precaution was unnecessary. Sophie was welcome here. He held no ill will toward her and wished her nothing but happiness.

The marquess turned away from the velvet-framed window. "My presence is required in London, so I will be departing tomorrow."

"You will not."

He arched a brow. His blond hair was a maternal trait, as were his blue eyes. His mother's angelic features were hardly touched by time and she remained a lauded beauty, the liberal strands of gray in her tresses adding maturity to her youthful appearance. Today she had dressed in soft pink, and she looked not much older than his score and ten years.

"Why must you be so difficult?" she lamented, shaking her head.

"You had a spouse and two sons. How can you not understand the duress placed upon a male alone in the company of three females?"

The dowager mirrored his raised brow. "My dear boy, if you think I am unaware of how often you pay for the dubious privilege of spending time alone with multiple females, you are sadly mistaken."

"Lord save me," he said dryly, moving to sit in the nearby gilded chair with its elaborately carved arms and curved legs. "The horror of discussing my carnal proclivities with you is upsetting my sensibilities. The urge to flee is now overwhelming."

She snorted. "Nonsense."

"I am departing tomorrow, Mother." He lounged, stretching his long legs out and crossing one ankle over the other. "This evening will be sufficient enough time to renew our acquaintance."

"And if is not sufficient," she asked with obvious hopefulness, "will you stay?"

Justin sighed inwardly. "I am not inventing the affairs I am required to attend to. I was not expecting visitors, so I made no accommodations for any."

"But these affairs could be delayed, yes?"

"I refuse to speak any further on the matter," Fontaine muttered, "to avoid saying something I may later regret."

His mother joined him, sitting primly on the edge of the opposite cream and gold settee. Her gown was showcased to advantage in the setting of the family parlor, which had been spared the attentions of a decorator for many years.

The baroque style of the room with its elegant moldings and lavish abundance of gilt soothed him. His lineage was old and a source of great pride. This room reminded him of those who had preceded him and strengthened his desire to do justice to those who would follow.

"I was so hopeful when you were courting Lady Julienne," she said morosely. "A shame she is a bit touched."

"Oh?" Both brows rose. "Desiring a love match is a sign of insanity?"

She lifted her chin. "Wedding for love is all well and good, but the girl hadn't the sense to fall in love with you, instead of that Remington scoundrel. I still cannot collect it. What was she thinking?"

The marquess looked away to hide his smile. "That is your maternal pride talking."

"It's common sense," she retorted, "which she is obviously lacking. It is in a female's base nature to choose the strongest, handsomest, most established male in the herd."

"Ah, my day improves," he drawled. "What a relief it is to learn that I am the most impressive bovine in the marriageable lot." He refrained from pointing out that Sophie hadn't selected him either, choosing to betroth an earl of far lesser circumstance.

"You are incorrigible." His mother shook her head, setting the pale gold and silver curls at her nape to swaying.

"And you wish to marry me off to your dearest friend's granddaughter. What does that say about you?"

"I never said anything about marriage," she argued, but her blush betrayed her.

Justin knew when it was best to let a matter rest, so he said nothing, choosing instead to think about Sophie and the scandal that ruined her.

"You have no cause to be nervous," the Countess of Cardington reassured under her breath. "We are among friends."

Lady Sophie Milton-Riley managed a shaky smile against the lip of her sherry glass. "Nervous, *grand-mère*? Never."

She was very nearly terrified, but refused to say so aloud. Her memories of Lord Fontaine were clouded by years and the distorted memories of a child. What she had were mostly impressions, those of a tall youth whom she'd fancied as a golden prince, albeit a rather stern one.

The countess shook her head and shot her "the eye," the look filled with love that said she did not believe a word she was saying. Sophie leaned over and pressed her lips to a wrinkled cheek. "I intend to enjoy myself. I promise."

"Good. Oh!" The countess straightened and her voice lowered. "Here he comes."

Sophie glanced up as the Marquess of Fontaine entered the lower parlor. Her breath caught, and when his gaze sought her out, she reached quickly for the pianoforte behind her for balance.

Dear God, had he always been so handsome?

He smiled, and she set her glass down before she spilled its contents.

How the devil could she have thought he was a prince? Princes were mortal. Fontaine was a golden *god*, with a body built for carnal sin, wrapped in the chilly infamous English hauteur she had never forgotten. How he used to intimidate her with that steely-eyed stare!

And how very different was her reaction to that same stare now.

Who knew aloofness and aristocratic arrogance could be such a potent lure when mixed with the body and face of Apollo?

There was a very substantial reason why the Marquess of Fontaine was not suitable husband material for her. Sophie was willing, however, to set aside such vital concerns for a moment so that she could admire him properly.

It was one of the few benefits to being a woman with a scandalous reputation. She did not have to lower her eyes and pretend that she wasn't struck nearly witless by his appeal. She could, instead, openly appreciate the male form approaching her with thoroughly masculine feline grace.

Sophie blew out her breath. Her childhood friend had grown into a man well worthy of the many hours Society dedicated to discussing him. He had always been an avid sportsman and his physique proved that he still was. His dark blue velvet jacket required no padding to enhance his broad shoulders, and his breeches were just tight enough to reveal powerful thighs, muscular calves, and . . .

She blinked.

Good heavens! She should not be staring *there*, scandalous past or not.

Jerking her gaze upward, Sophie focused on his lips instead. They were somewhat thin and given his inclination for . . . imperiousness . . . she had remembered them being rather stern. But they were nothing of the sort. Instead they were shamelessly sensual, curved in a way that teased a woman to make him smile. Or whisper shocking things.

Sophie's problem was that she enjoyed shocking things. They were much more fun than nonshocking things, hence the present state of her existence.

The moment he came to a halt before her it became extremely difficult to breathe properly. She bowed her head as she curtsied, hiding her confused frown. After all these years, he still unnerved her.

With a furtive gaze, Sophie watched as the marquess charmed her *grand-mère* into blushing, then he returned his attention to her. She hoped that she managed a semblance of a smile, but with her heart racing, she could not be sure.

"Lady Sophie," Fontaine murmured, lifting her gloved hand to his lips. "A pleasure to see you again."

She took note of his voice, which was deeper now and warm, so at odds with his rather formidable, icy exterior. How like him to be so starch-stiff and formal. And how like her to be so irritated by it. His composure had always goaded her to do rash things to break through it, and tonight was no exception. She set her hands on his chest for balance, lifted to her tiptoes, and pressed a quick kiss to his cheek.

"You look well, my lord," she returned, meeting his shocked gaze directly. Her lips tingled, forcing her to wrinkle her nose. She recalled suffering similar reactions to him when she was younger, which had prompted her to tell him that she was allergic to his arrogance. His reply, if she remembered correctly, had been a snort.

"Shall we?" the dowager marchioness asked, gesturing across the hall to the dining room.

For a moment longer, Fontaine stared at Sophie with a narrowed gaze, then he gave a curt nod and offered his arm to the countess.

The rest of the evening passed in a blur of casual discourse and more serious discussion regarding Lord Hastings and India. The meal was impressive and served over many courses. From the marquess's jest comparing the meal to the prince regent's now legendary banquet at the Brighton Pavilion back in January, Sophie collected that his lordship recognized the aim to keep them seated and talking as long as possible. She wondered how he felt about her visit and if he realized, as she did, that they were being paired. She needed to speak with him privately to know, and also to enlist his help. The dissuading of the countess and dowager was too great a task for one individual.

And so it was that Sophie found herself pacing outside Fontaine's private rooms after everyone retired. As apprehensive as she was about meeting with him alone, she forged ahead out of necessity. There was no other solution. She required his assistance in extricating them from this shameless matchmaking. They could not marry—a man of the marquess's station would never accept a woman in her circumstances, regardless of their past friendship—but neither could they simply point that out and be done with the business. The dowager and the countess knew everything, and it apparently had not swayed them. But if Fontaine was willing to work with her to prove her point, they could prevail.

She sighed and came to an abrupt halt before the door.

Fontaine was known for his impeccable deportment and faultless manners. She could not predict how he would respond to the gross deviation of propriety she had committed so many years ago. He had been polite and dryly charming at dinner, but they had witnesses then. Now they would be alone and perhaps his true feelings would be aired. She had suffered and survived malicious gossip and been ostracized. But Justin . . .

Sophie swallowed hard. Dear God, how would she bear it if he was cruel?

Of course, there was only one way to find out.

Sophie lifted her chin, squared her shoulders, and knocked on the paneled door.

Chapter Two

The moments that passed after Sophie knocked seemed an eternity. She forced herself to breathe in and out with slow, deep breaths and wait, rather than scamper back to her room and find another way. Finally the door was opened by a manservant who was most likely Fontaine's valet. The smile she gave him was both a greeting and an expression of relief.

"Good evening," she said cheerfully. "I wish to speak with his lordship, if I may."

There was a pause as the man blinked wide eyes at her, then a large hand curled around the top of the door and pulled it open further.

Fontaine came into view looking even better than he had at dinner. Then he had been fully, faultlessly dressed. Now he was sans coat, waistcoat, and cravat, the opening at his collar revealing honey-colored skin and a light dusting of pale blond hair. He looked relaxed and far less rigid than he had earlier, a softening her female sensibilities enjoyed far too much.

"Lady Sophie," he murmured, in the deep voice of a pure male. "An unexpected pleasure, to be sure."

"Might I come in, my lord?"

"This is my bedchamber," he pointed out.

She gave him a wry look. "Yes, I know."

His mouth twitched at the corners. "If you wish to compromise me, I must tell you that asking permission first is a rather odd way to go about it."

Sophie blew out her breath and tapped her foot impatiently. "Why must you always be so difficult? Have you any notion—"

He reached out and hauled her into the room.

Dismissing his valet, he then shut the door, enclosing them in a space that smelled strongly of him, a delicious blend of bergamot and tobacco that stirred her in ways she wasn't prepared for.

Needing distance between them, she stepped farther into his space. Her gaze drifted across the large, well-appointed chamber. Decorated in dark woods and shades of gold and brown, it reminded her of a lion's den and suited its master perfectly, as did the two matching, fully grown mastiffs who approached her.

"You've no need to fear them," he assured her. "They are quite gentle."

"Well, hello," she greeted, extending both hands. The massive fawn-colored beasts pressed their great muzzles into her palms and sniffed. Apparently finding her acceptable, they welcomed her with copious amounts of viscous drool. She glanced over her shoulder at the marquess. "What do you call them?"

"George and Edward."

"Truly? How unusual."

"They share their names with the two gentlemen who were with me when I purchased them as pups. Since both men felt the need to jest at length about salivating animals, I deemed them appropriate monikers."

"Lovely!" Sophie laughed, pleasantly surprised by his sense of humor, which she did not remember ever seeing much of.

She watched him step behind the screen in the corner and when he returned, gratefully accepted the damp cloth he offered to wipe her hands. "They are beautiful dogs."

"I think so," he said easily, watching her with a stare that made her feel slightly breathless. His intensity had always frightened her a little, although she could not collect why. He would never hurt her; she knew that like she knew the sun would rise in the morn.

Moving to one of the two wingback chairs in front of the fire, Sophie sat and tugged a footstool closer so she could set her slippered feet upon it.

"Please, make yourself comfortable," he teased, taking a seat opposite her. The way he filled the chair caught her attention. He did not sit with any sort of straightness to his spine, as she would expect. Fontaine lounged like a king of the jungle, his long legs stretched out and his back angled into the groove between the chair back and the wing. George and Edward studied him a moment, then shuffled over to the footstool and set their giant heads atop each of her feet.

"They like you," he said.

"I like them."

"I thought you hated dogs, or were afraid of them. Some such. You could not tolerate Lady Cardington's pet. His name eludes me now . . ."

"Max, and he was a beast. I like dogs, truly. But Maximillian was not a dog; he was a demon. He chewed up my best shoes and lifted his leg on my bedpost at every opportunity." She smiled suddenly. "But I am grateful for him now, because he works in our favor."

"Oh? How so?"

"*Grand-mère* refused to see how horrid that animal was. I tried to tell her, but my complaints fell on deaf ears. He was wickedly clever and always on his best behavior for her."

"So you invented a fear of canines?" The chastising shaking of his head was tempered by obvious indulgence.

"The feigned phobia served its purpose," she said. "And now it will be one of the many points of contention between you and me."

He grinned, and she was riveted.

Tilting her head to the side, Sophie contemplated her old friend with new eyes. How dashing he looked in his inelegant sprawl with his throat revealed to her gaze. He had always been uncommonly handsome, but the intimate pose made him seem overwhelmingly so. Where once he had been lean and youthful, he was now large and mature. His features were more angular, his gaze more knowing. Sophie could not shake the feeling that she had just walked into a predator's lair.

"So we are to be contentious." His lips twisted wryly. "I am not certain how to feel about so much effort being expended to avoid marriage to me."

"Relieved?" she suggested blithely. "If I left the matter to you, you would most likely pronounce that you'd never marry a woman such as me, and that would goad them to dig in their heels. I am saving you endless trouble."

"You believe I would never wed you," he repeated, frowning.

Sophie drummed her fingers restlessly against the end of the armrest. "Of course not. I would drive you to insanity."

"Perhaps I would like that."

"Stuff," she scoffed.

"Hmm . . ."

"Hmm?"

"Never mind. So tell me, how are you faring, Sophie?" The low, intimate timbre of his voice was slightly distracted, as if part of his mind was occupied with other thoughts.

She offered a small smile. "As well as can be expected, my lord."

"Justin," he corrected.

"Justin." Her gaze lowered to his throat, which she could not seem to resist looking at. "How are you? You look . . . well."

He tilted his head in acknowledgment. "Thank you. I am." There was a short pause, then, "How is your son?"

"Thomas is wonderful." Sophie smiled at the thought of him. "He's quite the loveliest thing in my life. But I shan't bore you with the details."

"If a topic interests you, it interests me. Does Thomas look like you?"

"No." Sophie frowned, startled by the marquess's words, which were delivered without inflection. "He looks like his father, thankfully. A blessing I appreciate immeasurably."

Lifting her hand, she rubbed at the space between her brows where an ache was building. She had been plagued with megrims in the months after Langley's passing, and the stress of her first outing and her unexpected reaction to Fontaine were bringing back echoes of that pain.

"I am sorry for your loss," he murmured.

"Thank you." Her hand dropped back into her lap. "But I have my son and I am tremendously grateful for him. He has been a brilliant light during a very dark time."

She had been faced with people who intimated that it would have been better had she lost the babe. The very suggestion angered her in a way nothing else could. To propose that the loss of her child would have been preferable to the loss of social standing was so heinous she could not credit it.

"Where is the boy now?"

"With Langley's younger brother—the current Lord Langley—and his family. Thomas visits with them often. He is a tangible piece of his father, and they cherish him."

"You are very brave, Sophie."

She studied Fontaine, attempting to discern if he was being facetious or not. She saw only sympathy. "No, I am not brave. Not at all. I have survived. That does not make me courageous; it is merely a testament of my stubbornness."

His mouth curved. "Call it what you like. I admire you a great deal. I doubt I would have weathered the storm near as well."

The combined effect of that smile and his praise left Sophie speechless. She was taken aback by how it affected her, warming her from the inside, loosening the tight knot of apprehension she had not known was there. When had his opinion become so important? Or ... perhaps it had always been important.

"I would not have expected you to be supportive," she admitted, her damp palms wrapping around the end of the armrests.

"Why not?"

"Because you were forever chastising me when we were children."

The marquess's eyes widened. "I was not."

"Yes, you were. I remember the incidences quite clearly, especially that day in the garden when you shouted at me and I nearly fell. Scared me witless."

"Are you referring to the time you were attempting to climb to the top of the pagoda?" He snorted. "It was you who scared the wits from me! I rounded the corner in search of you and there you were, hanging some distance from the ground by only your fingertips. My heart stopped beating altogether. You could have killed yourself."

She snorted back. "As if you cared for my health. It simply offended your aristocratic sensibilities to see a female engaged in such sport."

Outwardly, Justin was fairly certain he maintained his composure. Inwardly, he was stunned. Sophie could not believe that. Not truly. "Are you daft?"

Sophie blinked her thickly lashed green eyes at him. "Beg your pardon?"

"If you believe I wished to hold you back due to your gender rather than out of concern for the safety of your person you are sorely mistaken."

As she continued to stare at him as if he had grown two heads, Justin in turn stared at the ravishing creature who sat across from him and felt a bit ... addled. In his mind, he had held an image of her as she had looked the last time they met. She had been ten and nine, slender yet lushly built, her hair a riot of dark chocolate curls shot with striking strips of burgundy. Full red lips and those lovely eyes had rounded out the picture of a beauty on the verge of blossoming. He had watched her grow from a child to a woman, accompanying his mother on every visit to Lady Cardington's just to witness the transformation. Biding his time. Waiting for the day when she would be his.

A day that had never come.

His mother had been the one to tell him that Sophie had accepted Lord Langley's addresses. After that, he never returned to the Cardington dower house again.

In the years since, his memories had not aged her. She had been arrested in that moment in time. Because of this, the vision who greeted him in the parlor before dinner took him completely by surprise.

His mother was right. The years had been kind to Sophie, turning her youthful attractiveness into an intoxicating blend of innate sensuality and fully ripened curves. When she had kissed his cheek, the smell of her and the feel of her warm body so close to his had thrust home an undeniable truth—he still wanted her. This time with a man's desire, not a boy's infatuation.

And dear sweet Sophie apparently had no notion of the hunger she had awakened. Otherwise she would not be visiting his private rooms and reclining in a way that bared her ankles. He was in a riot of lust over that view, such as many a naked woman had been unable to incite in him. The desire to press his lips to that tiny part of her rode him hard. He wanted to push up the hem of her skirts and follow the length of her lithe legs with his mouth. He wanted to spread her thighs wide and lick inside her, drink her in, hear the sounds she made when lost in climax.

"My lord . . . Justin."

She squirmed slightly, and he realized his lengthening silence was making her uncomfortable. He forced himself to look away. "Yes?"

He heard her sigh. "I feel as if we are strangers."

"Does that disturb you?"

"Yes, it does. Is it possible that you might stay a few more days?"

Justin refrained from smiling. That had been his intent ever since she kissed him in the parlor, but it was fortuitous that she asked. "Why?"

He could see that she was attuned to the growing sensual awareness he felt building between them. Her gaze roamed often from the top of his head to his polished Hessians and back up again, the green irises dark with female appreciation.

But the rapid lift and fall of her chest betrayed her unease. She had not expected to desire him, and therefore had no defenses in place to manage the attraction.

Which worked perfectly for him. He would ensure that she remained unsettled and unguarded so he could slip inside her . . . in every way possible.

"Because *grand-mère* will never believe we are ill-suited if she doesn't reach the conclusion on her own."

His gaze narrowed. "Are we ill-suited, Sophie?"

Again she looked at him as if he were an anomaly she could not classify. "Don't tease, Justin. You know my circumstances make me unacceptable for you. Besides which, I would never marry a man who did not love my son as much as I do."

"I am curious," he said softly. "What type of woman would you deem 'acceptable' for me?"

Sophie tucked a loose strand of hair behind her ear and waved her hand, both gestures betraying her nervousness. "Someone such as Lady Julienne Montrose, I suppose." A flush spread across her cheeks.

"Interesting." Pleasure filled him that she had kept apprised of his activities. "Perhaps it will surprise you to learn that the qualities I most enjoyed in Lady Julienne were ones that reminded me of you—her ability to disregard the opinions of the *ton*, her mischievous nature, and warm sensuality."

"My lord!" Her hand lifted to her throat.

He offered a wolfish smile, relishing the chance to shock her for a change. "I am quite serious."

Her cheeks flushed. "You are not."

"Who are you trying to convince? You can save your breath if you are attempting to sway me. I know a passionate woman when I see one."

"This conversation is ridiculous." Her arms crossed over her chest. "I am trying to extricate you from this mess, and you are making things difficult as usual."

"As usual? I have always been accommodating," he said smoothly.

She snorted. "You have been driving me mad for years."

On this particular occasion, Justin was fairly certain that the reason why she was maddened was for just the reason he'd like and if assisting her kept her within his grasp long enough to act upon it, he had no objections. "How can I help you?"

"If you could manage to delay your departure for a few days, we could contrive ways to demonstrate how we are completely inappropriate for one another—such as your love for dogs and my dislike of them. Not simply because we are contrary progeny who refuse to heed the wisdom of our elders, but because we are a disaster together."

"A disaster?" By the time all was said and done, he would know every reason why she had never considered him for marriage. He would know everything about her, including all the ways he could make her come.

"Well," she shrugged, "something similar to that, if we have any luck at all. Imagine the fun! Eventually, they will retreat from their plans, hopefully before we cause any permanent damage."

Justin laughed.

And Sophie was captivated.

Merriment transformed him, thawed him. Fine lines spread out from the corners of his eyes, revealing how often he found amusement in his life. Suddenly, Sophie wished she knew the man who had earned those laugh lines, the private one. Someone he had recently become. Or perhaps he'd always had a hidden side? One she had failed to see?

The prickle of sexual awareness she had felt all evening intensified to the point where she was forced to rub her arms. She stared at him, unable to look away. His smile slowly faded, his expression altering to become fiercely intent. It made her shiver, that look. And he had been giving it to her ever since she'd entered his bedchamber.

"Have you been alone since Langley passed?" he asked in an intimate murmur.

"I have my son."

"That is not what I meant, and well you know it."

Sophie tugged her feet out from under George and Edward's great heads and stood. "Heavens, it's late."

Fontaine rose as well, and followed her to the door. She reached for the knob and was startled when he came up behind her, his palm pressed to the panel over her head preventing her from leaving. Caged by his big body, there was no way to avoid breathing in the scent of his skin. It was delicious, as was the warmth that radiated from him. He moved closer, pressing his front to her back. She began to pant. The knowledge that he was fully, impressively aroused was inescapable.

She was tormented by her confusion. Reconciling the seductive male behind her with the aloof boy she knew from the past was beyond difficult. There had been a measure of safety in the distance inherent in friendship. Now, the imaginings in her mind of the two of them as lovers bridged that gap.

"Your heart is racing," he whispered, his breath hot

against her skin. His tongue swept across the vein that fluttered madly at her throat. Her back arched and a startled cry escaped her.

"A portion of your response is desire." His open mouth brushed behind her ear and she shuddered violently. "But a portion of it is fear. Why? You must know that I would never hurt you."

Unable to speak, Sophie agreed with a jerky nod. His teeth bit gently into the tender flesh where her shoulder met her neck. Her knees weakened and his free arm came around her, banding at her waist to support her. Taking further liberties, his thumb stroked the side of her breast in a soothing rhythm that did nothing to calm her.

Sophie's eyes closed and her damp forehead rested against the door. His chest labored against her back, the heat of his body set hers on fire. Her nipples peaked hard and tight, aching. As if he knew, he cupped her breast and kneaded it. Her sex clenched in rhythm with his grasp and she grew wet, slippery and hot.

"Oh dear God," she moaned, quaking. How did a woman manage a desire such as this? She had lusted for Langley and relished his lovemaking, but those emotions had not reached this depth. She hadn't the experience required to control her responses. "You overwhelm me. I cannot think or breathe."

"And I am undone." His mouth was moving over her bared skin. Nipping, licking, biting. "This is passion, Sophie. Need and hunger."

"It is insanity, my l–lord." Her voice broke as he continued to fondle her intimately. "With a small ch–child dependent upon me, I cannot afford to go in–insane."

"There is only one cure," he murmured. "Shall we administer it?"

She shook her head, but lack of energy gave the movement no strength. "I do not understand . . . what is happening."

Justin breathed deeply. "We are becoming lovers, sweet Sophie. *Finally.*"

He tilted his head and took her mouth. She gasped at the contact, the tingling of her lips urging her to press them hard against his. Her angle was awkward, but she did not care. The kiss was perfect, his lips so soft, yet firm, the taste of him dark and delectable. She could not temper the ardent way she answered him. Her response was instinctual and greedy.

The groan that left his throat made her shiver, so filled with rough longing and ravenous need. He licked deep inside her, his tongue gliding back and forth against hers, the measured tempo blatantly erotic. She whimpered softly as tension coiled in her womb. He pulled back at the sound, breathing harshly. "Stay with me tonight."

Her lower lip quivered, her thoughts scattered and unable to settle. Justin licked the soft curve of her mouth, his touch so reverent it coaxed a tear to blur her vision, then slip down her cheek. He wrenched himself away. She felt his loss keenly; the lack of his warmth left her cold, the lack of his support left her shaky.

"Damn you." The look he gave her scorched. "I can make you stay. I can make you beg me to allow you to stay. But that is not what I want. You will give yourself to me. I will have you no other way."

Sophie turned to face him, lifting her fingers to press against her kiss-swollen lips. "You have always . . ." She reached behind her and gripped the knob.

"Always what?" he asked gruffly, the lust within him a palpable thing, barely leashed.

"Always been too much." With a quick pivot, she opened the door. "Good night, my lord."

She fled, leaving him standing there staring after her.

George whined softly. Edward paced at the threshold.

Justin knew just how they felt.

Chapter Three

"Lady Sophie said something to me last evening that perplexes me," the marquess murmured to his mother the next morning as they descended the stairs to the lower floor for breakfast.

"Oh?"

"Yes, she said I have always been 'too much.' I've no notion of what that is supposed to mean."

Her mouth curved innocently, an affectation reinforced by her pale ringlets and light blue gown. "Interesting."

He glanced aside at her. "Do you know what she is referring to?"

"Hmm . . . Perhaps she means to say you are overwhelming."

"Yes." Justin scowled. "She said that, too."

"Truly? How did I miss this discussion? I recall you two sat quite some distance from each other in the parlor after dinner."

"Never mind that," he muttered. "Can you explain what the devil she is talking about?"

She linked her slender arm with his. "When you both were children, she used to make up stories about you. You were a 'prince' most often, though sometimes when you were surly, you were cast as a toad or an ass."

He choked.

"I noted something in her stories. You were usually set atop an intimidating pedestal. A character who ruled over all with an iron fist and nary a smile. She would speak of you with awe."

Justin shook his head, frowning. "I was a boy."

"A very serious boy," she corrected. "You changed a great deal after your father passed on."

"I have a great deal of history to live up to."

"Yes, you do."

"She has a bastard child."

"Yes, she does." The dowager patted his arm. "Your father and I didn't wait either."

His eyes turned heavenward. "I could have lived my entire life without that knowledge, Mother, and been quite content."

"Stuff. Don't be prudish."

Heaving out his breath, the marquess prayed for the rest of his day to improve upon his morning. He had spent restless hours the night before contemplating Lady Sophie and her circumstances, and how he could have her.

Had she stayed the night with him, it would have been something he would have regretted as much as she. A man of his station could not marry a woman in her circumstances, she was absolutely correct about that. Which left him with only one option—to take her as his mistress. It was an offer he could not make to her, not to Sophie. He respected her too much to suggest such an arrangement; the mere thought sickened him.

But not having her at all was impossible. He *would* have her. He only needed to discern *how*.

His mother shot him a narrowed side-glance as they reached the parquet floor of the foyer. "I should like to see a man retain his virginity until marriage."

"How progressive of you," he murmured.

"With all your rumored excesses with females of unsavory reputation, I would think you'd appreciate a woman with a healthy appetite for sexual congress."

"I will not discuss anyone's sexual appetite with you, not mine and most definitely not yours." He steered her toward the dining room.

"Why not?"

"I would rather go to the tooth-drawer's," Justin muttered, "or wear a hair shirt."

He assisted her into her chair at the end of the table. "I had decided to remain in residence for a few more days, but that does not mean you should send for the parson. Do I make myself clear?"

The startled, yet hopeful glance the dowager bestowed on him over her shoulder made him smile and bend to kiss her cheek. God help him, he adored her, daft as she was.

That same kiss—when witnessed by Sophie as she entered the dining room—inspired tender feelings of a different sort. Her stomach fluttered madly in response. She came to an abrupt halt in the doorway, her *grand-mère*'s arm wrapped around hers.

"See?" Lady Cardington whispered. "A good man. Do not let that stiff-as-pudding exterior fool you."

Sophie could say that she wasn't fooled, not after visiting his rooms last night, but she held her tongue and shivered when he straightened and caught sight of her. The look he gave her flared instantly from innocuous to indecent.

"Good morning, my lord," she greeted, in a voice remarkably composed.

He approached them with that animal grace that made her breathing shallow. All the incongruities about him intrigued her so much. The unflappable deportment mixed with latent sensuality. The dry wit mixed with the wicked gleam in his eyes. Arrogantly arched brows over glances filled with pure male appreciation.

Such as the glance he was heating her with right at this very moment.

Sophie took a deep breath. She had chosen her day gown of soft green trimmed in darker green ribbon because it was her best. The long sleepless night had been spent wondering if the marquess's attraction to her had been spurred by the late hour or if he would still desire her in the light of day. Now that she knew the answer, she had even more to consider.

She held no illusions. Nothing could ever come of this attraction. A man of Justin's station could not marry a woman in her position and mothers did not become mistresses, at least not *this* mother. Despite this, she worried that she would succumb to his seduction if she remained under his roof. He had awakened a hunger in her that had gnawed at her all night. She could not take the chance that feeding it would not appease it.

"Lady Sophie," he murmured in that warm, rich-as-honey voice. "Lady Cardington."

Fontaine took her *grand-mère*'s arm and led her to the table. Sophie followed. Once the countess was seated, he turned to her. "Shall we?"

He gestured toward the covered salvers on the buffet. She nodded and joined him, taking in his fine form so elegantly displayed in brown breeches and coat, with a multicolored embroidered waistcoat to counter the austerity. It suited the man he had become, somber yet possessed of a more colorful side that he showed only rarely.

"You steal my breath," he whispered.

She looked away, afraid her expressive face would reveal too much. "Thank you."

"Thank *you*. Already my day is complete, now that I have seen you."

As Fontaine reached for a plate, Sophie reached for the pepper with a shaking hand. As she sprinkled the spice into her palm, she glanced at the two women at the table and noted that they were engrossed in a discussion. She exhaled sharply.

"Do you remember the time we picked flowers and I had a reaction to one of them? The pollen or some such?"

He stared at her quizzically. "Of course I remember. You sneezed for hours."

"Do you recall the treatment?"

"It was long ago."

"I changed my garments, blew my nose, and applied a cold compress."

"Are we reminiscing?" His mouth curved fondly and she was struck by guilt. "If so, I remember more pleasant memories."

"Forgive me," she whispered. Then she lifted her hand and blew him a kiss, which also served to blow pepper—

—right up his lordship's aquiline nose.

"Good God!" he shouted, staring at her in wide-eyed horror. Then he sneezed.

And sneezed.

And sneezed.

"Dear heavens," the dowager cried, pushing back from the table in a rush. "What is the matter with you, Fontaine?"

His reply was a sneeze. Then another. And another. He doubled over, sneezing like a madman.

Patting his back sympathetically and ignoring the fulminating glare his reddened eyes shot in her direction, Sophie said, "I cannot be certain, my lady, but it appears he is having on olfactory fit of some sort." She leaned over and stared at him, then leapt back when he sneezed violently.

"Heinous!" he gasped at her, covering his mouth in a vain attempt to curb his pulmonary spasms.

"What could it be?" the dowager asked, as she hurried over to them. "I have never seen him like this."

"He is having a paroxysm, obviously," the countess pronounced, joining them at the buffet. "A violent reaction to something that does not agree with his constitution."

"If he has never been this way before, perhaps it is my presence that distresses?" Sophie suggested.

"Ridiculous!" the countess and dowager negated in unison.

Sophie shrugged. "Of course you both would know better than I, but it seems that the offending smell would have to be recently introduced, and I just thought—"

She was cut off by more sneezing and offered a sympathetic glance that was met with a scowl. "It would probably be best for me to break the fast in my room. If his lordship improves, then we shall know it's me. Perhaps my perfume? He told me yesterday evening that it was—" she winced— "not to his liking."

"My lord!" the two women chastised, sounding every bit like offended mother hens.

"Vixen," Justin hissed.

"Fontaine!" the dowager protested. "It is not Lady Sophie's fault that your olfactory sense is overly sensitive. Personally, I think she smells lovely."

"He could be allergic to me," Sophie continued, raising her voice to be heard over the noise the marquess was making. "The removal of my person should rectify the problem. If he worsens, then we will have to search for another culprit."

Stepping gingerly away, Sophie noted the watery eyes and reddened nose of the Marquess of Fontaine, and felt odious. But an hour or so of discomfort could spare them a lifetime of regret. When considered in that light, her actions were somewhat less reprehensible.

"I do hope you feel better soon," she said to Justin, meaning every word.

His lordship replied with a galvanic sneeze.

"Has Lord Fontaine's condition improved?" Sophie asked her *grand-mère* as they sat in the private sitting room that bisected their two chambers. Decorated in pale blue and white with delicately carved furniture, it was a relaxing retreat, yet Sophie was anything but soothed.

"Yes." The countess sighed. "He felt better soon after you retired."

"Oh, good."

"It is not good. Not at all."

Sophie looked down at the book in her hands and felt awful to have caused the disappointment she heard in the beloved voice. "You can still enjoy your visit with Lady Fontaine. I can keep myself occupied."

"That is not the point. Fontaine is a powerful man who occupies the highest strata of society. His friendship is extremely valuable, and he has a *tendré* for you."

"He does not!" Sophie felt the blush sweep up her cheeks and into her hairline. How obvious was the attraction between them?

The countess shook her head. "Child, he may have grown past it now, but he was once quite smitten with you. Affection for first loves lingers for a lifetime."

"He was not smitten!" she denied vehemently, even as her heart leapt at the thought. "I would have known if he was."

"I wondered if you were blind to it." Her *grand-mère* sighed. "Why do you think he accompanied his mother so often? A man of his station had more important matters to attend to."

Sophie snapped her book closed and rose to her feet, agitated. "You are mistaken. He . . . he . . ."

"Do not think to say that he came because of his mother. Fontaine is not the type of man to be tied to any woman's apron strings." The countess abandoned her needlepoint on the small walnut table beside her, and linked her fingers in her lap. "Did you never wonder why he ceased to visit after your betrothal was announced?"

Sweat misted Sophie's forehead. "He was always so critical . . . so chastising . . . he—"

"Critical? Or concerned? You were forever involved in some scrape or another. You were angry and unruly, most likely due to the premature death of your parents. You took unnecessary risks and defied convention. I was worried about you, but knew that the more I intervened, the more you would resist. I expected you would outgrow such behavior, which you did. However, Fontaine was less patient."

"He wanted me to be someone I am not!"

"He wanted you safe. Did he ever ask you to curb your mischief? How often did he depart with ruined attire from following you into another mess?"

Spinning away, Sophie found herself breathing with difficulty, images from the past rushing forward in a deluge. "I don't know . . ." Her hand lifted to her chest and rubbed ineffectually at the ache there. She wondered if she had hurt him in her ignorance. It pained her dreadfully to think of it.

"He appears to hold no ill will toward you, and his support could do much to improve your circumstance. It is unfortunate that he has acquired intolerance for your person." Her *grand-mère* studied her a moment and then offered a smile. "Perhaps you could refrain from wearing your perfume?"

Sophie rubbed the back of her neck. "That will change nothing. We are completely unsuitable. He prefers blondes, such as Lady Julienne—"

"And you prefer brunettes such as Langley."

"Yes, well . . ." She had adored Langley, loved him madly, had thought him the most charming man in the world. But she lusted for the golden marquess. Hungered for him. Ached for him in unmentionable places. When he entered the room, her body hummed with energy that wanted spending in a bed.

But she was also frightened by that need for him. How could she, a woman of so many faults, live up to the expectations of a man who seemed to have no faults at all?

"Regardless," Sophie cleared her clenched throat, "I have Thomas, and Lord Fontaine requires a woman as different from me as night is to day. Even Rothschild washed his hands of me."

"Your brother is a self-centered idiot." The countess patted the vacant seat next to her on the gilded settee. "He will have his comeuppance one day. That is the way fate works."

Sinking into the proffered space, Sophie leaned into her *grand-mère* and set her head on the frail shoulder. The scent of jasmine made her eyes water, the memories of a less complicated time bringing sadness. Now she was looking at the past with new eyes, remembering earlier conversations with new ears, feeling new emotions.

Wondering what she would have done then, if she had known what she knew now.

Chapter Four

When the knock came to Justin's bedchamber door after dinner, the smile that curved his mouth was mirrored inside him. George and Edward immediately rolled to their bellies from their previous positions on their sides, then they padded over to the door at the same time Sophie's husky voice drifted to his ears.

Justin rose from the chair before the fire. "Show her in," he said to his valet, "then you may go."

Inside him, something wild coiled tight, prepared to spring. But when Sophie came into view with sad eyes and her lower lip caught nervously between straight, white teeth, it quieted abruptly. She was wound up as well, but not for the same reasons he was.

"Who knew such mischief could hide beneath the exterior of an angel?" he murmured, attempting to calm her with gentle teasing.

She was dressed in deep blue this evening, the cut of the bodice and sleeves so painfully simple that on a lesser woman, it would have been plain. On Sophie, however, it allowed her lush figure to take the stage. She had kept herself sequestered all day, tormenting him with the knowledge that she was under his roof, yet unreachable.

With her head bowed, she said, "I meant no harm."

Her palpable unhappiness disturbed him. "Why do I feel that you are upset about more than my inability to smell a blasted thing all day?"

"I am sorry about that, too," she said contritely, startling him by stepping closer and running the tip of her index finger down the bridge of his nose. The innocent touch nearly undid him. It was the first intimate connection she had ever initiated. "I thought only of escape."

"Escape?" he asked gruffly, his body reacting to her proximity and the scent of her skin.

She stepped back and clasped her hands. "Did I misunderstand our previous relationship?"

Justin arched a brow.

Sophie looked deep into his eyes, searching. "Have you ever contemplated walking on the surface of the moon?"

The other brow rose to meet the first.

"I never have," she continued, her tongue flickering out to wet her lips. "Not until this afternoon when *grand-mère* suggested that perhaps you once cared for me beyond mere friendship and I attempted to conceive of something more impossible."

"Sophie—"

Holding up a hand, she halted his speech. "If I wounded you, I never meant to. I was simply unaware. It never occurred to me that a man such as you would ever find me . . . would ever find anything—"

"Sophie—"

"You were always so damn perfect, so poised, so rigid . . . so . . . so . . . so *arrogant!*" She pointed an agitated and accusing finger at him. "Always ordering me about and correcting me and . . . and . . . and—"

Justin glanced heavenward, then snatched her to him and kissed her full on her indignant mouth.

"Mmpf . . . !" A weak protest died before it was born. She melted into him, all soft warm passionate woman.

Heat flared instantly, burning across his skin and setting

his blood on fire. Cupping her nape, he held her still, fitting his mouth to hers. Taking it. Possessing it. As he should have done years ago.

Her hands pushed at his shoulders, then slid up and over them, thrusting into his hair. He growled, maddened by the simple contact, aroused to bursting, his cock hard and throbbing. Cupping her hip, he urged her closer, grinding his erection into the soft flesh of her lower belly. She surged into him in response, feverish and ardent, her body writhing in his grasp. Her grip on his scalp began to hurt and he welcomed the pain. It grounded him. Otherwise, he feared he would pull her to the floor, push up her skirts, and show her how far beyond friendship his feelings went.

Sophie yanked her head to the side, panting. "I cannot breathe."

His mouth moved to her throat, then to her shoulder.

"Justin." Her hands roamed over the length of his back, caressing through the fine linen of his shirt. "You entice me to give what I shouldn't."

The sob in her voice struck him with the force of a blow to the gut and pained him as deeply.

With a growl, he pushed her away.

They stood apart, breathing harshly, flushed and disheveled. He ran his hands through his hair, feeling the sweat that dampened the roots. His entire frame was tight, tense, hard, his jaw clenched.

"I am at a loss," he said, his hands fisting. "I cannot have you, and yet I cannot conceive of not having you. Not when this," he gestured between them, "is all I can think about."

"I am so confused." Her green eyes were dark and fathomless. "I feel . . . for you . . ."

"Say no more. I am a man, not a saint."

"I loved him. He made me happy."

"It pleases me to know that you were content."

"I know it does." Her hand lifted and came over her heart. "I would not change my past because it gave me both beautiful memories and my son, and yet all day I have been haunted by imaginings of what could have been. Where would we be in our lives if I had known?"

"All this time, I thought you were aware and chose differently regardless."

"No." She held her hand out to him, but he did not take it, afraid of what he would do if they touched again. Her arm lowered slowly. "I have no wish to hurt you."

"This is not your fault, Sophie. Any guilt you might feel is unwarranted."

"There is no way for us to be together, is there?"

"No way that we could both live with," he said gruffly.

Cursing, he turned from her and crossed to the grate. He rested his arm on the mantel and stared into the fire, willing his burning blood to cool. He could taste her on his lips, smell her on his clothing. She was in the palm of his hand, yet he could not hold on to her. "I will leave in the morning."

"I cannot run you from your own home."

"I prefer it." His eyes closed. "I would smell you here. See you here. Want you here."

"Why? Why me? I make every misstep and you walk true."

Justin looked over his shoulder. She stood where he had left her, watching him, so heartrendingly beautiful in her yearning. "Who can explain the attraction between opposites?"

Her lower lip quivered, yet she stood tall and proud, undaunted by the unkind turns in her life. He wished he could shelter her from more pain and tragedy, but fate was cruel to him as well, mocking him for his youthful caution. He should have made clear how he felt years ago, and left no room for doubt or misunderstanding. All this time, he had thought she was never meant to be his, that she was not capable of deeper affection for him. Now he realized that he might have had his heart's desire, if only he had disregarded his pride and opened himself to her.

"You should return to your room," he murmured, looking away, resigned.

Silence filled the space between them. Only the sounds of the crackling fire and his rapid breathing offered relief.

"Justin . . . ?"

He heard the soft plea in her voice and his back tensed. She cleared her throat, causing his mouth to twitch. He knew that sound well. It was the sound of her gathering courage.

It was also the herald to mischief.

"I cannot be your wife or mistress," she said in a low, husky voice that warmed his blood like strong wine. "But for tonight . . . I can be your l–lover."

Justin spun to face her, flushing with avid lust and soul-deep longing. "Bloody hell."

Her lovely face took on that obstinate cast he adored. The tapers around the room burnished her, their golden glow gleaming off her creamy skin and glossy curls. "I want . . . I want . . ."

"Christ," he muttered, lacing his fingers at the back of his neck, "I know what you want. Do not give voice to it, or I may not have the strength to resist giving it to you."

Sophie stared at the marquess displayed in the alluring pose, his throat bared to her, his shoulders so broad, his arms flexing powerfully. She licked her lips, and moved toward him. "Why resist?"

"You owe me nothing."

"This is not about the past. This is about now, this moment, when I feel as if something in me is dying. I came to you tonight knowing this visit would lead to farewell, and yet now that we are agreed, I mourn. I haven't the strength to sleep alone tonight, aware that in the morning you will leave and I will not see you again."

His gaze narrowed. "You ask too much from me, Sophie. Better to wonder how it would be, than to know."

"Is it? Would it not be better to live on real memories,

than it would be to live on fantasy?" She rounded the wing-back.

"And what of tomorrow?"

"We can worry then."

He snorted and dropped his hands to his lean hips. "It is exactly that sort of thinking that lands you into trouble so often."

Lowering her voice, she moved with what she prayed was a seductive sway to her hips. "This time, I hope it lands me into your bed."

The groan that rumbled in his throat made her breasts swell further until they ached.

"I have a confession, my lord."

He waited. Alert. A predator crouched for the pounce. Sophie shivered, then embraced the driving urge she had to touch him, hold him, clasp him deep within her. Here, in his lair, with its earthy colors and dark, masculine appeal.

Dressed only in his shirtsleeves and trousers, he revealed a glimpse of the man he was in his private hours. A man she could have had. She regretted the loss, although she would not alter her past decisions.

"You see, my lord," she stepped up to him, coming to a halt a mere inch away, "your supreme self-possession is an irresistible lure. I want to crawl beneath it, see inside you, slip under your skin."

Lifting her hand, she set it over his heart and felt its frantic tempo. She was in much the same state; short of breath with raging blood. "When we were younger, I would sometimes shock you deliberately just to see beneath your exterior."

"You have always been under my skin," he murmured, pulling her into his embrace, where she wanted to be. He seemed to consider her carefully, then he cupped her cheek, staring down at her with a starkly intense gaze. "Be certain, love. Once we walk down this path, there is no turning back."

Sophie soaked in the warmth of his hard body and the

rich, spicy scent that clung to him. Just days ago, the thought of him had set her insides aflutter. She felt the same now, but for an entirely different reason. It was no longer the anxiety of reacquainting oneself with someone who had once been dear. It was anticipation and pure, heady desire.

"I have always admired you," she confessed, nuzzling into his palm. "My life has been in such disarray since the death of my parents, but you were so solid and immutable. Even as I provoked you, you strengthened and motivated me. Over the years, I often found myself imagining what you would do and considered that carefully before acting. I would not be the woman I am today had you not been in my life."

Heat flared in his eyes, and he pressed warm, firm lips to her forehead. "I am glad you thought of me."

"I never forgot you. And now . . . how easily you have turned my childhood awe into a woman's fascination. I was told you had the appearance of a god amongst men, but the tales failed to convey how seductive you are."

He snorted.

"Scoff all you like," she said. "It's true. Your voice makes me shiver and your presence inspires shockingly carnal musings."

"Do you imagine my mouth on you?" he asked roughly. "Everywhere? Do you imagine being taken on your hands and knees? Or bound and restrained for my pleasure?"

Her exhale was shaky and she clung to him for balance. Dear God, he sounded so primitive, blatantly defying his civilized exterior and reputation.

"I will *know* you, Sophie," he warned darkly. "I will know every inch of you, every curve and crevice. I will know you as no one else has ever known you. I will own you. Are you prepared to accept that?"

Sophie wondered at the change in him, the sudden seriousness of his bearing. "I want to be with you. However you would have me."

She turned her head and pressed her lips into his palm. The flutters in her stomach were riotous, causing her to quiver against him, but she was not afraid.

"My love," he murmured, his gaze bright with fierce adoration.

Following her heart, she surged into him, her lips bumping awkwardly into his.

A low, delighted chuckle rumbled in his chest at her eagerness. Then he cupped her nape and fitted his mouth over hers. Perfectly.

Sophie stopped breathing, arrested by the kiss. Her lips tingled and her ears rang, her skin flushed and her toes curled. As the world spun behind her closed lids, she leaned heavily into him. He paused, his lips moving along her cheekbone to her ear.

"Breathe, love," he admonished in a deepened tone that made her breasts swell.

His hand came up and squeezed the full, aching flesh. She inhaled sharply as he kneaded her, and then he took her mouth again, teasing her with gentle flicks of his tongue. Dizzy and unbearably aroused, she opened wider with a moan, shivering as he accepted the invitation with lush, deep licks.

The smell of his skin intoxicated her. She was beginning to love that unique combination of bergamot and tobacco. She already loved the feel of his body, so big and powerful. He dwarfed her, made her feel as if she was enveloped in warm, tangible safety. He was not pulling her under or drowning her. He was revealing the depth of his desire, and she was empowered by his admission.

With his hand on the curve of her hip and a low sound of encouragement, Justin urged her closer. Unresisting, Sophie slipped her fingers into the silky strands of his golden hair. The simple touch seemed to affect him strongly, made him shudder, and crush her slender body roughly to his hardness. Their mouths sealed together, so that each labored breath was shared.

Heat swept across her skin in a prickling wave. Perspiration dampened her forehead. She began to writhe against him, goaded by a physical sense of urgency she had never felt before. He hummed soothingly and attempted to calm her, but there was no help for it. She wanted his bare skin pressed to hers, his body straining over and inside hers.

Her arms fell to his hips, then her hands slid up the length of his spine. The muscles of his back tensed to rockhardness beneath her fingertips, despite the linen that separated her touch from his flesh. Her returning kiss became more feverish, the rushing of blood in her ears near deafening.

All the while his mouth drank from hers, the frantic movements of her body in stark contrast to the deep, luxurious pace of his kiss. He cupped her buttocks and rocked her into him, the lewd, blatant carnality of the gesture shocking her and inciting her further. Tension coiled tightly in her womb, becoming a deep hunger that fueled her growing desperation.

"Easy," he rasped, gentling her with calming strokes of his large hands. "Or we won't make it to the bed."

Part of Sophie's mind comprehended that he was threatening to make love to her in this very spot. Her body, however, clearly felt the venue was not an issue, blindly seeking to appease the insane need she felt to eat the man up like a tasty dessert. To nibble on all the hard lengths of muscle she felt beneath her palms, and to lick across what she imagined was rough satin skin. She nipped at his jaw and he groaned, the provocative sound filled with lustful longing. Tugging at his clothing, Sophie attempted to work her way to the man within.

"Sophie." Emotion thickened the normally clipped accents of his voice. He continued to fondle her breast and she whimpered as she grew wet with desire.

His thumb stroked across her thrusting nipple, and she released a thready cry. Her knees gave out and his arm at her waist tightened, locking her against him. His erection strained into her lower belly, goading her to rock into it. His responding growl excited her unbearably. The expert manipulation of her breast became more aggressive as one thickly muscled thigh intruded between her legs.

"Justin," she breathed.

"Tell me what you want."

"You."

Lifting her feet from the floor, he carried her to the bed.

Chapter Five

Justin found his hands shaking as he worked to release the buttons that held the sapphire gown to Sophie's lush body. She was fidgeting with impatience, as she was often wont to do, and he smiled, his chest filling with a deep, tender ache.

"Hurry," she urged, glancing over her shoulder at him, her green eyes heavy-lidded with passion.

"You still have no notion how to wait for the things you want." He softened his statement with a quick, hard kiss to the top of her shoulder.

"Would you prefer me to have patience when I want you?"

"I have waited a lifetime." Sliding his hands into the gaping back of her gown, he cupped her shoulders, then pushed the garment off and onto the floor. "Perhaps you should know a little of what it feels like to want something and be denied."

She turned into his embrace, clad only in a sheer chemise and silk stockings. He inhaled harshly at the feel of her pressed against him. "I never denied you," she murmured, nipping at his chin with her teeth.

Crushing her soft curves into his painfully aroused body, Justin buried his face in her short-cropped curls and breathed her in. The smell of her was delicious and he laughed softly.

Sophie pulled back slightly to look up at him.

"The way you smell appeals to me," he replied to her silent query.

She blushed, but her eyes sparkled with mischief. "What would you do if you were truly allergic?"

"Make love to you in a bath. Or pin my nose."

"You would not!"

"You doubt me?" Cupping her buttocks he tugged her into him, pressing the throbbing length of his cock against her.

Her gaze lowered to his throat and her hands lifted to pluck at his collar. "Would you . . . undress for me?"

"Of course." Justin smiled. "Will you assist me?"

Nodding, she reached for the placket of his trousers.

"Ah, love," he murmured, exquisitely tormented by her proximity and the knowledge that in moments she would be naked and arching beneath him. "You always did move directly to the point."

"I want to see you." She was nervous. He could see it in the way she worried her lower lip between her teeth. But she was eager, too. Open. Curious. He cupped her face in his hands.

"I am yours," he promised, his thumbs brushing over her cheekbones. "You have no need to be uncertain with me."

He tensed as the backs of her fingers brushed tantalizingly over the bulge of his erection. He was so hard for her it was painful and he groaned in relief when his cock sprang free of its confinement, coming to rest heavily within her palms.

"Is this mine, too?" she whispered, tracing the veins that pulsed along the length of him.

"Does it please you?" He grit his teeth as she stroked him with both hands.

"Yes. It suits you."

Justin managed a choked laugh. "How so?"

"It is large, proud, and arrogant."

"How the devil can a penis be arrogant?"

Sophie looked up at him from beneath long, dark lashes. Her thumb slid over the head of his cock, the journey eased by the drop of semen that collected there. "Look how ready he is. I am not certain he will wait for me."

"Continue fondling me like that and he might not."

He began to disrobe, but she did not release him, her fingers caressing him with such gentleness he was amazed he didn't come. By the time he was bared to her, perspiration covered his skin in a fine sheen and his seed leaked copiously, coating her hands.

"Undress," he said urgently, tugging his aching ballocks down to stave off an imminent release. He watched in an agony of lust as she removed her stockings, then frowned as she crawled on top of the bed. "The chemise, as well."

She shook her head. "I would rather wear it."

"No." Justin did not intend for the word to come out so harshly, but damn it all, he wanted her naked beneath him. Her skin to his.

Sophie arranged herself like a sensual feast, her lithe body sprawled across the many pillows that piled against his headboard. The last remaining vestige of her attire was so sheer, he could see the shadow of her areolas and the impatient thrust of erect nipples. Between her legs a dark triangle lured him, enticed him. But it was not enough.

"You deny me?" He frowned, hating the material that separated him from his deepest desire.

The fingers of her right hand fidgeted with the lace that framed the neckline. "I am not young. And I have had a child. In this instance, I believe wondering is better than knowing."

Sophie knew the moment understanding dawned. Fontaine's eyes widened and he stilled, taking stock before acting, as was his way. She leapt before looking. He looked before leaping. It was one of the many things she appreciated about him.

She watched him move to the bed, eyeing his powerful masculine beauty with hunger and infatuation. He was so lean, yet muscular. Perfect. Everything about him was perfect. And she was so imperfect.

He took a seat on the edge of the bed, and cradled one of her hands within his own. "I am grateful for your beauty," he murmured. "It arouses and amazes me." His mouth curved in a slow smile. "But I adored you when you were gangly."

"I was never gangly!"

"You were." His smile widened into a grin. "No breasts or hips. Just tall and reed-thin. And I adored you. I adored you with mud on your face and food on your chin and twigs in your hair."

"I never had food on my chin!"

"You did." He crawled over her, his knees resting on either side of her hips, his cock right where she wanted it . . . if only he would lower his body six inches or so. "It is *you* who captivates me, love. Your impulsiveness, your vitality, your lust for life. You have no fear. You see what you desire and grab it with both hands. I admire those qualities about you because I lack them myself. I am overly cautious and sometimes take too long to act, a fault that has cost me dearly."

Her hand lifted to cover her mouth and hide the trembling of her lips. She knew he referred to losing her to Langley and her heart ached. She made it a point to regret nothing in her life. If she proceeded with an action, it was because she was decided. But she regretted having caused him pain, even though she had done so unwittingly.

"So you see," he continued, collecting the hem of her chemise and tugging it upward, "while I am thoroughly smitten with your exterior, it is your interior that won my deeper regard."

Sophie arrested his movements with her hands over his.

He met her gaze squarely, his brows lifted in silent challenge. She knew that look well, and it made her smile. She took a moment to marvel over how comfortable she felt with him, as if they had been lovers forever, then said, "Allow me."

With her heart full, she sat up and pulled her chemise over her head. It was not as easy as she would hope, her insecurity around the marquess a lifetime habit. The change in position put their torsos in close proximity, and she shivered slightly as she felt the heat of his skin. Releasing a deep breath, she settled back against the pillows and lifted her chin.

His gaze was so hot it made her perspire. Her eyes closed as Justin touched her stomach just above her pelvic bone. She did not have to look to know he followed the mark left by her pregnancy. The mattress dipped and swayed as he moved away from her, and her eyes burned at the unbearable intimacy. A moment later she jerked in surprise when his open mouth pressed to the spot, then moved upward, his tongue slipping into her navel. One hair-dusted leg hooked over hers and tugged it aside, opening her thighs to his avid touch.

"Justin!" she gasped, arching as he parted her and stroked her with his fingertips.

His mouth moved to her breast, brushing along the side, kissing the faint marks that marred the under curve. "Christ, you are so beautiful."

Her arms lifted, embracing him, as he found her nipple and engulfed it, suckling strongly. A callused fingertip circled her clitoris, then dipped lower to slip inside her. She cried out and bowed upward, straining, her body echoing the contractions of his mouth around his plunging finger. Aroused by his praise and gentle ministrations, Sophie felt herself softening, opening, becoming slick with welcome so that every thrust of his hand sounded wetly in the room.

Lifting his head, Justin watched her, giving her no room to hide. His skin was flushed, his eyes fever-bright, his lips parted with harsh, panting breaths.

"I used to imagine you like this," he confessed in a husky whisper, withdrawing from her depths, only to return with two fingers. Stroking along her inner walls, rubbing, caressing, making her writhe. Her nails dug into his forearms, her nipples peaked hard and painfully tight.

He kissed her, absorbing her cries into the heat of his mouth. "If you open your legs wider," he whispered, "I can fuck you deeper."

His crude wording first startled her, then inflamed her. Squeezing her eyes shut, she spread her thighs shamelessly, hungrily accepting the deluge of sensation after the last few years of numbness.

"No, look at me," he murmured, his throbbing erection a hard pressure against her leg. "Let me watch you."

Sophie relented, unable and unwilling to deny him, feeling safe with him in a way that made such sharing possible. Her eyes locked onto his, her body quivered against his, her gasps mingled with his, until she cried out. Falling into orgasm with a hot rush of tears. Clinging to his big, hard body with all her strength. Grateful he was with her, just as she had always been grateful when he was at her side.

"Justin," she whimpered, rubbing her tearstained cheek against his. "Darling Justin."

He came over her, the ripples of his abdomen glistening in the candlelight, the muscles in his arms flexing as he held his weight aloft. "Put me inside you," he rasped, his chest heaving as if he had run a great distance.

Touching his lips with the fingertips of one hand, she reached down with the other and positioned him. His breath blew hot against her skin as he rolled his hips and eased into her.

She tensed as he breached her, her lungs seizing as the first thick inches spread her wide.

"Hush," he murmured, freeing one hand to stroke down her side. Reaching beneath her thigh, he pulled it up, anchoring it on his hip so that the pressure lessened. "You were made to hold me."

He settled more of his weight on top of her, pinning her down, forcing her to accept his leisurely pace.

Senses that had been dazed by her recent climax, flared to renewed life. "Please," she begged, squirming. "Please hurry."

"You never had any patience, love."

She moaned as he sank deeper. And deeper. So slowly. Taking his time. Finally, with a breathtaking lunge, he filled her to the hilt, his thighs shaking violently against hers.

"Christ, you feel good." His forehead pressed to hers. "Perfect. No! Don't move . . . be still . . . allow me a moment . . ."

Near mindless with lust, she rocked her hips restlessly, pushing him deeper into her, but it wasn't enough. Not nearly.

Justin brushed her damp curls away from her forehead. She stilled, staring up at him, arrested by the sight of the deep hunger and longing in his eyes. He made no effort to disguise it. Here, in this moment, Sophie saw inside him such as she never had before, finding the man beneath the collected exterior.

"Kiss me," she whispered. "Please, kiss me."

"Yes," he murmured, his lips lowering to hover over hers. "Yes."

As their open mouths met in a passionate mating, he withdrew from her drenched sex and then slid home, the thick head of his shaft rubbing inside her just as his fingers had. Her kiss grew frantic, her desire near maddening. Her nostrils filled with the scent of his skin and their joint arousal, urging her to action. She pressed her heels into the mattress and lifted to meet his next downward thrust.

He growled when he hit the end of her. "I want this to last."

"No! Dear God, no." Sophie grabbed his buttocks and urged him to pump faster. His firm ass clenched within her palms on every downstroke, the feel of him propelling his cock into her so erotic she began to plead softly.

"Whatever you want," she promised in a rush, desperate to give him pleasure, desperate to break through his iron control. "Anything you want . . . *please* . . . faster . . ."

Justin pulled back and lunged hard, pounding deep. "Is this what you want?"

"Yes! Yes." She writhed upward, straining with him, her body moving as a thing separate from her mind, driven by an animal greed that should have shocked her. Instead, she was empowered by it.

Embracing her need for him with all the passion she possessed, Sophie took him as hard as he took her, accepting the fierce driving thrusts of his cock with no restraint. Relishing the sounds of his guttural cries of pleasure.

Then he plunged into the root, swiveling his hips to grind against her. Her neck arched, her eyes flew wide. "Justin?" she gasped, taut as a bow, suspended on the edge of something wonderful.

"Come, Sophie," he crooned breathlessly, stroking in measured rhythm. "Come, and I will come with you."

Arms around his neck, she pressed her cheek to his and shivered into orgasm with his name on her lips. As he promised, he followed, holding her, loving her, supporting her.

Just as he always had.

Chapter Six

Justin sprawled naked atop the counterpane, one arm tucked behind his head, the other holding Sophie close to his side. The fire in the grate burned low, the tapers extinguished. Her fingers wandered idly across his chest, and her leg was tossed over his. As far as heaven went, he was fairly certain this was it.

"What is your life like with your son?" he asked.

"It's wonderful." Her tone held a soft breathy quality of happiness. "Every day is an adventure. You never know when you will find a toad in your bed or a grasshopper loose in your dining room. Some nights there are monsters in the armoire and on others, there are faeries in the air."

"I would enjoy that, I think."

He felt her smile against his skin. "You will be a wonderful father, I'm sure. I realize now that it was only my own insecurities that made me feel as if you looked unfavorably upon me. You were merely trying to protect me from myself. I think you will be somewhat of a mother hen, fussing after your progeny and taking great pains to ensure their safety."

He snorted.

"And that snort," she commented. "I used to think it

was arrogant and dismissive. Now I collect that you make that noise when you are embarrassed by praise."

"Provoking wench. Is the only way to keep you from teasing me to make love to you? You are much more agreeable then. Tractable even."

She hugged him tightly. "You are quite good at the business, you know. I did not know that I could . . . feel like *that* . . ." she exhaled in a rush, "while you are inside me."

He looked down at her. "An orgasm?"

"I have had them before," she amended quickly, lifting her head to look at him. With her face framed in a riot of short, dark curls, and her eyes bright, she looked younger and happier than when she had arrived. Pushing his fingers into her hair, he massaged her scalp, finding deep joy in his right to touch her as he wished.

"But not during intercourse?" He smiled. "I hope you enjoyed it. I intend to repeat the experience as often as possible."

She sighed forlornly. "I would love to stay, but time draws short. The sun will rise soon."

He cupped her cheek. "Only hours separate my body from yours."

Sophie pushed up, baring her curves to his gaze. In the faint orange glow from the banked fire, she looked like a pagan sexual goddess. His cock twitched in appreciation of the view.

"What are you saying?" she asked with a frown.

"I am saying that I will have you again tonight, if not before then. Do not be startled to find yourself in a secluded corner with your skirts around your waist."

"You said you were leaving!"

Justin arched a brow. "That was before you asked me to bed you."

She gasped. "I will not be your mistress! I have a child who shares my life."

"You insult me," he said, swinging his legs off the edge

of the mattress and standing. "I would never ask that of you." Collecting his black silk robe from the armoire, he shrugged into it, then moved to the grate. "Do you truly believe that I would think you were sufficient for fucking, but not for wedding?"

"I cannot marry you!" she protested.

He blew out his breath and kept his face averted to the fire. It would not do for her to see him wounded. Though it was ridiculous to feel that way, he knew. He had known from the moment he acknowledged what he must do, that she would fight him tooth and nail. "That sounded like a refusal."

"Oh, do not be daft!" she muttered. "Marriage to me would ruin you."

"Allow me to worry about that."

"What is the matter with you?"

He finished stoking the new coals and rose from his crouch. "Sophie—" His voice fell to silence as he faced her. She had pulled on her discarded chemise and knelt on the bed with her hands cupping both knees. He thought her the most glorious creature in the world.

His gaze moved away from the flashing green eyes and came to rest on the Fontaine crest carved into his headboard. Immutable resolution filled him. Sophie was where she belonged and he would fight to keep her with every breath in his body.

"You are a model of respectability," she continued, warming into a full-blown heated debate, "and an admired member of the aristocracy, and I am an example of how far one can fall from grace."

Justin crossed the distance between them, caught up her hands and pulled her from the bed. "Lady Sophie Milton-Riley," he said with all due seriousness, "would you do me the great honor of becoming my wife?"

She stomped her foot. "No, no, no, you mad fool. You said there was no way for us to be together that we could both live with, and you were of sound mind then. Obviously sexual congress disturbs your brain functions in some way. You need sleep," she pronounced. "Once you wake, you will see how insane your proposal is."

"I love you."

"Dear God." She gasped and bent over slightly, as if struck.

"I have always loved you."

Sophie shook her head violently. "You are mistaking the remnants of orgasm with elevated feelings. You did not feel that way before sex."

"My love." He pulled her into his embrace. "We would not have had sex, if I did not intend to marry you. I asked you, quite clearly, if you were prepared to be owned by me. You agreed."

"That is not what you meant!"

"It was. Kindly remember that *you* are the impulsive one in this pairing. I am the one who considers all aspects in great detail."

Sophie pushed at his chest in a bid for freedom and he released her, knowing that she would pace in her agitation. It was quite comforting to know her so well.

"You might grow to love me," he said, watching her.

"I already love you," she snapped.

He grinned.

She glared. "But that is the worst of all reasons to wed!"

"I *will* marry you, sweetheart, so you should accustom yourself to that fate posthaste. I lost you once. I refuse to lose you again."

"Justin." She heaved out her frustration, striding back and forth in front of the fire, oblivious to the way the backlighting revealed every inch of her delectable form. "Why must you always be so difficult? I will not allow you to sacrifice yourself for me."

"Yet you intend to sacrifice our love for me?" He shrugged

out of his robe and went to her, tossing it about her shoulders to keep her warm. "Where is the fairness in that?"

She stopped, her gaze dropping between his legs. He saw her swallow hard. "You would resent me after awhile. Society will never accept me, and that would reflect upon you. I would become a great hindrance. That would be unbearable for a socially active man such as you."

He lifted her chin so that their gazes met. "Not having you would make me more wretched."

"You've no notion." Her eyes were luminous with unshed tears. "It is not pleasant to be relegated to the fringes."

His hands settled on her shoulders, then slid down to her elbows. "Do you trust me?"

"You know I do."

"Then trust me to manage this."

"How?"

"I will find a way," he promised, sliding his hands beneath his robe to circle her waist and lift her off her feet. The feel of their bodies touching made his heart leap and then race madly. His cock swelled between them, and her breathing quickened. The instant, intoxicating, wildly uncontrollable hunger that flared between them was delicious.

To feel so alive, to be loved by the one woman whose affection he had needed for so long, to have the opportunity to correct the greatest error of his life . . . it was all together nearly enough to make him shout with joy.

But the weight of their dilemma hung over them like a dark cloud. They were both highly aware of the imminent thundercrack and the downpour of censure that would follow. The only certainty was this moment, these last hours before dawn.

So he determined to relish them. He stepped toward the bed with his precious Sophie in his arms. She clung to him, her mouth at his throat, kissing and nibbling in a way that drove him to madness.

Laying her on the chocolate velvet counterpane, he followed her down, brushing the edges of the robe aside so that he could cup her breasts. His open mouth lowered, surrounding her nipple through her chemise, his tongue flickering across the tightened peak. He rested on his side, freeing his hand to slide down between her thighs. She opened without reservation, baring her cunt to his reverent caresses. A deep sound of praise rumbled up in his chest, vibrating against her skin as he continued to suck deeply at her breast. He parted her and stroked through the slickness he found, both hers and his. With two fingers he pushed into her, feeling the soft-as-satin walls tighten and release as he pumped in and out.

The sounds she made as he pleasured her were music. Her breathless pleas were aphrodisiacs. The feel of her hands in his hair and on his shoulders made his heart clench with longing. Wrapping his leg around hers, Justin ground his cock into the soft flesh of her outer thigh in a vain effort to relieve the desperate ache.

Then he gave up and levered over her. Kneeling, he draped her legs over his thighs and pushed her chemise up over her breasts. "My God," he breathed, undone at the sight of her dishevelment. The wanton pose was the realization of his deepest carnal fantasies. "You are so beautiful."

His fingers caressed her from breast to cunt in featherlight adoration.

"Please," she cried, wiggling delightfully.

"Shh," he soothed, gripping his cock and angling it down to the tiny slitted entrance to her body. "You should watch, love. It will excite you."

Sophie pushed up onto her elbows and stared at where they almost joined. Rolling his hips, he eased into her, sinking into hot slick silk. The sight of his penetration moved them both. He hardened and grew thicker, she began to pant and flooded with moisture so plentiful it bathed his cock. As he had before, he took his time, memorizing every moment. The final surge to the root made him groan and grind against her, shoving himself as deep into her as he could go. She was stuffed full of him, a fit so perfect it made him want to howl with pleasure.

Her cunt fluttered rhythmically, betraying how close she was to coming. His thumb to her clitoris, he pushed her over, gritting his teeth as she milked his tortured cock with strong pulses.

"Yes," he growled, watching the orgasm move through her, watching her fall helpless to the passion that had gripped him alone for so long.

Only when she settled limply into the pillows did Justin begin to fuck her. Holding her hips, he withdrew to the tip, then thrust hard and deep. Out. In. Powerful, driving strokes straight into the heart of her. Hearing the sounds of flesh slapping against flesh, feeling the heavy weight of his balls striking the firm curve of her ass, listening rapturously to Sophie's sobbing pleas for more. Always more. He made no effort to coddle her sensibilities. She had to know how it would be between them, had to understand that while he loved her with a gentleman's heart he would fuck her with a man's primitive desire.

And she loved it. Loved him.

Justin's skin misted with sweat, then dripped with it, and still it went on, his fingertips bruising her flesh as he held her down. Pumping her to orgasm again so he could see the startled pleasure drift across her features and the way her green eyes dazed in the throes. As she convulsed around him, he released his control, tossing his head back with a guttural cry. The climax shook him, making him shudder and jerk violently with every hard, thick spurt of his seed inside her.

His jaw ached with the force with which he clenched it and he lowered into her open arms with gratitude. Nestled against her breast, he listened to her heart's desperate beating.

"I love you," she whispered, stroking the perspiration-slick length of his back. "Whatever happens, know that I return the depth of your affection."

"I will marry you," he returned, kissing the nipple closest to his mouth. "And I will know how you feel, because you shall tell me every day."

She said nothing, but her silence spoke a sad farewell.

Justin closed his eyes, and began to plan.

Chapter Seven

Freshly bathed with his hair still damp, the marquess paced in his study with his hands clasped at the small of his back. The hour was early, Sophie was still abed in her own chamber, having left his rooms just before dawn. He had hated that parting, temporary though it was. Hated that they could not be lazy and lie abed all day, wrapped up in each other.

"My lord, you summoned?"

He paused, turning to face the countess and his mother as they entered. He greeted them, gestured for them to sit on the settee, and then leaned back against the front of his desk.

With his arms crossed, he asked, "When you both conceived of this matchmaking scheme, did you consider all of the many impediments to marital bliss?"

The women shot furtive glances at one another.

"We've no notion of what you are talking about," his mother said finally.

Narrowing his gaze, the marquess studied his mother's gown, a near garish mix of flowery profusion that she somehow managed to make attractive. "Lady Sophie has declined my proposal of marriage."

Twin smiles spread across the two faces before him.

"Bright girl," the countess said with laughter in her voice, "I would not wish to be sneezed upon for the rest of my life either."

His mother grinned. "And this will spare your dogs from certain separation from you."

"I've no notion," he said dryly, "how I have retained even a modicum of sanity after spending most of my life around you three troublesome females."

"Forgive us, my lord," Lady Cardington said, blinking in an exaggerated show of innocence. "You must collect that we were under the impression that you and Lady Sophie did not suit."

His mouth curved. "If you think I am too proud to admit that you were correct, you shall be disappointed." Justin knew the effort his mother must be exerting to contain a crow of delight.

"So you wish to wed her?" she asked.

"Yes."

"And what of the boy?" the countess asked.

"He is a part of Sophie. His position in my life will equal hers."

"Oh, this is wonderful!" his mother said, clapping her hands gleefully.

"Yes, yes!" agreed the countess.

Affording the two a moment to relish their near success, Justin's gaze drifted around the room. Decorated in various shades of gray and blue and filled with stained walnut furnishings, it reminded him of a stormy day. He found himself contemplating what Sophie would think of such a somber setting. He wondered what shades she might have chosen. A lighter palette, he imagined. One more cheerful to suit her carefree personality.

He was madly in love, obviously. When a man spent his quiet moments reflecting on a woman's taste in decor, there was no denying it.

His mother's spine straightened and her face took on a

suitably serious mien. "Does she display a similar interest in you?"

"Yes." He rubbed his jaw, remembering the feel of Sophie's mouth moving across it with ardent kisses. "But she refuses to wed me with her tattered reputation. Somehow, we must make her acceptable. I assume you both would have considered this before pairing us."

The countess sighed. "She requires a great deal of support and something that would make her irresistible."

"You must first begin with Lord Rothschild," his mother instructed. "Restoring her brother's favor to her would be of immense help."

Justin nodded. "Yes, of course." He had considered that this morning while bathing, and believed he knew how he might convince the earl to bend in this.

"Then we must find something sensational, something that will make it much more advantageous to accept her than it is to snub her. Truly, if that Princess Caraboo creature can manage the task, our darling Sophie can do the same."

"Dear God." He cringed. "We want her to be acceptable, not a blasted curiosity!"

"No, no, of course not," Lady Cardington agreed. "We are simply pointing out that nearly anyone can become a welcome and celebrated personage under the right circumstances."

"I will leave those machinations up to you," he said, shaking his head. "That part of the affair sounds as if it needs a female mind to concoct it. But whatever mischief you conceive of, I want to hear of it before you act. Do I make myself clear?"

Two heads nodded in unison.

"I am departing shortly to attend to the matter of Rothschild." He pointed a chastising finger at both of them. "Keep Sophie out of trouble until I return."

"Yes, my lord."

He moved toward the door, pausing to kiss his mother and the countess on their cheeks. "Thank you," he murmured. "I owe you both a great deal for your meddling." "We do not meddle!" the dowager protested, affronted. Shaking his head, Justin departed.

A sennight later, impatience was riding the marquess hard as he vaulted down from his carriage in front of the impressive three-story columned entrance to Remington's Gentlemen's Club in London. Taking the steps two at a time, Justin strode swiftly through the watered glass double doors held open by black and silver liveried footmen. As he handed his hat and gloves to the waiting attendant, he took stock of his surroundings. Lucien Remington was acknowledged as a man of impeccable taste, and he ensured his establishment's position as the most exclusive in England by continuously updating the decor. Remington did not follow prevailing inclinations in design. He set the standard for them.

Justin noted the multitude of improvements with a suitably appreciative eye. The lay of the rooms remained the same. Straight ahead was the gaming area, which was the center of all business. From there, one could access the stairs to the fencing studio, courtesans, and private rooms above. The pugilist rings were on the lower floor. To the left, the bar and kitchen. Justin's destination—Lucien Remington's office—was to the right and he turned in that direction without further delay.

"Good afternoon, Lord Fontaine," the secretary greeted, leaping to his feet from his position behind a desk. He reached for the knob of the nearby door and opened it, ushering Justin in with due haste.

Remington glanced up at the intrusion and stood upon recognizing his expected visitor. "My lord." He bowed slightly in welcome.

"Remington."

The marquess's gaze swept across the room. The first thing one noticed upon entering was the carved mahogany desk that directly faced the door. The second, was the massive painting that hung above the fireplace. From there, the lovely Lady Julienne smiled, her dark eyes bright with happiness and love. Two strapping lads with the dark hair of their father stood behind either shoulder, and a young girl with the golden hair of their mother sat at her feet.

"Your wife grows lovelier by the day."

"I couldn't agree more." The softening of Remington's features as he glanced at the portrait revealed how deeply he loved his wife, a gently bred earl's daughter who had rejected Society in favor of a love match with a bastard. Once Remington had been a gazetted rake, his black-as-pitch hair and irises a unique shade of near purple had been irresistible to most women. Now he was known as a man unfashionably devoted to his spouse.

"You are a fortunate man," Justin said, feeling no ill will. Julienne had made the best choice for her happiness. Yes, marriage to him would have afforded her the social status due a woman of her breeding, but he knew that he would not have made her as content as Remington did.

"Yes," Remington agreed, "fairly impressive for a mongrel, some say."

Justin returned his attention to his host, finding Remington's lauded eyes filled with laughter as he alluded to the time when they had been rivals for Julienne's affections and Justin had disparaged Remington for his common breeding.

"You have not yet forgotten?" Justin asked, taking a seat before Remington's desk. The surface was littered with piles of paperwork, betraying the breadth of Remington's empire. The product of a long-standing romance between a demimondaine and a duke, his obscene wealth had been hard-won and was a source of great envy.

"I will never forget it, my lord." Remington moved to the row of decanters on the nearby console. "The moment those words were spoken, it was an uphill battle for you to win Julienne. I am not usually grateful for aristocratic arrogance, but in this case, I have made an exception."

Accepting the proffered libation, Justin smiled. "You will be surprised to learn the reason why I am here today, Remington. I do wish I could preserve the look on your face when I tell you."

"Hmm . . ." Remington resumed his seat, held his snifter in both hands, and arched both brows expectantly.

"Lord Rothschild is a member of your club, is he not?"

"Yes. Of course."

"Excellent. Perhaps you have extended credit to him in the past?"

Remington's gaze narrowed. "Where is this leading, my lord?"

"To a file of information, I hope," Justin said blithely. "You see, I wish to marry his sister, who is quite ruined. I would wed her regardless, but the obstinate woman refuses out of concern for me. She was disowned by Rothschild when the scandal broke and I am certain that adds to her reticence. Therefore, I must persuade him to accept her back into the fold. Publicly and dramatically."

His smile turned into a grin as Remington's face took on a noticeably shocked cast.

"For clarification, Fontaine: Are you asking me to disclose private information about a peer so that you may extort his cooperation in order to marry his scandalous, ostracized sibling?"

"Exactly! Extraordinary, is it not? Who would have guessed that I would one day do something so dastardly? And with such glee?"

"Not I," Remington said wryly. "I begin to think I was lucky that you conceded Julienne so easily."

Justin considered the man across from him carefully. "Oh?"

"You said you would fight for her, yet you never truly

did. You could have been a grave threat to me, had you chosen to be."

"She was in love with you and you made it clear that you reciprocated her feelings. You both had my reluctant sympathy. I did think she was daft to choose you, however. Gads, to think of the social heights she could have achieved as my wife!"

"Ah, now I recognize you, my lord," Remington said, laughing. Setting down his snifter he pushed to his feet and moved to the shelves on the wall to the left of the grate. Some action on his part exposed a hidden doorway, which in turn led to a hidden gallery. Remington disappeared into the opening, and a moment or two later he emerged with a thick file. He whistled low. "For your first effort at extortion, you selected a fat bird."

"Truly?" Justin stood, startled to realize how relieved he was. "Is there information I would find useful?"

Remington's mouth curled slightly at the corners. "Plenty."

The marquess crossed the room, set his glass down on the small table near the settee, and accepted the file. As he skimmed the contents, his mouth fell open. He shot a glance at Remington. "Damnation, how do you acquire such knowledge?"

"I have my ways," Remington said evasively.

"Have you such detailed observations about others?"

"When necessary."

"Bloody hell."

"The information I hold is quite safe, I assure you. Aside from my man-of-affairs, you are the only person I have ever allowed to see a personal file."

Justin nodded gravely. "I owe you a debt of gratitude."

Remington waved the comment away with a careless gesture. "Consider it my debt paid for doing your least to win Julienne."

"I should like to take some notes, if I could."

"Certainly."

A few moments later, after an attendant was summoned with fresh parchment and quill, Justin sat on the settee before the grate. A brief flash of light caught his eye, and he bent to investigate. When he straightened, he held aloft a lone tin soldier. The mental image of Remington's children here with Lady Julienne made him smile.

"Remington?"

"Yes, my lord?" Remington glanced up from his paperwork.

"Would you be so kind as to compile a small list of merchants I might visit to purchase amusements for a small boy?"

Remington's gaze moved to the toy and he grinned. "Certainly."

Justin nodded his gratitude, then returned his attention to his most pressing task and began to write.

First, to his mother:

> *. . . plan a dinner party. Make certain Lady Cardington and Lady Sophie are in attendance. Also invite the following . . .*

Then, to Lord Rothschild:

> *. . . requires a discussion regarding a matter of grave importance to both of us . . .*

And finally, he began to transcribe the most grievous, valuable, and intriguing information of that held in the file. All the while he thought of Sophie, wondering what she would think of the man he had become—one willing to go to any length for love.

Chapter Eight

Fontaine pulled his mount to a halt before the Earl of Rothschild's London townhouse. He imagined he should feel out of sorts or ill-at-ease at the very least. Instead he was determined and sure of his intent. In an hour or so, his life would be firmly set upon the path of his choosing. There was no way to avoid feeling triumphant about that.

Passing the reins to the waiting groomsman, the marquess climbed the short stairs with a decided spring to his step. Within moments, he was announced and shown into a large sitting room that boasted walls of pale gray woodwork inset with panels of grayish-green damask and a ceiling that was the canvas for an impressive mural featuring fat cherubs frolicking amongst fatter clouds. The overall impression was one of affluence, but Justin was well aware that, in this instance, appearances were deceiving.

"Lord Fontaine."

Turning his attention to the man who approached him, Justin noted the assured stride and uplifted chin of Sophie's brother. They were very much alike, the two Milton-Riley siblings. Physically similar in coloring and bearing, both tall and slender, yet there was a gulf between the two so wide they were nearly strangers to one another. Justin suspected it was due to the fact that they had been raised apart. Rothschild had been sent away to school, while Sophie resided with her *grand-mère*.

"Lord Rothschild," he greeted.

"An unexpected call," Rothschild said, returning the avid scrutiny with narrowed green eyes.

"Though not unwelcome, I hope."

"That remains to be seen, does it not? Grave matters are rarely pleasant."

Fontaine smiled and sank into the nearest chair, a narrow settee covered in soft green fabric and backed with intricately carved wood. "I have come bearing honorable intentions toward Lady Sophie."

The earl's eyes widened. A brief shocked silence filled the room, and then he threw his head back and laughed.

Bending down, Justin reached into the leather satchel he had set on the floor at his feet. He carefully withdrew the documents his solicitor had drawn up at his behest and passed them over. Rothschild's amused gaze turned to one of bewilderment as he accepted the proffered packet and settled into the seat opposite.

For a time, the only sounds in the room where those of pages turning and the ticking of the clock. Justin waited out the earl's reaction to his demands by studying the contents of the room, looking for any item that might match the articles mentioned in Remington's file.

"Dear God. Who arranged this farce?" Rothschild asked finally.

"I beg your pardon?"

Lifting his head, the earl blinked in obvious confusion. "I would not have thought you likely to be involved in a mockery of this magnitude. What wager did you lose to be pressed into this?"

"I am entirely sincere," Justin assured. "I wish to wed your sister and you shall make that possible."

"Are you serious?"

"Quite."

"Bloody hell." An incredulous silence filled the room for a long moment, then the earl snorted. "Have her, if you so desire, but the stipulations you make in this agreement are the ravings of a madman. I am free of her as it stands. I've no need to part with anything of value in order to accomplish that."

"True. I appeal to your gentleman's honor."

"You waste both of our afternoons with this nonsense." Rothschild stood, tossing the packet onto the small table between them.

"I ask only for the items that belong to Lady Sophie. I've no desire for anything beyond that."

"I will not simply hand them over to you, Fontaine, which will necessitate a lengthy courtroom drama while you attempt to prove ownership. You may have lost your head over Sophie, but I think there are limits to the amount of scandal you are capable of tolerating."

Justin's mouth curved grimly as he reached back into his satchel. He watched as the earl crossed the room to stand before the window. Rothschild appeared irritated, yes, but his frame also vibrated with a barely perceptible anxiousness that betrayed his concern. The earl was not ignorant. He would know that leverage of some sort was involved. The man was bluffing, as all gamblers were wont to do.

"I had hoped to keep this exchange on pleasant footing," Fontaine said easily, leaning forward to set a sealed document atop the table. Although he was completely focused on the nuances of the earl's physical reactions to his increasingly aggressive salvos, he kept his own exterior relaxed and innocuous.

Rothschild glanced over, his verdant gaze dropping to the tabletop. His hands were clasped at his back, stretching the dark broadcloth of his coat across his shoulders. Unlike many who found that addiction to gambling and the drinking of strong spirits went hand-in-hand, the earl was trim, fit, and known only as one who liked to wager on just about anything. Sadly, he wasn't very good at it.

Sighing, Sophie's brother returned to his previous seat to inspect the new offering and Justin turned his attention to a small statue that graced one of several artfully arranged bookcases. The many volumes that lined the shelves were displayed in every possible fashion—on their sides, spine outward, and front-facing. In between, various antiquities waited to be admired and coveted.

It was not long before the earl made some hideous noise that was something between a strangled gasp and a sob.

"By God!" Rothschild sputtered. "Where did you get this information?"

The marquess shrugged. "I have my ways."

"You cannot prove any of this!"

"Do I need to?" Looking at the earl, Fontaine raised both brows in silent query. "What a deucedly nasty business that would be. Of course, it might be worth it. Your scandal might take some of the attention away from mine. Yours is decidedly more lurid, I think you will agree."

Rothschild's face flushed with anger and embarrassment. "You do not understand my position."

"Oh, I think I do. You and Sophie were bequeathed a modest collection of Egyptian antiquities by a French relative, and you are presently using them to guarantee your markers."

"So, you see, I must retain them."

"No, *you* must see that I do not care about your predicament. I might have been more accommodating had you shown even a modicum of support for your sister when she needed it most, but you did not, so I shall not." The marquess rocked back on his heels. "Instead I shall drag you unwillingly up to my estate in Northamptonshire where you will dine with your sister and several highly esteemed members of the peerage who happen to have a fascination with antiquities. You will support her now, as you did not previously."

A cold, hard edge entered Rothschild's eyes. "You think you can make her suitable? You are delusional."

"I think I can make her an Eccentric, and that, Rothschild, will make her acceptable to other Eccentrics. It is a beginning."

What followed was a tedious hour of complaining, cajoling, and conniving that resulted nevertheless in Rothschild ordering his valet to prepare for a journey north. With such a disagreeable companion in tow, Justin anticipated a miserable trip, but as he watched the loading of the earl's trunks onto the rear of his coach, he was grinning from ear to ear regardless.

"Dear heavens, he's done it!" the dowager Lady Fontaine cried.

She lifted her gaze from the boldly slashed penmanship of her son, and smiled at her dearest friend. She had gratefully accepted the invitation to join the countess and Sophie on their return to their residence, despite her concern that her removal from Northamptonshire would delay word. She should not have worried. Fontaine had written directly to the Cardington dower property, having anticipated her inability to wait out news alone. "He has convinced Lord Rothschild to assist us."

Lady Cardington clapped her hands, the tension that had gripped her slight frame upon the arrival of the post dissipating with a relieved smile. "His lordship has hidden depths. Of course, we both knew that."

"Yes, we did." The dowager refolded the short missive carefully. "But now we have work to do, Caroline."

Blowing out her breath, Lady Cardington set her shoulders back. "What is required of us?"

"We are to arrange a gathering." Leaning forward, the dowager passed the letter over. "I have no notion how we shall manage the guest list he has demanded."

Caroline rose from her floral slipper chair and moved to the walnut escritoire in the corner where her spectacles waited. "We shall lie and elaborate." She gazed out the window to where Sophie walked beside Thomas in the rear garden. "We need only to entice them to come. The rest we leave to Fontaine and Sophie."

"Did you truly attempt to climb to the top of the pagoda?"

Sophie glanced down at her son with a sheepish smile. "I did."

"I am glad I was not here to see it," Thomas said, gazing up at her with Langley's dark eyes. "I would have been frightened for you."

"Then perhaps you can understand why I was so frightened when I found you attempting the feat yourself."

"I thought you were angry."

She set her hand atop his unruly chocolate brown waves. "No, not angry, darling. Terrified."

Looking at the structure, she remembered fragments of the day when Fontaine had caught her hanging from the roof's edge.

"By God, you mad creature!" he'd cried, just before he wrapped his arms around her waist and pulled her free, spilling them both to the grass in a tangle of limbs.

He had been shaking with fury, or so she had believed at the time. Now she realized how he must have felt and her heart hurt. How could she have been so blind to his feelings for her?

She sighed. She suspected she knew why. Confusion at the loss of her parents and the lack of connection to her only sibling had made it difficult for her to perceive affection. She had been angry at the world, and therefore saw only anger returned to her.

"I have been invited to visit the Fontaine estate again," Sophie said, dropping her hand to link fingers with Thomas's grubby ones. They rounded the corner and she gestured to a crescent-shaped marble bench beneath a tree.

"I like Lady Fontaine."

"So do I." Although it was Justin who had requested her return in a short but sweet note that offered a chance at happiness. However, there was more at stake than her feelings. "Would you be upset if I went?"

Thomas appeared to consider the question carefully. "You have been sad since you returned."

Sophie blinked, startled that he had been perceptive enough to notice. "I miss a friend."

"Will you see your friend again when you go?"

"Yes."

"Then I will not be upset, though I will miss you."

With watering eyes, Sophie pulled Thomas into her lap and hugged him tightly to her. He wriggled and squirmed, protesting indignantly. And then he settled into her arms with an exasperated sigh.

"Thank you," she said, when she had collected herself.

He squeezed her back and then climbed off her lap. "Since I cannot climb, can we catch insects?"

"I suppose."

With a whoop of joy, Thomas led the way to the nearest bush. And for the first time in a very long time, Sophie felt hope.

Chapter Nine

Sophie jumped when the knock came to the door of her guest chamber in the Fontaine manse. She was not high-strung by nature—energetic, yes, but prone to nerves, no—but on this occasion she could not help it. When she had arrived that afternoon she'd taken note of the Rothschild crest on the travel coach in the drive. For the first time in many years she was sharing the same roof as her brother. In fact, she was fairly certain it was the first time they had been in the same province since their parents had passed on.

She rushed to the door and pulled it open. "Lady Fontaine," she greeted as she saw who called on her.

The dowager was already dressed for dinner, her slender figure encased in cream colored satin skirts capped with a forest green bodice. Her blonde hair was artfully curled and her wrists, ears, and throat were adorned with brilliant emeralds rimmed with diamonds. Altogether, she presented a picture of elegant, affluent, mature beauty, and the care she displayed in her choice of attire was a vivid reminder of how important tonight would be.

"Lady Sophie."

Dipping into a swift curtsy, Sophie hoped she hid her disappointment. As focused as she was on Rothschild, she was equally focused on Fontaine. To know that he was so close . . .

to imagine him relaxed in his den, the place where he had loved her so ardently and so skillfully . . .

Her body thrummed in response to her yearning, and she released her breath in a rush. She had hoped to find him on the opposite side of the door, although she had known it would be far too risky an action for him to take with so many guests about. Her silly heart did not care about the reasonableness of its expectations. It cared only about its infatuation with Justin.

"Do not tax yourself worrying," the dowager said with a reassuring curve to her lips, misunderstanding. "I am duly impressed with Fontaine's arrangements and feel comfortable advising you to leave everything within his capable hands."

Sophie nodded. "I trust him."

"Of course you do. He is a most trustworthy man. He does nothing in half-measure. You can be certain that he has no doubts regarding the outcome of this evening. He would not risk your unhappiness."

Sophie lifted her chin and smiled. The thought of her love for Justin straightened her spine and strengthened her determination to make the night a success, whatever he had planned. "I will make him happy."

"I know you will." The dowager gestured down the hall. "I offer you the use of my abigail and my rooms for dressing. Everything you need awaits you there."

It was odd that the dowager would see to such a task herself, rather than sending her maid to Sophie, but Sophie didn't question the offer, or how it was presented. She simply expressed her gratitude and followed Lady Fontaine down the gallery until they reached their destination.

Stepping into the lovely suite of rooms decorated in varying shades of gold, wine, and pink, Sophie was immediately arrested by the profusion of boxes set atop the chaise. Big and small, it appeared that every size and shape imaginable was represented.

"I took the liberty of peeking," the countess confessed. "Fontaine has excellent taste. I hope you agree."

The thought of wearing garments selected by the marquess caused a low quiver of excitement in Sophie's belly.

"He also spent much of this afternoon upstairs in the nursery," Lady Fontaine continued, "finding and setting aside his favorite toys from childhood for Master Thomas."

Sophie's eyes stung at the mental image those words evoked. The countess seemed to understand. After a gentle squeeze of Sophie's shoulder, she departed the room in silence.

Riveted in place, Sophie allowed the tears to fall. She could not have foreseen that she would fall in love again, but there was no doubt. She was giddy with it.

The door reopened and then closed behind her. The sudden flare of awareness across her skin revealed the identity of her visitor.

She inhaled deeply, then turned to face him. Justin lounged against the closed portal in a sultry pose so rakish it aroused a hot, carnal longing. He had loved her body long and well, and she craved more of the same.

"My lord," she breathed, dipping into a slow curtsy. She could not move any faster. The sight of him made her heart race until she felt dizzy. She stared, drinking him in, unable to do otherwise. He was different now than he had ever been. The infamous, chilly hauteur was nowhere to be found. He was warm and vibrant, the air around him charged with energy.

"My lady," he returned, the corner of his mouth lifting as he straightened and came toward her. Dressed in tight breeches, white waistcoat, and artfully tied cravat, he was devastatingly handsome. The effect he had on her was so powerful that despite the gloves he wore, when he lifted her hand to his lips, her skin tingled.

"You mustn't look at me in that manner in front of the others," she whispered.

"In what manner?"

"As if you are besotted."

The slow curving of his sensual mouth made her heart race. "I have always looked at you this way. After all these years, I cannot change it now."

"Justin . . ."

"You must be unaware of how you look at me. I may look besotted, but your returning perusal is indecent."

"Indecent?"

"As if you wish to lick me from head to toe, and nibble on everything in between."

The scent of starch and bergamot teased her nostrils. He was so close, she could feel the warmth that radiated from him.

"I do wish to do that," she admitted.

Her confession elicited a groan from deep in his throat, followed immediately by the banding of his arms around her and the lifting of her feet from the floor. Tilting his head, he took her mouth with a passion that stole her wits. Sophie could only cling to his broad shoulders and kiss him back with like desperation.

He pulled back with a deep timbral laugh, turning his head when she pursued him for more. "I did not come here for this, love."

Sophie stuck her lower lip out in a pout, and he nipped it playfully with his teeth. "Did you miss me?" he purred.

"Sometimes." He arched an arrogant brow and she wrinkled her nose. "Most of the time."

Fontaine grinned.

"All of the time," she amended, blushing.

"How lovely you are when you blush," he murmured in an intimate, possessive tone that made her toes curl. He pressed his lips to the tip of her nose and then set her down.

"What have you planned?" she asked, studying him for signs of unease. She found none.

"In the family parlor, you will find Lady Cardington

entertaining an elderly gentleman who is endlessly fasci-
nated by a small statue, which I collected along with Rothschild from his London residence. In return for promised
access to study the thing, he has agreed to school you on its
finer points."

"A statue?"

"Yes. A small part of a larger collection of valuable antiquities that belongs to you."

"To me?"

"Yes." His blue eyes laughed at her. "My darling, I adore
you."

Sophie shook her head with a smile. "You must."

"Once you feel comfortable enough discussing the subject, the three of you will join us in the lower drawing room
where your brother will greet you as if you are both fond of
one another. Can you follow along with the ruse?"

"I can do anything if it means you will be mine."

Justin reached for her again. In the decidedly feminine
surroundings of his mother's suite, his blatant masculinity
was even more compelling. "I have waited a lifetime for
you to want me."

"I will want you for a lifetime." She cupped his cheek,
her thumb drifting across the cleanly shaven skin. "Will
that make up for the delay?"

"Hmmm . . ."

"Something else, then?" Her hand slid around to cup his
nape. There, the silky smooth ends of his hair curled around
his collar and tickled her knuckles. She pressed her lips to
his ear and whispered, "Some licking and nibbling, perhaps?"

"Yes," he said hoarsely, his body hard and tense against
hers. "That might do it."

"So . . . I am to greet Rothschild as if we are the closest
of siblings," she repeated, "and discuss my heretofore unknown antiquity with feigned knowledge, and then?"

"Then we will spend the evening listening to Rothschild

enlighten us about your collection while pretending that we knew everything he is saying prior to him saying it. The other esteemed gentlemen will weigh in with their thoughts and eventually one of them will have the poor manners to yawn, freeing us to retire."

Sophie wriggled seductively. "And then?"

"Minx."

"Will you be mine then?"

"I have always been yours."

"You will make me cry," she sniffled.

"No." His smile was wicked. "I will make you limp with pleasure. Then I will make you my wife."

Chapter Ten

Justin slouched before the fire in his bedchamber with a brandy-filled goblet in one hand and George's head nuzzled in the other. He watched the blue flames in the grate and thought of Sophie, so dazzlingly beautiful in the gown he had wheedled out of the modiste. It had cost him a bloody fortune to convince the woman that the garment would receive more attention on Sophie than it would on the woman for whom it was originally made. But he would gladly pay the amount a hundred times over to have the same result.

The countess and his mother had wanted something sensational, and he would like to think he had managed to accomplish that.

The soft knock he waited for finally came. Leaping to his feet, he startled the dogs and spilled his libation as he set it hastily on a table as he rushed past. Justin threw open the door and his heart clenched.

"Sophie."

She said nothing, but words weren't necessary. Her dazzling smile was enough. He looked quickly to the left and right, to be certain she was not seen, then he caught her hand and pulled her into his bedchamber.

He locked the door and shooed the dogs into the sitting room. When he turned back, he found her waiting where he had left her. With great, joyful strides Justin caught her up and lifted her high. She set her hands on his shoulders and threw her head back, laughing as he spun them about.

"I began to despair," he said, setting her on her feet so that he could pull her into his embrace. "I thought perhaps I would not see you until morning, a delay I would find unbearable."

Sophie's eyes gazed luminously up into his. "As if I could stay away," she whispered. "I was near desperate to be alone with you all evening."

"Well then, I forgive you for making me wait," he said magnanimously, making her smile.

"I love you, you arrogant man." Cupping his nape, she pulled his head down to steal a kiss.

For a moment, he allowed her the lead, then the scent of her skin and the feel of her body inflamed him. Her soft mouth was parted and moving feverishly against his.

Breathing hard, he somehow managed to wrench his head away. "Will you consent to marry me now?"

"How can you ask questions at a time such as this?" she complained. "We have been apart for weeks on end."

"I've learned extortion has its uses. My title, which usually lures women in droves, is a deterrent to you. But you seem to enjoy my body well enough. If I have to withhold it from you to gain your acceptance, I will do it. Much as it will pain me."

The soft glaze of lust in her eyes turned to rich amusement. "I still cannot collect how you extorted that performance out of Rothschild this evening."

He grinned. "What do you think of that?"

"I think my influence is already corrupting you." She cupped his cheek in the palm of her hand. "Was he telling the truth?"

"About the value of the antiquities bequeathed to you? Yes. Rothschild has been using them to guarantee his markers, which are not inconsiderable."

"All that excitement displayed over that little statue . . . Incredible!"

"Quite. Adventurers such as Belzoni have fueled the great interest in such things, fortunately for us. Your collection, while small, is priceless." It took some clever maneuvering on his mother's part to lure both lauded experts in the field and members of the peerage who were avidly engaged in the topic to his estate in Northamptonshire on such short notice. But somehow the task was managed, resulting in a dinner party that would not be forgotten for some time. "You are now an eccentric collector of some means, which grants you a bit more license."

"And my once barren social calendar has become filled with numerous invitations to display the rest of my private collection."

"Once word spreads, you will scarcely be able to keep up. As long as those items can be seen only through you and not a museum, you shall be in some demand."

She shook her head. "How did you learn of Rothschild's deception?"

"I have my ways."

"My darling." Sophie lifted to her tiptoes and pressed a kiss to his chin. "How will I ever do you justice?"

"Never mind that nonsense. Simply say yes." He rocked his hips suggestively against her. "I have something you want and I am quite desperate to give it to you."

Her laughter was music to his ears. "Yes, you wicked man. Yes!"

Sophie rubbed her breasts into his chest, brushing his lapels open so that only the material of her bodice and chemise separated her nipples from his skin. The brazen advance undid him, bringing to life fantasies he had cherished in his youth and again as a man. She gazed up at him seductively beneath long, thick lashes. "Now, will you take me to your bed?"

He growled and lifted her, taking the few steps necessary

to reach the nearest wall so he could pin her roughly against it. She gasped softly at the impact, her arms at her sides, her hands pressed palms down against the damask.

"The bed is too far away," he said gruffly, shrugging out of his robe.

"Dear God," she breathed when he stood naked before her.

He stroked himself, lengthening and thickening his cock, watching her pupils dilate with a similar desire to the one that raged within him.

Impassioned, he caged her between his arms, his mouth at her throat, his teeth nipping the sensitive skin. "Pull up your gown."

He felt her swallow hard beneath his lips. "*Here?*"

"Yes, here. I want to lick you, Sophie love," he purred, his hands moving all over her, rediscovering all the curves and valleys of her body. "I want to put my mouth on you, eat at you, kiss you between your legs—" he took her mouth with lush, deep flicks of his tongue—"just like this."

"Yes." Her head fell to the side, baring her throat to him. He felt her hands between them, pulling up her skirts. Her movements brushed against his cock, and his jaw tensed. His gut cramped tight, lust warring with deeper, more powerful emotions.

He reached down and cupped her, parted her, finding her cunt slick and hot and soft as satin. He tested her with a gently probing finger, the feel of her grasping tissues pushing him beyond any hope of restraint.

"Bloody hell." Sinking to his knees, he lunged for the pulsing flesh between her legs and covered it with his open mouth.

Sophie jerked violently at the shocking sensation of a lover's kiss in her most intimate place. Her senses were overwhelmed with the sight and smell of him, her heart racing at the boldness of his actions. The growling sounds he made as his tongue flickered desperately over the clenching opening of her sex made her knees weak. He held her upright and draped her leg over his shoulder, giving her the support she needed to bear the exquisite torment while opening her further to his relentless demands.

Her fingers dug into the wall. The sounds of the ticking clock and her labored exhales were muted by the blood roaring in her ears. She looked down, watching the way the fire reflected in the golden strands of Justin's hair. He held her open with his fingers, nuzzling his parted lips against her, worshiping her with reverent kisses. The sight of her gown held to her waist and the beautifully built man on his knees before her was deeply, searingly erotic.

"I need you." Her eyes slid closed and her hot cheek pressed against the cool damask. "Please . . ."

Justin tilted his head and pushed his tongue deep, the slight roughness of early stubble on his chin rasping against the sensitive skin of her inner thighs. She keened softly at the shallow, teasing plunges, nowhere near satisfying, but wonderful nevertheless. In and out. Piercing her hard and fast. He ate at her with near ravenous hunger, groaning in a way that made her cup her breasts and squeeze, fighting the aching swelling.

"Please," she begged, twisting and arching, rocking into his mouth. "Please . . ."

He altered position, moving higher, his agile tongue fluttering rapidly over the tight bundle of nerves that begged for his attention.

The surge of release hit her hard.

She cried out and clung to his perspiration-slick shoulders as the climax stole her wits. He continued to torment her, to lick her on the outside and the inside, pushing her to orgasm again. This time she could only whimper as her sex spasmed madly.

"Beautiful," he praised, his voice husky and low. "I believe I shall do that every day."

Flushed and panting for air, Sophie was still quivering

violently when Fontaine pushed to his feet and carried her to the bed.

Laying her on her side, he exposed the back of her gown and began to free the long row of buttons. The task was a lengthy one, giving her the time she needed to return to herself. When she was finally nude and he was levering over her, she was ready, her arms and legs opening wide in welcome. His lean hips settled against her, and his arms—so strong and warm—embraced her in a cocoon of bergamot and tobacco-scented male that she never wanted to leave.

How quickly her need had reached this level. And yet she did not doubt her feelings. Or his. They were simply there, inside her, feelings of connection that had made separation a misery. Talking with him and being with him were gifts she had always enjoyed. Now lusting for him was a state she had come to crave in her life. Waking in the morning and knowing that the new day would have him in it brought her a kind of joy she had thought never to feel again. It was not the same sensation as she had felt for Langley, but it was every bit as wonderful. She knew Justin so well, and more important, he knew her so well. Better than anyone, she thought. And he loved her in spite of her faults, or maybe even because of them.

"Share your thoughts," he murmured, as the broad head of his cock lodged at the entrance to her body.

She set her hands on his shoulders. "I want to make love to you in the sunshine so I can see every inch of you without shadow. I so love to look at you when you are inside me."

The smile he gave her was warm and wicked. It made her breath catch and her heart leap. "Ah, love. Promise me you will always be wild."

"Because of you," she breathed. "You make it safe for me to take risks. You always have."

He pushed the first thick inches of his beautiful cock into her and she gasped, her back arching upward as her body attempted to contain such pleasure.

"Sophie . . ." A violent shudder coursed the length of his frame.

She panted, writhing beneath him. "Th–that feels delicious."

It was more than Justin could take, that throaty praise. He held her hips down, and plunged deep.

Sophie's broken cry as he hilted had him groaning in near pain. She was tight as a fist around him, and swollen from his previous ministrations.

"Hold still," he ordered hoarsely, sucking in air like a man too long under water. Her cunt was rippling along his cock, sucking him deeper, luring him to forgo courtesy and fuck her until neither of them had the energy required to go on.

"I can't bear it," she sobbed, scratching him, struggling in her impatience, urging him to ride her to the finish.

Christ, but he loved it. Loved her. Had always loved her. He relished having her, owning her, and the way everything in his world had altered irrevocably because of her. His future, so orderly and well planned just weeks ago, was now an adventure waiting to happen.

His thighs flexed against hers as he kept her pinned, and fucked her slow and deep. Rolling his hips. Making her beg more, because it drove his lust higher to hear how desperately she craved his body inside hers.

"Justin," she moaned, arching her breasts upward to press against his chest, their skin sticking together with the sweat of their exertions. His head lowered, his lips fastening on a tightened nipple, his cheeks hallowing as he drew on her in long pulls that mimicked the stroking of his cock inside her.

He rode her at length, thrusting between her spread thighs in a lazy, sensual rhythm, feeling her climax again. And again. Such a passionate woman. Her body quaking beneath his, stirring his ardor further until the sheets were fisted in his white-knuckled grip and he was driving powerfully into her. The tension coiled in his shoulders, slid down his spine, and gathered at the base of his aching cock. He was so hard, so ferociously aroused, he almost feared the impending orgasm.

When it came, it tore guttural cries from his throat. Killing him. He shuddered violently and she clung to him, his darling Sophie. She whispered to him, anchored him, so that the violent spewing of his seed inside her was not the loss of his soul, but the merging of hers to his.

He pumped hard and fast into her, taking her over the edge with him.

Fitted to him, the other half of a whole.

With her cheek on Fontaine's chest and her legs intertwined with his, Sophie spoke of her son. Countless moments of joy and discovery.

He listened quietly, his hands stroking down the length of her spine. "I wish I could alleviate your concerns."

"You will," she said, her mouth curving against his skin. "I adore you. I fail to see how anyone could not."

She felt his cock twitch against her thigh and raised her head to meet his gaze. Sprawled against a pile of pillows and lying amid monogrammed white sheets, the marquess was unbearably handsome. He looked disheveled and thoroughly sated, an appearance that flattered him so well she found her passions rising along with his. His big, hard body was a finely wrought instrument of pleasure, and the golden skin that covered the lean lengths of muscle was so sensitive to her attentions. She could make him groan with the slightest of touches. "Will I always be able to rouse you with a compliment?"

"You rouse me by breathing, love." He winked and scratched at the center of his chest. "And I adore you, too."

Sophie stared at him a moment, comparing the warm man whose bed she shared with the cooler, more reserved boy she remembered.

"We should depart as soon as possible," he said. "I would like to meet your son."

"How soon?"

"As soon as we can urge our guests to depart."

She kissed his jaw in silent gratitude. "Good. I miss him."

"I know." He hugged her tightly. "You will be together again as quickly as I can manage it."

She heard the faintest trace of worry in his tone, and understood how hard this must be for him. How would she feel, were he to have a child to win over? Knowing how deep the bond between parent and child was, and wondering if she would ever be even a small part of that connection, or if she would forever be an unwanted intrusion. It made her love him all the more that he was willing to make so many changes to his life and take so many risks just to be with her.

Pinching the sheet with two fingers, Sophie tugged it downward until the edge reached his upper thighs and his cock was bared to her gaze. A quick glance upward found him watching her with eyes that glittered in the near darkness.

"I want to kiss you here," she said, circling his cock with gentle fingers. "Such as you did to me."

"Feel free." A hint of laughter had replaced the apprehension in his voice.

The sound made her smile.

"I've come to be wary when you wear that mischievous look," he said.

Sophie fluttered her lashes innocently. "Mischief? Me?"

"Ha!"

She crawled over him and settled between his spread legs. The pattern of his breathing changed, became faster as the muscles in his thighs tensed. Her breasts brushed against his skin and his breath hissed out between his teeth. The power she held to give him pleasure was heady, as was the sight of his body, which aroused her to a fever pitch. Her hand closed around him and angled his throbbing cock to meet her eager mouth.

"Christ!" Justin arched off the bed as Sophie's soft, wet lips surrounded him.

He had been serviced this way countless times, yet it had never felt like this. He was ready to blow. After his recent galvanic orgasm, he should be able to enjoy a lazy climb to the peak. Instead, he was gritting his teeth to prevent toppling over.

"Umm . . ." she purred, lifting her head. "I like this. I believe I shall do this every day."

He choked. The sight of her mouth poised just above his cock was a fantasy he had cherished for years. To think of such pleasure daily . . . "You'll kill me."

"You'll bear it." Sophie pumped her hand and his hips jerked.

"Bloody hell!"

Cum beaded the tip of his cock. He watched in an agony of lust as her tongue came out and licked up the drop. The sound she made, one of deep pleasure, made his balls draw up.

"Suck it," he groaned, reaching for her, cupping her cheeks so that he could feel her mouth open. He felt his hardness through the softness of her cheek, and gasped as her tongue lifted and stroked the sensitive underside of his shaft.

The next he knew he was writhing atop the linens, his jaw aching with the force with which he clenched it, his arms tense and fingers cramped as he forced himself to hold her gently.

Sweet Sophie was driving him insane, her hungry mouth sucking and sucking, her cheeks hollowing with every drawing pull, her head bobbing in a wild, unrestrained rhythm as if loving him this way was for her pleasure alone.

Dear God, he was going to die. He was muttering and

cursing and begging, wanting her to stop. Wanting her never to stop.

Her gentle fingers cupped his tight sac and squeezed gently, rolling his balls, heating them with the warmth of her palm. His eyes widened with the knowledge that he was about to come, his throat working to warn her, but no sound came out.

With the last of his strength he pushed her away. Her response was a growl and hard, deep suction.

He came like a geyser, groaning, blasting deep into the welcoming depths of her mouth. Her hand urgently stroked the length of him that would not fit inside her, pumping his cum up the shaft to spill over her working tongue. She wouldn't stop, the demented female, taking to him to heights of pleasure he'd never reached, then carrying him back down with long, savoring licks.

The mattress cradled him as he sank into it, devastated. Then it was Sophie who cradled him, her lush body coming to rest over his, her cheek settling over his madly beating heart.

"I love you," he whispered, his damp face nestled in her fragrant hair, his arms hugging her close. "Christ, I love you so much."

He felt her press a kiss into his chest. He gazed up at the canopy above them and basked in his contentment. The days ahead would bring challenges, but if the nights ended thusly, he would bear them all with nary a complaint.

"I will make you happy," he promised. "I will do my best to make Thomas happy."

"I know, my love," she crooned.

"But," his tone was a warning, "if you ever blow pepper up my nose again, I will take my hand to your arse."

"Perhaps I shall like that," she teased mischievously.

His cock twitched wearily, insanely interested despite being spent. "Bloody hell."

Chapter Eleven

The day promised to be bright and beautiful the morning Justin began his campaign to win over the young Master Thomas. His mind was occupied with possible things to say, suggestions for activities they could share, answers to questions that may be asked of him. It was a dreadfully taxing business, this. The happiness of his fiancée rested on his ability to bond with her child. It therefore meant a great deal to him.

He intended to give the boy an active and prominent role in the wedding, but that plan would only succeed if the child was willing. To that aim he intended to make a nuisance of himself until they were friends. Of course, the emotions behind the plan were nowise near as simple as that.

He was nervous such as he had never been. Standing before the mirror that morning, he had rejected several cravats and coats, trying to picture himself through a five-year-old child's eyes. Would Sophie's son find him distant and hard to approach, as some adults did? Would Thomas resent him for winning some of his mother's affection?

Filled with concerns and doubts, Justin took a deep, fortifying breath as the golden-bricked manor house came into view. Despite his mental preparations, he felt in need of a stiff drink by the time he reached the end of the front drive.

He dismounted and handed the reins to the waiting groomsman. Then he took the steps to the front door two at a time. Before he could knock, the portal swung open and Sophie was launching herself into his arms. His heart stuttered at the feel of her and he crushed her close.

"My lord," she greeted, lifting to her toes and kissing him full on the mouth.

"Stop that," he admonished, glancing nervously over her head. "What if he sees you?"

"My darling." Her eyes sparkled. "How I love you. Thomas is in the nursery and cannot witness my affection."

"You might be surprised. When I was his age, I was never where anyone would expect."

Common courtesy dictated that they share tea with the countess first and so they did, both of them enjoying the obvious happiness Lady Cardington felt over their union.

And then it was time.

With her fingers linked with his, Sophie led him up to the nursery on the upper floor.

"Ready?" she asked when they reached the closed door.

"Yes." As he would ever be.

She pushed the portal open and entered. "Tommy," she called, her voice pitched sweetly.

"Hmm?"

The distracted sounding reply made Justin smile. He stepped into the sunshine-filled room and found the source of his anxiousness seated innocuously on an English rug surrounded by a legion of tin soldiers. Nearby, on the window bench, a governess knitted quietly.

"I would like you to meet someone," Sophie said, sinking to a crouch.

The small, dark head lifted, revealing handsome features and big brown eyes. Justin tensed as Thomas turned his head and found him, steeling himself for an unknown reaction.

Sophie made the introductions.

"Hello, Master Thomas," Justin said carefully.

"Hello, my lord." The boy's inquisitive gaze dropped to the marquess's riding boots. He frowned, then looked back at his toys.

Justin thought he had been summarily dismissed, which tied his stomach in knots, then Thomas picked up a soldier and held it out to him. "This one has boots like yours."

"Oh?" Bending at the knees, Justin accepted the offering and remarked, "So he does. How lucky I am to have such boots."

Thomas smiled. The gesture was Sophie's in miniature, and Justin's chest tightened. He sank the rest of the way to the floor.

"You can play with the red ones," Thomas said magnanimously. "I shall be blue."

"Thank you. I should like that very much." Justin glanced at Sophie. She blew him a kiss that went straight to his heart, then rose and moved to the bookcase.

"Shall I read you both a story?" she asked, in a voice huskier than usual.

"Yes! The fables." Thomas glanced at him. "You do enjoy fables, don't you, my lord?"

"I do."

The child beamed. "Excellent."

And so it was a beginning. Auspicious, to be sure.

Epilogue

Tiptoeing carefully through the maze in the rear garden, Sophie shivered slightly at the thrill of being hunted. Somewhere, her husband was searching for her. She knew that the longer she kept him waiting, the hotter his blood would run. Just a sennight ago, she had managed to evade him for almost a half hour, and when he'd caught her . . .

She stifled a moan as sudden lewd images filled her mind and made her lustful. She would never look at the alcove near the music room in quite the same way again.

A twig snapped, and Sophie dropped to a crouch. She waited with bated breath, then, when she felt certain the way was clear, she crawled through a small gap and emerged in the neighboring row.

"Caught you!"

Screeching, Sophie flailed slightly as she was hauled to her feet, then the maze fell silent as Justin smothered her protest with a deep, possessive, toe-curling kiss.

"Umm . . ." she moaned, rubbing against his big, hard body. "You, my lord, give perfect kisses."

He pulled back far enough to reveal his silently chastising arched brow. "Do not attempt to distract me from your mischief, Lady Fontaine. A woman in your condition should not be crawling through bushes."

"Nonsense!" she protested.

"It is not nonsense. Shall we ask Thomas how he feels about your activities?"

Sophie pouted. "You have me at an unfair advantage. The two of you are always joining forces."

"Because we love you. He is desperate for a sibling, as you well know since he has plagued us for one since the day we wed." Justin pressed a lingering kiss to her forehead. "You mustn't overtax yourself, love."

Wrapping her arms around his lean waist, she rested her cheek against his heart and sighed. "I am only a few months along. Besides, I feel the need to point out that sharing your bed can be far more strenuous."

That comment earned her a gentle swat to the derriere. "Insatiable wench." He linked his fingers with hers and led them out of the maze. "I beg to service you with my mouth and have you plead for my cock until I can either do as you ask or never manage a moment's rest."

"You have a divine mouth," she murmured, hugging his arm. "I love it, as I love all of you. But that other part you mention is . . ." Sophie purred softly. "Well, it is quite irreplaceable."

He shot her a scorching side-glance, and she grinned impishly in reply. They approached the manse with rapid strides, their eagerness to be alone and as close as two people can be goading them to haste.

"My lord! Come swiftly!"

They paused at the sound of Thomas's cry. Turning their heads, they found him standing at the edge of the garden.

Just beyond him was the stream and by the looks of his wet pants, muddy sleeves, and beleaguered-looking tutor he had been enjoying himself immensely there. George and Edward sat on their haunches to the left and right of him, guarding him as they'd been doing since the first night the three had slept under the same roof. They shared his room now, which suited everyone perfectly.

Justin lifted his hand and waved.

Thomas rimmed his mouth with both hands to amplify his voice and shouted, "I found a five-legged frog!"

The deep pride revealed on her husband's face brought tears to Sophie's eyes. Being *enceinte*, she was more emotional than usual, but the depth of affection Fontaine bore for her son had moved her from the beginning. It was one of the many reasons she loved him as she did—with every breath in her body.

"We must go see this wonder of nature," he murmured.

"Yes, my love." She lifted their linked hands and pressed a kiss to his knuckles. "We must."

"Pregnancy suits her," the dowager marchioness said to her dearest friend as they admired the handsome family from their vantage on the rear terrace.

"Most decidedly," Lady Cardington agreed, stirring sugar into her tea.

The gentle summer breeze pressed Sophie's golden muslin skirts to her body, revealing a softly swelling belly. "I cannot tell you how it affects me to see her so happy. She was deeply grieving when she carried Thomas. It was difficult to see such a happy event marred by such despair."

The dowager offered a sympathetic smile. "She is an admirable woman, Caroline."

"And your son is an admirable man, strong enough to make decisions with his heart and disregard those who have smaller minds. I knew they would be perfect together." Shaking her head, Lady Cardington rearranged the cashmere blanket that warmed her legs. "Those two. You do realize that I have never looked at pepper the same way again?"

"Oh, dear heavens, neither have I! But you did warn me."

"Yes. She was a fanciful child. Always concocting some mischief or tall tale. I had thought that light within her had died with Langley, but Fontaine's affection has restored it."

"And Sophie has shown him a different view of the

world that has altered him for the better. They are well-met. Of course, you and I knew that from the beginning."

The two women leaned back in their wrought-iron chairs and shared a secret smile.

"Beautifully done," one said to the other.

The laud was apropos of both of them.

THE RUBY KISS

Noelle Mack

Chapter One

London, 1856

Susannah was wearing the corset. From his vantage point, looking in her window from the balcony of his townhouse next door, Carlyle Jameson could see it and more. What a glorious woman.

She heaved a sigh and Carlyle almost stopped breathing. Still partly concealed by the camisole that she wore underneath it, her full breasts were nicely cupped and lifted high by the frilled top.

His gaze moved to the ribbon rosebuds sewn into the frill, which put him in mind of nipples he could not see. Carlyle had to adjust his trousers when Susannah toyed absently with one rosebud, waiting for Lakshmi, her Indian maid, to finish loosening her laces in back.

Susannah slipped a hand beneath the ribbed silk, rubbing her skin. "One can scarcely breathe in these things," she said over her shoulder to the maid, "though this one is pretty."

Carlyle would have to agree. The corset was dangerously pretty. Lakshmi had concealed a fortune in gems in it before all three of them had left India never to return. Susannah had no idea and he had only found out afterward.

The maid had hidden the thing among the clothes in Susannah's trunks. Once in London, Lakshmi had confessed everything and shown the corset to Carlyle, whom she regarded as her protector. He had been in a way. But he had no idea what to do about the gems, and told her to put it back where it was.

Certainly he had never expected to see Susannah wearing it. Or any other corset. A few minutes ago, thinking she was at the theater, Carlyle had come out onto the balcony that overlooked the back gardens of their side-by-side houses and happened to glance that way.

The dangerous corset fit her perfectly. In fact, it was a marvel of its kind, a hybrid of British rigor and a very Indian love of ornament, made of pink silk. Each of the ribbon rosebuds had its own stem of seed pearls, further adorned with openwork leaves and fanciful tendrils and hundreds more seed pearls covered the corset's numerous ribs—applied by Lakshmi in hopes of interfering with a woman's fine sense of touch. The padded ribs concealed rubies and sapphires, while the ribbon rosebuds hid diamonds from the mines of Golconda, six in all.

He wondered why Susannah had donned it tonight—perhaps it was only a whim. Her maid could not very well refuse her.

Susannah plucked at a thread too fine for him to see. "Oh dear. A few of the pearls have come loose."

The maid circled around her to look, clucking with distress.

"I shall fix it. You cannot sew by candlelight, Lakshmi."

The maid begged to differ, apparently, murmuring something he couldn't hear that made Susannah give in. "Oh, if you must. But wait until morning—I insist. Perhaps the sun will appear tomorrow."

Ah. He heard the sadness in her voice. The gray skies and cold, rainy weather of England oppressed her. That was to be expected for someone who had lived all her life until now in the sensual, enfolding heat of India.

He watched as Lakshmi came around her mistress to unhook the front of the corset and remove it. She folded the thing with some difficulty—it was quite stiff—and set it on the chest of drawers. Then she hovered nearby, not wanting to leave the room for reasons Carlyle could certainly understand.

He had to smile. Kind to a fault, Susannah was waving her maid away.

"That is all the help I need, Lakshmi. Thank you. You may go to bed."

The Indian woman nodded and withdrew, casting one last glance at the corset. With her gone, Carlyle felt even more like a bounder for continuing to watch Susannah. He too glanced at the corset on the dresser, as if that gave him a reason.

Hah. You would trade all the gems in it—no, all the gems in the world—for a kiss from Susannah. One perfect kiss. But the gems are not yours and neither is she.

He looked back at her. Now clad in only a thin camisole from the waist up and billowing petticoats from the waist down, Susannah seated herself before a mirror mounted on a small table and began to unpin her hair. Down it came in waves of rich, dark brown that made Carlyle long to feel its heavy softness running through his fingers.

How delightful it would be to kiss the nape of her neck until her lips parted. Her eyes would close with dreamy pleasure . . . Carlyle chided himself again for thinking such things about her, innocent that she was.

Susannah picked up a brush and began to run it through her hair, her beautiful breasts moving with every stroke.

He was mesmerized—and he was on fire with lust. Her rounded rump, evident even under several petticoats, shifted on the padded stool as she leaned forward, pouting at her reflection, idly brushing her hair back over her shoulders. The brown waves fell to her slender waist.

Susannah set down the brush and picked up a bottle of eau de cologne, squeezing its tasseled bulb to spray a fine mist over her bosom and neck. Her dampened camisole made her nipples stand out underneath it, as pink and tight as the ribbon rosebuds on her cast-aside corset. She shivered, chilled by the draft from the open window behind her.

Carlyle would have walked through a brick wall at that moment to have her, to claim her body, to hear her whisper words of love in answer to his own . . . he shut his eyes to regain his equilibrium, breathing deeply.

He opened them. Susannah was reaching out through the open window to close the shutters. Thank God she did not see him, even though he was less than ten feet away. Lit from behind, her upper body was a curving silhouette beneath her camisole. With her hair tumbling around her face, her expression held a mysterious tenderness, as if she expected a lover to come to her that very night.

Then, reaching out with both hands, she pulled the shutters in. He heard her latch them, then close the window.

Carlyle sighed. He would have to be careful to make no sound when he went inside.

Susannah settled herself once more on the padded stool, rubbing her bare arms to warm them. The fragrance of the garden, even filtered through the sooty air of London, had brought to mind a night in India.

She and Carlyle Jameson had been waiting for the moon to rise in an open-air pavilion of pierced stone, looking out over a reflecting pool. A palace musician began an evening raga, whose haunting melody reached its climax just as the moon appeared, casting silvery light over the water.

It had been a magical moment—and she had almost thought then that Carlyle would kiss her. But, watched as they were by her old ayah a few yards away and a couple of miscellaneous aunties pretending not to notice a thing, he had only smiled.

She had been rather put out, although she could not say that Carlyle had refused her, since she hadn't offered him anything. As she remembered it, she had been explaining the intricacies of the Indian musical scale . . . and then suddenly she'd thought about being kissed. By him.

She still wanted him to. But he seemed to want to marry her off to the highest bidder in London, something she was not at all sure she desired.

Growing up in a maharajah's palace in Jaipur, Susannah had enjoyed a great deal of freedom, especially since her mother, a girl of eighteen when she had married Susannah's father, had died so young. She'd had the benefit of an excellent, if somewhat improvisational education and the run of the maharajah's library, which boasted innumerable volumes, some quite rare and some quite scandalous, on every subject under the sun, including love.

Love. Had she found a chance to sin—she hadn't—she would have been only an auntie away from discovery. There was no end of them in India, where families were large and there was no such thing as privacy.

Certainly Carlyle was the only man she had ever wanted to kiss. The feeling was so strong that it had surprised her. They talked freely, spent happy hours in each other's company, but he kept a courteous distance, perhaps because he was fifteen years older. She had been just twenty-one then, with no experience of life beyond India, save what she could learn from the illustrated London magazines that sometimes reached Jaipur a year or more after the news in them was truly news.

Good or bad, the world beyond the palace walls had seemed too distant to worry about. Her father's death had changed all that. Her heart had been shattered.

Almost too numb to feel anything, she'd been grateful for Carlyle's guidance. He'd followed Mr. Fowler's instructions to the letter and brought them all from India to this bewildering city, where she knew no one well besides Carlyle. He saw to it that she had whatever she needed and her father's name opened some—but not all—doors. Alfred Fowler had earned a measure of fame dealing in gems, and the maharajah had kept him on retainer for just that reason. He'd made a small fortune that would have lasted a lifetime in India. But not in London. Therefore, she must marry.

Susannah looked at her reflection as she began to brush her hair again, singing under her breath, an Indian melody from long ago. A lonely woman awaited her lover, who did not come to her—oh, how did it go? The words escaped her. After many months in London, she had forgotten a great deal. There was no one to speak Hindi with, and Lakshmi preferred the dialect of her village.

By a happy accident, on one of their recent excursions, her maid had found a few of her Rajasthan countrymen selling carpets in a cluttered shop. Lakshmi had chattered eagerly with the buxom wife of one, promising to return to the unfamiliar lane into which they had ventured, but Susannah could not remember where it was.

She would have to get a street map of London and try to retrace their path. It would do Lakshmi good to be among people who understood her, to eat familiar food, and be made welcome. The maid was gawked at whenever she went out, and she preferred to stay in the house, hovering over Susannah in a way that was not healthy.

Lakshmi was growing thinner and more nervous each day. Susannah suspected that her Indian maid was indeed lonely. But what future was there for her here?

That was a question she might as well ask herself. Susannah put down the brush. She had gone along with Carlyle's programme, if it could be called that, of social events and introductions to eligible men, realizing without him telling her that her father probably would have brought her back to London eventually and done the same thing.

Her father's banker controlled the sum that had been left to her, waggling a finger and counseling prudence every time she saw him. Her requests for money had to be made in writing and in person, which was a nuisance. She supposed it was better than having to beg a husband for money, but even so . . .

She sighed. Susannah had yet to meet a man in London she liked. The raffish Englishmen she'd known in India were very different, adventurous by nature, and not well suited for husbandhood. If pressed, she would have to count Carlyle among them.

She had not been quite sure then what he did to earn his living, and she still wasn't sure. Her father had mentioned that the young officer had some connection to the East India Company, that he showed great promise, that he had an excellent head for business and was thoroughly trustworthy in all his dealings, but precisely who employed Carlyle Jameson or why was never made clear to her.

The details of the day she had met him—and all the time they had spent together—were still clear in her mind. By contrast, she had very little memory of the months after her father's death, but perhaps that was to be expected. Yet Susannah knew her father would not have wanted her to mourn overlong—he had loved life and hoped she would find happiness.

Was it wrong to wonder if that might be found with Carlyle? She liked everything about him, including just looking at him. He had dark hair that was almost black and gray-green eyes; and he was strongly built and tall, far taller than many Englishmen in India, who seemed to wilt in the heat upon arrival and never recover. It might be said that he thought a trifle too highly of himself, but a single defeat at chess had curbed that tendency on the day they had met.

He had seemed so startled when she checkmated him. Susannah had explained her strategy, pointing to the chessboard.

"I placed my bishop here—and a knight there—so that you perceived an attack where there was none, Mr. Jameson. You wasted precious time and too many moves on an imaginary enemy. And so I conquered."

He had given her a wry look that acknowledged as much, but he managed to smile at her. "Well done, Miss Fowler. You are a sly one."

The remark had piqued her. "That is not a compliment."

"It is the truth and the mischievous look in your eyes is proof enough."

"Then I must accept it." She'd packed away the chessmen in an ivory box, handling each piece with care. She looked up and caught him admiring her.

Carlyle cleared his throat, embarrassed. "Hmm. I would be happy to play once more. I thought I was rather good at the game."

She'd inclined her head, twirling a wayward strand of dark brown hair around her finger. "You are. But I have had lessons from the maharajah's teacher. The Indians invented chess, you know."

He possessed some skill at the game, but he was too bold by nature to be brilliant at it, a sword-waving warrior rather than a strategist. Susannah smiled to herself. Boldness was a very appealing quality. And she hadn't minded winning so often. She knew it was not because he let her.

Her father and his eccentric friends—a mélange of races— were nothing like Carlyle, preferring to sit and smoke cheroots and talk about old times. But the newly arrived Englishman preferred to ride and shoot and charge around in the open air, seeming to sit down only when he wanted to recount his adventures or challenge her good-humoredly to another match or simply to listen to her talk.

His company was a very great pleasure. They often went into her favorite haunt, the maharajah's library, when he sought to find out something about the land he had come to. Perhaps that had been only a pretext for getting to know her. It had worked.

Susannah had instructed him in all things Indian, naively not realizing that he was just as interested in how she looked by moonlight as he was in evening ragas . . . until that moment she had wanted him to kiss her.

She liked to think that he had somehow planted the suggestion in her mind. After all, he was handsome and gallant, and love was a game he could very well beat her at, especially when he was the only Englishman around. He had competition here in London—of a sort. The men she had been introduced to thus far were extremely dull by comparison.

At least she could choose, unlike an Indian bride. It was unfortunate that none of the possible candidates had interested her. But she had been polite, exceedingly so, to all of them.

Susannah stifled a yawn. Eventually she would marry. Women did. But she hoped she would not end up with a husband like the fellow occupying the seat next to hers in the theater box tonight, an acquaintance of Susannah's half-aunt. He had dozed off before the second act. She and Mrs. Posey left early.

The prospect of attending an unending series of social occasions with her elderly chaperone was not a pleasant one. Susannah frowned. Mrs. Posey exhorted her to think of her future—but did that mean becoming the wife of a man she could never love? To be truthful, she doubted that she could find one who would love her.

She sensed the disapproval in the whispered comments about her "background," as her life in India was referred to by the more narrow-minded. Some seemed to regard her as positively exotic, though she looked as English as any of them. And it had been a rude shock to find out that an excellent education was considered a drawback in a woman.

It occurred to her that her father would have told them all to go to the devil. She might just do the same some day, given a cup of strong punch. Carlyle would laugh, she knew. Oh dear. Why had her father not simply left instructions that she was to marry *him*? She supposed he was penniless. That was why second sons got packed off to places like Rajasthan.

Still, it was Carlyle she hoped would come to call, his boots she wanted to hear upon the stone steps of the townhouse in Albion Square, his face smiling down at her that she wished to see.

He continued to keep a courteous distance, though, which discouraged her. Susannah frowned, not wanting to think about it. She attacked the clutter upon the dressing table, tucking engraved invitations back into the mirror frame, putting her brush and comb back on their silver tray, and capping the jar of sweet-smelling powder. She collected her hairpins and put them in a china dish, then looked about for something more useful to do.

There was the corset. There was no reason for Lakshmi to fret over such a minor repair. Susannah could sew the pearls on just as well.

She rose and got her sewing basket from inside the wardrobe, taking out a shawl to cover her bare shoulders too. Wrapping it carelessly around herself, Susannah looked in the sewing basket for her half-spectacles, which she put on, catching a glimpse of herself in the mirror again.

Fie. She looked like an old maid. She pouted in a way that would have amused her father, and picked up the corset from the chest of drawers.

Once settled in the armchair, a small pair of scissors in her other hand, she looked for the pearls that hung by a thread and found them. She could not decide whether to snip the thread or save it, and while she was thinking, accidentally jabbed the sharp point of the scissors into one padded rib of the corset.

A flash of dark red made her suck in a breath, thinking she had cut herself without knowing it. She squinted at her thumb. She hadn't. She squinted at the corset. But she had— there was a drop of dark red blood. Yet the pink silk was not stained by it, which was odd. She touched the drop and realized that it was hard.

Very odd.

Susannah sat up straight and the shawl fell off her shoulders without her noticing it. She squeezed the slash in the silk. A ruby popped out and fell in her lap, glowing red against the white material of her petticoat.

What on earth . . . ? She ran a fingernail along the rib. Another ruby fell out, then another. When she was done, there were twenty in all. She left them in her lap and held up the corset to count the ribs. There were ten on each side of the front hooks. Now that she had emptied one rib, the others felt suspiciously stiff.

She cut a small, almost invisible slash into a rib on the other side. The channel yielded twenty sapphires of a vibrant dark blue. By midnight, she had taken hundreds of small precious stones out of the corset. Her petticoat was filled with winking blue and red points of light.

She smiled ever so slightly, looking down at them. Anyone else who'd stumbled across unexpected treasure would have been agog with excitement, but Susannah knew enough about gems and gem-dealing to keep quiet—and to keep her discovery to herself. She dipped a hand into the stones and let them cascade through her fingers.

Her father had sometimes allowed her to look at and even play a little while with his cache of gemstones and pearls, but he'd kept a watchful eye on her and on his precious stock in trade. Most of it was destined for the workshop of the palace artisans, to be set into rings and dagger hilts and turban brooches and ceremonial objects. The maharajah liked to dazzle his subjects—it was expected of him—and rewarded his courtiers with such things, to say nothing of his concubines.

Alfred Fowler cared very little for gems, except for the price he could get for them. He was a shrewd trader, buying low and selling high. Very high. When she was older, he'd told her that it was best not to keep such things around. She'd feared for him and for herself, but he'd said the maharajah would kill anyone who dared to steal from his treasury.

He had shown her the ingenious hidden compartments in his traveling cases and trunks, but he never put the real goods in there. The compartments were filled with paste jewels and lacquered beads that resembled pearls to satisfy a thief.

While traveling on business, he preferred to conceal gems and pearls inside belts and the seams of his clothes, so nothing could be taken from him—without the use of force, of course.

Someone had thought along similar lines and stuffed the pink corset in the same way. The gems were of high quality as far as she could see, but she would need a jeweler's loupe to assess them properly. There was one somewhere in a wooden chest filled with mementoes of her father. Susannah picked up the largest ruby, wondering if her father had planned to smuggle the gems out. It would not be the first time Alfred Fowler had done such a thing.

Taking opium for the pain of his final, wasting illness had made him ramble, and he had told her of many things that were best forgotten. But he had said nothing of this. Ought she to ask Carlyle? Or was it possible that Lakshmi had hidden the gems there?

She could not imagine why or where the girl might have got them. Had Lakshmi sewn the corset? It was possible— the embroidery was distinctly Indian in design. Susannah had come across it this morning when she was clearing out a drawer, finding it at the bottom. She had admired it with a trace of puzzlement, not remembering where it had come from or who made it. Several of the palace women had worked to provide her with clothing that was suitable for England, and it had all been packed for her. But that was months ago.

She held up the corset and looked at it closely. It was cleverly fashioned and the embroidery was very fine.

The Indian maid had seemed nervous when Susannah discovered the loose pearls, but then she'd been flighty and distracted for the last few weeks.

It was all very strange. Susannah's forehead furrowed when she thought back to the time of their departure from India.

Carlyle had insisted that Lakshmi accompany them to London when another girl would have done just as well.

Now that she thought of it, she'd heard the maid's name muttered in connection with some court scandal around the time of her father's death. Out of respect for Susannah's feelings, no one had said much. There were so many scandals in the palace anyway, where gossip was rife, especially in the zenana, where the concubines lived.

If only she could remember more.

It hardly seemed possible that a village girl like Lakshmi would have thought of concealing gems in such a way. Susannah doubted that her maid had ever seen a corset before coming to her. Lakshmi had been the servant of the maharajah's favorite, whose shapely body was never pinched and poked by such beastly things.

Susannah rose, tossing the corset onto the bed before she folded the heap of rubies and sapphires in part of her topmost petticoat. She bent to pick up her evening shoes from the floor.

Numerous as they were, the gems could be easily hidden under paper stuffed in the toes, the shoes put back in their box, the box returned to the bottom of her closet, and no one would be the wiser.

She sat down on the bed and let go of the petticoat she had been clutching to sort out the stones, putting the rubies in the left shoe and the sapphires in the right.

Once she'd found tissue paper and crumpled it into the toes, she put the shoes away. She would not wake Lakshmi, who was not likely to tell the truth if she were confronted. Even if the maid had not smuggled the stones, she had hidden the corset. But someone had to have put her up to it.

The only likely culprit would be Carlyle Jameson. Susannah went back to the bed and dragged the crocheted afghan from its place at the foot of the white comforter. She tucked her feet under it, still thinking. There could be a good reason for Carlyle having the gems. Her father might have given them to him as payment for taking care of her. But having and hiding were two different things.

If they were indeed her father's gift, Carlyle might not have wanted to tell her. She supposed he wouldn't want her to know that he had been well paid for his services on her behalf, being an officer and a gentleman and all that.

Hmm. Perhaps there was a better word than payment. Alfred Fowler was not above out-and-out bribery when it served his interests.

So that was why Carlyle had been at such pains to get her out of India and handle every complication of introducing her into society—it was a rewarding job in every sense.

Bah. And she had thought he liked her. Another thought occurred to her. The corset was hers and, for now, so were the gems. If Carlyle Jameson didn't own up to what he had done, she might as well sell them. Of course, she would not do so until the mystery of how they got there in the first place was solved. But she would have them appraised. Just in case she got to keep them.

She had no doubt of their value. Susannah jumped up from the bed and put the corset on top of her sewing box.

She would either wear it or keep it with her. She preened a bit in front of the mirror, putting on a haughty smile. The fantasy of being a very wealthy woman—who didn't have to marry anyone—was deliciously wicked.

In the house next door . . .

Lost in reverie, his long legs stretched out in front of him, Carlyle Jameson stared into the fire. Red, orange, hot pink—the intense colors of the licking flames reminded him of India. He was trying not to think of Susannah in that damned corset.

Perhaps it was a lucky thing he had chanced to see her tonight, for more reasons than one. It was time to remove them. She need never know. Once the rubies and sapphires and diamonds were sold, Lakshmi, a pawn in a cruel game that had now played out five thousand miles away, would be set for life. Once he had found out about the gems, he'd thought they would spirit the corset out of Susannah's bedroom, remove the jewels, and put it back. She would be none the wiser, and they could sell them.

But Lakshmi had been skittish and uncooperative. Understandably, she was afraid of the maharajah, to whom the gems belonged, even though the old fellow was a few continents away. Still, it was very likely that they had been followed by his agents and were being watched.

Perhaps he should not have waited so long. But Carlyle had been leery of selling the stones right away if the least breath of scandal would have hurt Susannah's chances. So much time had gone by that he thought it was now worth a try—but he could be wrong. Very wrong. A dagger-wielding assassin was not likely to listen to the very good reasons why Carlyle had kept Lakshmi's secret or that he had not smuggled the stones out of India in the first place.

Lying low had seemed the best thing to do. Lakshmi had

hidden the corset in yet another place, but it seemed that Susannah had found it somehow, put it on, and liked the way she looked. So had he. His groin ached with the memory.

But she had that effect on him anyway, quite without trying.

Passing by earlier in the day he'd found Susannah poised on the doorstep, quite properly dressed. She'd waved as she'd waited for the carriage which would take her and her chaperone, Mrs. Posey, a whiskery female of great age and impeccable reputation, twice around the park to see and be seen.

It had occurred to him that they would not be gone long. It was about to rain. He thought he might call upon her.

Somehow the modesty of her costume had only added to her allure. Susannah had been wearing a high-necked dress of light gray silk with a subtle stripe in a darker gray. He remembered every detail. The stripes, nipped in and narrow at her waist, widened over her bosom in a distracting way.

Still stunned by seeing that very bosom nearly bare just a short time ago, Carlyle shook his head and put the delectable vision out of his mind, feeling a little ashamed of himself. He had promised her late father to take very good care of Susannah. To that end, he had brought her back to England and rented fully furnished houses side by side—one for her and one for him, with an eye to propriety and her safety. He had seen to the matter of her father's will and her inheritance, and other financial concerns, and enlisted her only relative to help him launch Susannah in society—in short, he had done everything he could for her.

As much as he liked Mr. Fowler, Carlyle knew he had been artfully persuaded by him—the man had played upon his sympathies with uncommon skill. Knowing that his illness was terminal, Mr. Fowler had put his affairs in order.

He provided Carlyle with letters of introduction, and more important, a generous letter of credit, charging him to spare no expense to establish his motherless daughter in society.

Carlyle, who had rather a reputation, realized that the older man knew nothing of it. He had pointed out that he was not the best choice for such a delicate assignment, but Susannah's father had replied that he was the only choice: there were no other Englishmen in Jaipur.

The man was dying. Carlyle could not very well tell him no.

Before that sad day came, Mr. Fowler drew up a declaration of guardianship himself, should anyone look askance at a worldly fellow of thirty-eight traveling with an unmarried woman of twenty-three. Whether the document was legally valid was an open question, but it looked impressive, bristling with gold seals and stamps and inky signatures, tied up with a thin red ribbon.

Mr. Fowler had made himself clear. His beloved Susannah could not be left in Rajasthan. Without a father or male relative to protect her, she would fall victim to intrigues among the women in the zenana, forever squabbling to advance themselves and their offspring in the regard of their aging ruler. Many would no longer feel obliged to be kind to the young English girl who had been raised among them.

As Carlyle well knew, a solitary female in that faraway land had few choices in life. Susannah might have ended up drifting from rich household to rich household as a governess, earning a pittance teaching the children of the East India Company families or Rajput princelings whose papas wished them to acquire a proper British education. But she would soon fade away into poverty and isolation.

His second promise to Mr. Fowler was turning out to be rather harder to keep: He was to find a suitably well-to-do Englishman of good character, although it had to be someone who would not ask too many questions about her somewhat unusual upbringing, and marry her off. Carlyle hated the idea.

Susannah would not discuss the subject with him in any case. He wondered why. An advantageous match was what every young woman dreamed of, or so he had heard. He was not the marrying kind himself. Nonetheless, she went out to balls and plays and dinners dutifully enough, escorted by Mrs. Posey. A distant half-aunt of hers, who lived in the country and seldom came to town, had charged her London friends to invite Susannah to anything attended by persons in trousers, to improve her odds.

Carlyle seldom went along. The easy familiarity of their relationship—they had known each other for more than a year in India—might have put off prospective suitors. Her father did not seem to have considered Carlyle himself as a suitable candidate for a husband, although he liked and trusted him, praising his intelligence and pluck and so forth, as so many did.

It did not matter. Whatever his sterling qualities, Carlyle was a second son who had gone to India to seek a fortune which had eluded him thus far. All the same, he might make one someday; she would have to marry one.

The odds were in her favor. In London, Susannah was an unknown, which made her all the more intriguing. She dressed beautifully—well, she was beautiful to begin with—and tailored her conversation to the company, which amused Carlyle, who had pegged her as a remarkably independent sort from their first meeting. But she seemed to have grasped that her late father's wishes were as good as a command.

In the weeks since they had come to London she had been quite ladylike . . . almost prim. His fault, in a way. He had been a perfect gentleman, Carlyle thought ruefully. Not like him. Not like him at all. But he was determined to be satisfied with polite chitchat and discreet lusting after Susannah, and that was that.

A spark escaped the grate and Carlyle stamped it out with the toe of his boot, frowning.

If it were up to him, her lovely body would not be confined within the acres of material that constituted proper attire for a well-bred woman in the reign of Queen Victoria. In Jaipur, Susannah had floated about in gauzy, simple dresses. No swags, no furbelows, no bothersome drapery—it was simply too hot. No stiff petticoats—the climate wilted anything starched within seconds.

To preserve her complexion, she had favored widebrimmed hats of light straw, delighting him on the first day he'd seen her with a flirtatious peek from under the brim of one.

Her eyes were large and blue, fringed with dark eyelashes. The fierce sun that beat down upon her hat made tiny dots of light dance on her cheekbones and the look she'd given him made his breath catch. He'd had to fight the impulse to raise a hand to her face and gently brush the light away.

She was impossibly pretty. He'd thought so even after she trounced him at chess later that same day, sitting inside a pavilion of pierced stone in the maharajah's enclosed garden. Susannah had added insult to injury by pointing out that he had not been paying attention. Of course not. How could he, faced with so lovely an adversary?

And so she conquered. More than she knew.

After that day, they had played many more times, and he was far more watchful, but almost never won. In the ensuing months, they had become good friends, progressing to fond flirtation, but no more than that. Susannah was young and headstrong, a volatile combination. His respect for her father—and his own wish to steer clear of complicated romantic entanglements—meant that Carlyle kept a certain distance.

Until that night by the reflecting pool when he had almost kissed her.

She had looked enchanting in the moonlight, her blue eyes wide and expectant, her hands folded demurely in her lap. But he could not bring himself to touch his lips to hers—and in the end, it hadn't mattered.

As her father grew increasingly weak, she spent all her time with him, until the inevitable. Clad in black, wrapped in silent grief, she never complained through the overland journey out of the Rajasthan hills to the coast and the long sea voyage home. Indeed, she had scarcely looked at him during those months until the stormy day they had arrived in London.

The fire before him now was not warm enough to make the memory less dismal. Carlyle crossed his arms over his chest and his legs at the ankles, thinking back on it.

A driving rain had drenched them all as they disembarked, and the carriage Carlyle had arranged for by post was nowhere to be found. The docks had been utter chaos, crowded with ships and shouting men unloading passengers and goods. Crowded into a leaking hackney cab, they'd jolted off to Albion Square. The fellow on the box had grumbled loudly because Susannah would not let him whip his horse.

Chilled through, holding up the bedraggled skirts of her traveling costume, she had gone upstairs immediately, assisted by her Indian maid. Lakshmi, who knew English but rarely used it, spoke soothingly to her in dialect.

He had wished he understood. The two women seemed so homesick and so ill-at-ease in London. As for himself, Carlyle was content enough. He could soldier on anywhere, it seemed. But he would be happier if Susannah was as happy as she'd been in India.

Alone in his house, he was keenly aware of her presence right next door. Hmm. She was probably swanning around in white linen petticoats and that nearly transparent camisole. He imagined her putting one foot on a needle-pointed stool—did she have one?—and unrolling a stocking.

Carlyle shifted in his chair.

He mused upon how lovely she had looked in that gray striped dress—a subdued color that marked the transition from one stage of mourning to the next. Her father was adamant that she was not to go about in black for long. Mr. Fowler had told Carlyle to find her a fashionable dressmaker as soon as possible, cost be damned. He paid no attention to the younger man's statement that he knew of none.

The long and the short of it, the half-aunt helped Carlyle find a dressmaker and everything else a young unmarried woman might require, including Mrs. Posey for the sake of decency, and a hairdresser who visited weekly, a few servants and a carriage to convey her about town, stabled in the mews behind the row of houses on her street. All quite necessary for husband-hunting, the half-aunt assured him. Compared to it, bagging tigers was easy sport.

So far no one had proposed. As her guardian, he would have had to listen to any such declarations, expecting some to come from men who were far older than he was. But he could not simply claim her for his own, although there was no one to forbid it.

He had made promises to a dying man—one did not renege on such vows. And Carlyle had no chance of inheritance. His married older brother, the earl, was in robust health and disapproved of life-shortening vices such as drink, while indulging freely in life-enhancing ones. Carlyle was an uncle several times over to nephews born on both sides of the blanket.

His role as Susannah's protector was eminently respectable in all its particulars, despite what had happened tonight. By mutual agreement, Carlyle even had a key to her house, but he did not come and go as he pleased.

Ah, if only he could. Carlyle thought that he still would not go so far as to steal a kiss but . . . he would not refuse one.

She would never do such a thing. A good reputation was hard-won and easily lost, as he knew only too well. But a man might dream all the same.

He drummed his fingers on the armrests of his chair. If Susannah was sitting on his lap, looking very pretty and not very proper . . . wriggling just a bit . . . The thought made his groin tense and he sat up, feeling rather too warm. Carlyle looked at the clock upon the mantelpiece.

He dismissed his sensual fantasy as he stood and stretched. Perhaps a breath of fresh air would clear his head. He could not and must not take advantage of his role as her guardian. She trusted him. As far as the corset was concerned, he was blameless. Of course, if she found the gems hidden in it, she might think otherwise.

It was time to get rid of the evidence, so to speak. And it was not as if Susannah would wear such a fancy corset often. Stealing it would be easy enough. Carlyle headed off to his solitary bed.

Chapter Two

Several days later . . .

The sun shone in upon the breakfast table, making every-thing on it look irresistible. Susannah lifted the lid of a speckled brown teapot and sniffed the rising steam. It had steeped long enough. She poured a cup.

There was toast in a rack, country butter, coddled eggs in porcelain cups, and her favorite treat, Devonshire cream with cherry jam. The little glass dish of jam caught the light and sparkled like . . . . like rubies, Susannah thought. Which were safely hidden upstairs in the toe of her left shoe. At the moment, she would rather have the jam. Susannah believed in breakfast, and she was in a very good mood.

The sun was out. But that was only one reason. She was formulating a plan to find out how the rubies and sapphires had come to be in her corset.

Carlyle would know. Whether she had to kiss or kick the information out of him remained to be seen. For now, she was going to repair the thing and think it over.

She ensconced herself in a chair and put a napkin over her lap. Her hair was loosely pinned up and her morning gown, a paisley print, fell in loose folds over her knees—she did enjoy being uncorseted. But Susannah had brought the pink corset downstairs with her, and a sewing basket, as she still had not finished its repair.

She lingered over the meal, sipping tea. The new downstairs maid cleared the dishes from the table and swept the toast crumbs into a silver crumb-catcher. "Thank you, Molly. That will be all."

The maid looked up, surprised to be addressed by name, let alone thanked. She only nodded and disappeared with the tray.

Susannah set down her teacup and picked up the corset, spreading it out before her. It was easy to flatten now that the hidden gemstones had been removed from the ribs. She traced a finger over the elaborate embroidery, admiring the seed pearl embellishment, and wondered again who had done it.

Reaching for the sewing basket on the floor, she unfolded the corset set atop it onto the table, then took out a pincushion, spools of thread, and a needlebook, setting everything out.

She jumped in her chair, startled by the knocks on the front door. The maid went to answer it and Susannah heard Mrs. Posey's familiar wheeze.

"Good morning then. And where is Miss Fowler?" Directed to the front room, Mrs. Posey waddled in. "Ah, there you are. But you are not dressed for the out-of-doors."

Susannah looked at her, puzzled—and then she remembered. They were to go to the Chelsea physic garden. She had entirely forgotten.

"Well, well, no matter. I can make myself quite comfy while you dress. Is that dark girl about?" Mrs. Posey looked at the gorgeous corset spread open on the table with indifference, too nearsighted to see much without her spectacles. "You shouldn't be mending. Put her to work after she gets you ready."

"Lakshmi is ailing," Susannah said. There was a noticeable edge in her voice. "She is still in bed. I am worried about her."

"Now then, she only wants to sleep late. You mustn't let a servant get the upper hand," Mrs. Posey said. "Especially not a foreigner." The older woman sank into an overstuffed, rather shabby armchair, which had been sat upon and sat upon until it was relatively soft, unlike most of the furniture in the house, which was good for one's character. Those who did not sit up rigidly straight on horsehair upholstery were doomed to slide off it.

"Ahhh." Mrs. Posey sighed with appreciation. The chair was in the direct path of the sunlight, which made her eyes blink and then close. Susannah had flung open the triple layers of window hangings, a very un-English thing to do. Still, she so disliked the entombed effect of a properly curtained room that she did it every chance she got.

She made no reply to Mrs. Posey. Given the warmth of the sunlight and the cushioned arms of the big chair, her chaperone might very well drift off, and Susannah would be spared the excursion, although the physic garden was a pleasant place. But she had no wish to be lectured on the many uses of lavender.

Sure enough, Mrs. Posey dozed off within minutes. The ticking of the clock in the room punctuated her soft snores, and Susannah returned to her repair of the corset.

She threaded a thin needle and began to mend the small slashes in the ribbing where she had removed the stones. The sound of footsteps on the marble floor of the small entry hall reached her, but she assumed it was Mr. Patchen going about his morning routine, directing the airing of rooms and the polishing of banisters and other important tasks.

A deeper voice than his made her jump. "Good morning, Susannah. Forgive me for not knocking. Your manservant left the front door open. I saw him go down to the kitchen just before I came in."

She looked up, startled to see Carlyle Jameson looking through the open door to the room where she sat.

"Oh—hello." Was it scandalous for a man to look at a woman who wasn't his wife if she was wearing a morning gown? He seemed to like what he saw, so she had probably broken yet another unwritten rule. However, the loose garment and its intricate print revealed much less of her than a fitted dress would have done. She hoped Mrs. Posey would not wake up and pin her with an accusing look. She pointed to the sleeping old lady, hoping Carlyle would take the hint.

"Ah, I see you are not alone. Very good." His voice became softer. "Then it is entirely proper for me to call upon you."

"I don't know about that," she answered quietly. "But come in."

This unexpected visit would require her to think quickly. His reaction when he caught sight of the corset would tell her something.

Looking down at it, Susannah thrust the threaded needle into the pink silk again and began to sew. Prim and proper. She felt anything but in her morning gown. The circumstances seemed far too intimate, despite the presence of Mrs. Posey. They might have been lovers, meeting in the morning after a night of . . . Susannah, a virgin, which was as it should be, wondered nonetheless about *nights of.*

Keeping her gaze upon her work, she heard Carlyle cross the thick carpet, his footsteps muffled now. He came around the table and took the chair opposite her. His nearness was unsettling.

Her body, unconfined, betrayed her. Susannah felt her nipples tighten, stimulated by the loose material that brushed them each time she made a stitch. His gaze never left her face—she could feel it.

It was not as if they had never sat at a table together—they had, often, and faced each other across chessboards with their knees nearly touching. But the open-air pavilion and the lofty marble halls of the palace kept everything light and breezy, unlike the hothouse atmosphere of a London parlor on a warm day. Perhaps flinging the curtains open had not been such a good idea after all. A touch of sepulchral gloom would be just the thing for cooling off her wayward thoughts.

Susannah stopped sewing and looked up into his gray-green eyes. Carlyle regarded her with the calmness of a cat—a very large cat, handsomely dressed in a light coat of dark wool and immaculate linens beneath a sober vest, clothes that did not hide his physical vigor and manly health.

He did not speak for a moment, holding her gaze, sitting quite still except for his large, sinewy hand, which tapped restlessly on the table as he smiled at her.

At last he looked down. Susannah noticed *something* flicker in his eyes—she decided it was shock—and felt a flash of satisfaction. So he had seen the corset before. Just as she'd suspected.

He lifted his hand from the table to adjust his collar. "Would you mind if I took off my coat? It is rather warm in here."

"Not at all."

Carlyle nodded and stood to remove the light wool coat. Susannah could not help but admire the power and grace of his tall body as he did so, looking intently at him when the sleeve of his shirt did not seem to want to part from the sleeve of his coat.

He tugged at it, not glancing her way. Fie. The most ordinary gesture or movement of his caused her to stare. She attempted a serene air, casting her eyes down to her work and putting a pin in her mouth in a seamstressy way.

Carlyle put the coat over the back of his chair and sat down again. "What a very appealing picture. Johann Zoffany might have painted you, Susannah. A woman *en déshabillé*, sewing a corset."

Corset. The word seemed to hang in the air between them, suggestive and sexual. Susannah told herself that it was only an article of clothing and there was no need to simper or blush about a mere word.

All the same, he or someone known to him had seen fit to stuff this very corset with hundreds of gems. She glanced at him for only a fraction of a second . . . and immediately regretted it.

The intelligent regard in his eyes made her think that he knew precisely what she was up to. Susannah felt her cheeks turn pinker than the silk she was sewing and she almost swallowed the pin. She hastily removed it from between her lips, aware that he was watching her closely. "I am not familiar with that artist."

He cleared his throat. "Zoffany painted the luminaries of the London theater and the great courtesans, then went to India to do portraits of native princes and the resident British. Before your time, my dear, but your father might have known Zoffany's work."

"He never mentioned the man."

Carlyle did not seem offended by her blunt reply. "Oh. Well, it was just a thought."

She would have to be blunter. "Hmm. I would prefer that you do not address me as *my dear*."

He looked a little pained. "I used to in India. You did not mind it then."

"We are not in India now."

"No, we are not." His voice was neutral and his steady gaze remained on her face. "You don't like London, do you?"

"Not very much."

Carlyle nodded. "I expect the endless parade of potential suitors is beginning to depress you. But I am sure someone will offer for you."

Susannah fumed. Would he never notice the corset? Did she have to wave it like a flag?

"Someone whom you might come to love," he added.

Perhaps he would receive a bonus, if that unlikely event

should occur. "Have I no other choice in life?" Her vehement question seemed to take him aback.

He shrugged his shoulders, rubbing a hand thoughtfully over his chin. He had been well shaved, she noticed. A faint scent of bay rum came to her unwilling nose. She sniffed in reverse to get rid of it.

"Well, if you do not wish to marry, you can subsist on the income from your inheritance for some time," he said at last, "if you can live modestly."

"Hmph." She waved a hand at the furnishings of the cluttered room. "I could live without all this, certainly. The British Empire raids the world simply to fill its parlors with useless bric-a-brac. Looking at it makes me want to run away."

He smiled slightly. "If the money must last, there will be no travel, no servants, no extravagances. That might prove difficult for a girl who grew up in a palace."

"My dear Carlyle," she began, forgetting that she had asked him not to call her *my dear*. "I did know it wasn't my palace."

"But you seemed somewhat—" He pressed his lips together for a second, not wanting to say something that would upset her. "Somewhat unaware. Everything you needed appeared as if by magic."

"My toys were mine. And when I was older, my books and my piano. My clothes, of course. It is true that I wanted for nothing, but I had very little I could call my own."

"And yet you were content."

She nodded. "Yes."

"The happy empress of your own domain."

Susannah shot him a wry look. "Are you saying that I was spoiled?"

"No, no. Not at all." Carlyle leaned back in his chair.

Liar, she thought, nettled. *Do not make yourself so comfortable.*

"Do you know, I once saw you leading a flock of peacocks about the palace grounds. You certainly looked like an empress."

She waved a dismissive hand. "Peacocks, bah. I would rather have twenty thousand pounds a year."

His mouth quirked up. "And so would we all. By any means possible."

"And what means would those be?" Her tone was barbed. "Men are free to do what they will. A woman is not."

He studied her intently for a long moment. "Don't worry so, Susannah." His tone was kind enough, but she could hear the hypocrisy underneath. "If your dowry is not spent it can be invested in the funds and that will help. You should do very well."

She raised an inquiring eyebrow. "How well?"

"That remains to be seen," he said.

Indeed it does, she thought. Carlyle would make a handsome sum if he sold the rubies and sapphires. If they were his. She was no closer to finding that out than when he had walked into the room. His bland assurances were not comforting.

Susannah crossed her legs and swung her foot under the table. Kissing the truth out of him would be nowhere near as satisfying as kicking him.

"But should you wed—"

"I shall never—ow!" She jabbed her fingertip by accident with the needle and a tiny drop of blood welled up. Susannah put her finger in her mouth and sucked before she thought of what she must look like.

"How do you know?" Carlyle's eyes shone with amusement. "Should I ring the maid for a sticking-plaster?" he inquired. "You would not want a bloodstain, however small, on your best corset."

At long last they had come back to the corset. Good. But her finger was throbbing. It was amazing how much a little sting could hurt.

"No," she said at last, removing her finger from her

mouth. A childish cure but it had worked. There was no more blood. His last statement piqued her. "How do you know that it is my best corset? Have you seen the others? Have you been skulking about my boudoir?"

He looked uneasy, which pleased her very much.

"Certainly not. But this corset is a very fine one, perhaps one of the most beautiful I have ever seen." He was talking fast. "The embroidery is unique and—"

"It sounds like you have made a thorough study of the subject of corsets," she said, a distinct edge in her voice.

"No, not really. Of course, one is much like another. It all depends on what's inside them." He gave her a smooth smile.

She gave him a narrow look in return. He was not to be trusted. She ought not to care. But she did.

And why is that? she asked herself, supplying an annoying but astute reply in an instant: Because you used to trust him. And you hoped he cared for you.

But those days were gone forever and she had changed. She was no longer a giddy, sheltered girl half in love with a dashing officer. She was a woman who had to make her own way in a cold and unfriendly metropolis, because the dashing officer was looking out only for himself. The corset in question—hers—had contained a small fortune in gems of uncertain provenance—his.

She amended the thought, but only to be realistic. Being fair had nothing to do with it. The gems were probably his. She still didn't know for certain.

It occurred to her that his very coolness gave away his guilt. Staying silent, she folded the corset lengthwise. His smooth smile faded away.

Susannah had a sinking feeling she was about to be bested at a cat-and-mouse game. If Carlyle Jameson knew anything about the gems she'd found, he wasn't going to confess.

They had talked at cross-purposes, and she felt deeply irritated. More with herself than him, however. She had bungled a heaven-sent opportunity to find out who'd hidden the rubies and sapphires. But then he had taken her unawares. Still, he could not have known she would be here, sewing away on the corset.

He glanced again at the corset she clutched. "Put it away. A lady keeps such things well hidden."

Susannah glared at him. "Are you saying that I am not a lady?"

"Not quite."

"Oh! You are insufferable!"

Furious with herself for seeming interested in what he thought, she gave a sharp shake of her head and her hair tumbled down. Susannah let it alone. Pinning it back up would mean looking for the hairpins on the carpet and that would mean bending down and he might very well interpret that as some sort of surrender.

Her agitation made her breath come faster. She parted her lips to speak but could think of nothing at all to say.

His eyes widened for a fraction of a second. "I was only teasing you, Susannah. I meant that you are young yet, and not quite a lady. But . . . may I say that you are lovely?"

What blather. And how humiliating. Mrs. Posey was probably feigning sleep and listening to every ridiculous word. Susannah rose swiftly, clutching the folded corset within the folds of her gown. "Go to the devil!"

He stood up very quickly. Susannah flung the corset at him. He caught it with one hand, tossed it aside, and backed her into a corner by the window where the sleeping chaperone could not see them if she awoke.

He was too fast to fight off and in an instant Carlyle silenced her with a kiss. It was not a brief one. His lips were inexpressibly tender, and the sensation of being swept off her feet and held in such strong arms was a thrill. His powerful thighs pressed against her and her body arched into his.

Instinctively—she had no other word for the shamelessness of it—she pressed her soft breasts against a linen-clad chest that was hard and warm, feeling her hard nipples grow harder still. Susannah slipped one hand over his heart without thinking, feeling it beat faster while she permitted him every liberty that a kiss had to offer.

He caressed her back, then slid both big hands down over her hips and bottom, pulling her closer still to him. Still kissing him back, Susannah struggled not to moan. She was entirely bare under the gown and he seemed well aware of it, handling her with very masculine skill. The sheer pleasure of it was nearly too much for her. Scared but wildly curious, she reached around to feel his hard buttocks. Oh, no. He was rigid. She moved her hands up quickly to his waist and felt those muscles tighten.

And all the while his mouth was on hers. So that is a kiss, she thought dazedly, when he broke it off and held her head close to his shoulder, stroking her tumbled hair. He bent to her, rubbing his head against hers like a huge cat.

No—no. It wasn't *a* kiss. It was *his* kiss.

Confused as she was, Susannah did not suppose that every man kissed in such a way that his partner might well swoon with pleasure.

She put both hands on his chest and pushed him away. Something had changed forever in that magic moment when he had claimed her lips. She belonged to him in some indefinable way that infuriated and frightened and thrilled her beyond measure. Gasping a little, touching a finger to lips swollen by the ardent pressure of his, Susannah backed away from the corner and from him.

Carlyle watched her, a troubled look on his handsome face. He too seemed to be fighting for breath, but he stayed where he was. After a moment, he bent down and picked up the corset. He said but one word as he threw it to her.

"Catch."

Susannah didn't even try. She watched the crumpled pink corset unfold as it fell to the floor once more.

Mrs. Posey emitted a wheeze and the folds of flesh around her eyes squinted into wrinkles. But she did not open them, not just yet.

Carlyle took his coat from the chair, taking his time about putting it over his arm. "Thank you for allowing me to share your morning. It has been a very great pleasure." He coughed. Susannah stared at him incredulously. "I do hope you enjoyed our conversation as I have. Good-bye."

Susannah clapped a hand to her cheek. How could she have been so foolish—and how could he have done what he did with no resistance from her?

He made a half-bow before she came up with answers to those questions. "I will see myself out."

She stood there and watched him go, the coat slung over his broad back. Unwillingly, she took him in, from his tousled dark hair to his boots. His confident stride extended from the muscular buttocks she had shyly touched, moving in rhythm with long legs that had captured his prey: Her.

He was gone. She heard the front door shut.

If only she had a fraction of his confidence. Or should she call it arrogance? She had been planning to kiss or kick what she wanted to know out of him, and he had beaten her to it.

But what a kiss. What a man. He was capable of anything. She almost . . . admired him for it.

Susannah picked up the corset once more, moving to the open door to hear if he had gone. He was exchanging pleasantries with Mr. Patchen. As if nothing at all had happened.

Her ire rose up again and she reminded herself how much she hated losing as she paced, her rapid strides quickening as she thought. More than ever, she was convinced that he had hidden the jewels in the corset.

The kiss had blindsided her. Owing to her regrettable curiosity to find out what happened next—what she had felt while clasped in his arms no more than that, surely—Susannah had not been able to winkle the truth out of him. He would be exceedingly wary from this moment on.

Carlyle had bested her without even trying. She hated him. Suddenly, madly, deeply.

"Now who was that, Miss Fowler?" asked the old lady in the chair, yawning. "I seemed to have dozed off. Did I miss anything?"

He waited until he reached the end of her street to put his coat back on. He'd stalled as long as he could in her front room, hoping to get a better look at the corset, but the fire in her eyes told him that she was very close to flinging something breakable—a china vase, perhaps—that would have woken Mrs. Posey.

He had seen a small cut in one of the corset's ribs when he'd sat down. And the thing had been limp—Susannah folded it easily. Therefore, she had removed the rubies and sapphires that had made it stiff enough to stand up by itself. There was no doubt in his mind that she suspected him of using her personal belongings to smuggle jewels, and despised him for it. It was too bad, but explaining Lakshmi's predicament would reveal more than that unfortunate young woman wanted the world to know.

Spouting off about the paintings of Zoffany had distracted Susannah just long enough to make a second quick study of the corset. He was sure that she had not found the diamonds inside the ribbon rosebuds nestled in the corset's frill, and that fact meant he breathed a little easier as he walked away from Albion Square. But only a little.

Though there were only six diamonds, Carlyle happened to know that they were worth far more than the rubies and sapphires. He might have to resign himself to Susannah keeping those, especially since she had found them. The diamonds, however, were a different matter. They were much prized by the maharajah, who boasted that they had once belonged to a Mughal emperor. In an offhand conversation about the old fellow's love of baubles, Alfred Fowler had said the same thing and added that they were a set, perfectly matched for extraordinary brilliance and clarity.

The maharajah had unwisely bestowed them upon his favorite, who had given them to Lakshmi in secret, and they were the stones, Carlyle knew, that the old fellow was most likely to want back. The diamonds had been easy enough to conceal, from what he could make out of Lakshmi's tale.

Bloody hell. Carlyle told himself it was only a matter of time before she found the diamonds, too. He would have to get them first and try to figure out some way to return them to the maharajah. That process would take months and was sure to cause no end of ill-feeling—meaning he would have to explain everything to everybody eventually. The prospect was daunting.

She very well might try to sell the rubies and sapphires—certainly she understood their value. If he told her that Lakshmi had removed them from the maharajah's palace, she might not. But it was difficult, if not impossible, to predict what Susannah would do.

The smaller gems were in her possession and possession was nine-tenths of the law. And they were worth a fortune, and what woman would not want to control a fortune of her own? It was becoming increasingly clear that she valued her independence more than he'd thought. That was only one reason why marrying off Miss Fowler was a thankless task, he told himself. Of course, the candidates thus far had been a lackluster lot. He could not blame that entirely on the half-aunt.

Carlyle had arranged several of the introductions, relying on recommendations from friends at his club, and choosing the safest-seeming men, in deference to Mr. Fowler's last wishes.

Yet he knew quite well that they were not suited for her, a curious fact he could not deny. He didn't understand it, but he was not inclined to soul-searching. Carlyle prided himself on being a man of action.

Still, her happiness was important to him. They had been fast friends in India. If he had been the unprincipled seducer and corset connoisseur she now seemed to think he was, they would have been lovers.

But nothing had happened. She was too young and too headstrong and too innocent—a volatile combination in every way. And her father had been his good friend. Carlyle considered his sexual attraction to Susannah quite understandable, but he also prided himself on his self-control.

He turned the corner, took a deep breath, and summoned up every ounce of it he had.

If she really did not wish to marry, then he might as well let her have the little gems, so to speak, and sell them to provide for herself. She could not prove he had put them in the corset. He hadn't. She might ask why she hadn't told him right away. He couldn't, that was all there was to it.

Time would pass. It seemed unlikely that she would accuse him outright of smuggling and even less likely that she would swallow her pride and ask him to explain. No, most likely she would simply sell them quietly through an intermediary—and get a good price, too. She *was* the daughter of the famous Mr. Fowler and that counted for something.

Her misguided suspicions concerning him were something that he would have to live with. He hated the idea that, as of this morning, she thought less of him for something he had not done. Especially since she had looked so astoundingly sensual in that flowing dress, her hair tumbling over her shoulders, her lips parted as she tried to think of something vile to say to him. He'd had to kiss her. Did she even know how irresistible she was?

The thought crossed his mind that he might have fallen in love with her. Hmph. He wanted to laugh and made do with a wry smile.

A little sweeper at the curb saw the smile and seized his

chance to beg a penny from a man in a good mood. Carlyle found three shillings in his pocket and dropped them into the lad's grubby hand.

"Aow—thank ye!"

"Carry on," he replied absentmindedly.

"Good day and good luck to ye, sir."

He would need it, because he did intend to get the diamonds back. Keeping a straight face while he had simultaneously teased her and pricked her pride had been the only way he could think of to distract her. The combined effect of remembering how she had looked in it last night—and finding that part of the treasure was no longer in it this morning—had been almost too much for him.

She was sensitive enough to read his mind—perhaps she had. The damned corset had been right under his nose. All he thought of was the diamonds once he realized the rubies and sapphires had been removed. God only knew where a woman would hide so many gems. They could be anywhere and everywhere.

He would have to find a way to get her out of the house somehow—and soon—and get the six diamonds out of the ribbon rosebuds. And those would have to be sewn back up just so, or she would notice that the corset had been tampered with again.

Carlyle frowned. He had never threaded a needle, never sewed so much as a button. He would have to enlist Lakshmi's aid once more. The Indian maid would be terrified of being caught once she knew that Susannah had found the other gems.

Poor Lakshmi had many things to fear. Serving as go-between for the maharajah's favorite and her young lover had been an awful mistake. The unfaithful favorite had given her the gems, prying them from their settings and ruining all her jewelry as a final act of rebellion against her lord and master. She had told Lakshmi to flee the country, knowing they both faced the ultimate penalty.

Carlyle had felt sorry for her and for the favorite, and his judgment had not been the best. At the time his overwhelming concern had been for Susannah. Had he but known . . . et cetera. But he hadn't.

What to do? If he succeeded in finding the corset in Susannah's bedroom, he could not just take it to his tailor's and have him or his busybody wife mend the opened rosebuds. The fellow was entirely too friendly as it was, always inquiring into Carlyle's life and loves.

And what if Susannah wore it night and day, instead of hiding it?

Preoccupied, he went hurrying down an unfamiliar street crowded with shops. Carlyle slowed his steps. Looking into windows would be a pleasant enough distraction. He came to a jeweler's. Bright little things winked at him from the boxes on display. Good God. No. He moved on to the next shop, a tobacconist's, and clasped his hands behind his back, studying the humidors. They were brown. They were square. There was one in a rectangular shape. He found their very plainness soothing, but there was a limit to how long a man could stare at mahogany boxes.

Onward he went. The shop next door to the tobacconist's sold prints and engravings. He glanced idly at the display in the main window. There was one of a lady in the elaborate gown of an earlier historical period, powdered hair piled high, bosom popping out of her tight bodice—

Don't look, he told himself.

An odd little man, his hands thrust into the pockets of a shabby coat, sidled up and leered at the same print. Carlyle sighed. He had fallen low indeed if this was the company he was keeping.

He stepped well away from the fellow, examining a group of botanical prints in the side window. Apples. Quinces. Pears—ah, that one was particularly nice. He peered through the glass, reading the fine engraved script beneath the two nicely rounded pears in the picture: *Cuisses de Nymphe.*

Nymph's thighs. He almost groaned aloud and then remembered the odd little man not far away, still leering at the prints. Judge not, Carlyle told himself, lest ye be judged. He had been reminded of Susannah by a colored engraving of fruit that was suitable for a Methodist's parlor. He strode away, swiftly putting as much distance as he could between himself and all stimulation.

He finally stopped in a park and sat down on a bench under a tree. Carlyle was beginning to realize that his brains were still addled by his unexpected glimpse of Susannah last night. But why? He was a grown man, not some randy lad, achingly stiff and stupid after just one look at an unclad woman.

And yet the mere sight of her had undone him. He was almost jealous of the damned corset, if it was possible to be jealous of an inanimate object. *It* was able to encompass her slender waist just as he wished to do with his hands, *it* had the privilege of cupping her beautiful breasts, *it* was warmed by her silky skin—he had no doubt that her skin was silky. At his level of amorous expertise, Carlyle was good at guessing such things.

He wanted to caress her with all the skill he possessed, wanted to rain kisses on her bare shoulders, wanted to tease her sensitive nipples, wanted to fondle her glorious rear with both hands, then beg permission to touch her as intimately as she might wish—damn, damn, damn. Right now he wanted to shoot himself more than anything. He could not have her.

Susannah knew that dressing herself would be a bit of a struggle, but she vowed to do it, even if her corset—*the* corset—ended up going on crooked. She could tighten the crisscrossing back laces before putting it on over her camisole and then take a deep breath and hook it in front somehow. It had lost much of its stiffness since she'd removed the gems. She might even be able to breathe.

She had looked in on Lakshmi, who still slumbered in

her narrow bed in the chamber under the eaves, though it was past noon. Susannah had no idea what ailed her, but it seemed that the very least she could do was go out and purchase a tonic from the apothecary or medicinal herbs to make up a posset.

She was thankful that Lakshmi was not suffering from fever, but had no idea what her illness might be. Would an English doctor prescribe the right remedy? Susannah doubted there were any practitioners of Indian medicine in London.

The physic garden could be just the place to find something that would help her, though Mrs. Posey might say something disparaging about Lakshmi again. Susannah resolved to sack her if she did. Unfortunately, she would have to be replaced and there was no shortage of chaperones for hire.

Susannah, who had left Mrs. Posey to her knitting in the front room, began to make a mental list.

First, she had to help Lakshmi. She decided to ask the Rajasthani family they had met—she would have to find them somehow. Or, first she had to talk to a dealer in precious stones—she knew just the fellow, she would write to him today—and have the rubies and sapphires appraised.

She wondered what Carlyle would have done if she'd simply spilled the stones on the table in front of him and asked where they had come from and what they were worth. His face had been close to expressionless when he saw the pink corset. Provoking of him. Perhaps he was a better strategist than she had thought. It all depended on what game he was playing.

Two days later . . .

Her face hidden under an overlarge bonnet—she had added a veil for good measure at the last minute—Susannah waited on the step for the clerk on the other side of the shop door to unlock it from the inside. Not wanting the servants to know about this confidential errand, she had traveled most of the way here via horse-drawn omnibus, a jolting journey that exhausted her, until she got out in Oxford Street and walked the rest of the way, looking in the shop windows along the way.

This shop's wares were not shown in the window. Indeed, there was no window and there were no goods sold here—only skill. Rough gemstones were cut, faceted, and polished behind the heavy doors, and sent back to those who had purchased them elsewhere.

The narrow lane was a warren of similar shops, some at street level and some within the taller buildings that loomed over the old ones.

She heard repeated clicks and then the door suddenly swung open. An elderly clerk peered at her doubtfully.

"I am Susannah Fowler," she said.

"Of course. Mr. De Sola told me you would be coming. My memory—" He tapped the side of his head. "Please enter." He stepped to one side of the door, peering up and down the empty lane.

She looked where he was looking and thought she saw the shadow of a man melt back into an alley. Had she been followed? The idea was frightening. No one besides Carlyle knew that she had found the stones. She looked again and saw nothing. The clerk was far too frail to deal with ruffians, but she supposed that a watchful eye was better than nothing. There was undoubtedly a burly fellow somewhere on the premises. Anything to do with jewels carried a risk of theft and worse.

She went in, lifting her veil over the bonnet, and was greeted by another man, white-haired and short, who came out from an inner office. Behind it, she guessed, was the cutters' room, where rough stones were assessed, sometimes for months, before the final decision to cut was made.

The man who greeted her was soft-spoken and utterly

unassuming. But she knew he was Moise De Sola, the man who had cut and faceted the legendary Gulbahar diamond and several of the largest jewels in the royal collection. Still, one might pass him in the street and never remember him. He gave her a kindly smile and clasped her hands in his.

"My dear girl." His voice had a slight accent. "It is an honor to meet the daughter of Mr. Fowler. You are as lovely as your father said, very like your mother. I cut the diamonds for her wedding ring, you know."

"I didn't." The ring had been buried with Georgina Fowler. She had never seen it.

Mr. De Sola sighed. "So much time has passed. I did not see him often after they left London—before you were born, Miss Fowler. But he sent many stones to me. Your father had an eye for beauty."

"Yes, he did." Her voice quavered. It was odd to hear her parents spoken of in a place where they had once been, perhaps standing where she was right now.

"I grieved to hear of his untimely death so far from home. But here you are—" He stopped when he saw an inadvertent tear trickle down her cheek. Susannah dashed it away.

"My apologies. Perhaps I should not have mentioned such sad things. But so many memories came back to me when I received your letter in yesterday's post—your father was a very interesting man. A rough diamond himself." He patted her shoulder. "My little joke."

Susannah composed herself. Though she had never been here, meeting someone who had known her father stirred emotions that she had kept firmly in check.

"Thank you, Mr. De Sola." She looked about her. The office was as her father had described it. Solid, plain chairs were set around a desk in the center of the room, which held grooved trays covered in black velvet. A jeweler's loupe rested on one, along with a pair of thin, long-fingered tongs with padded tips.

"What do you have to show me, my dear? I know you are here on business and we will close soon. It is Friday— our Shabbat. I must be home before sundown."

"I have some stones. I–I am not sure where they come from." She blinked a bit. The gaslight fixture that hung from the ceiling cast a circle of brilliant white on the desk, leaving the rest of the room in semidarkness.

"Please, sit down," Mr. De Sola said.

Susannah settled herself in one of the chairs, coming as close to the desk as she could without getting in the light. She took out two bulging envelopes of light paper that she had folded around the rubies and sapphires, and opened them, pouring the stones into a mingled heap.

"Some stones? I would say there are more than a hundred." He smiled again. The old man put the loupe to his eye and picked up a stone with the slender tongs, separating the rubies from the sapphires, and examining them one by one.

She had seen her father do the same thing many times and knew the process would take awhile. Mr. De Sola said nothing. He set aside the largest stones for a more careful look and arranged the rest in two neat rows of red and blue.

Then he studied the largest, five in all, for several more minutes, holding them carefully in the tongs and turning them this way and that under the light.

"Very interesting," he said at last. "I have seen these before. I think I cut these two rubies. The flaws and inclusions are where they were on the shank of the stone—where their setting would conceal them."

"Oh." Susannah gave him a surprised look. She had not expected him to recognize the stones. But he was well known for his uncanny ability to do so. There simply were not that many large, fine gems in the world.

Mr. De Sola took the loupe from his eye and set down the tongs. "All of them are of the highest quality. The rubies are from Burma—as you can see, they are the color of pigeon's blood, the most valuable. The sapphires are certainly from Kashmir. That cornflower blue is unmistakable."

He regarded her with a serious air, his white eyebrows lifted high over his dark eyes. "All of them have minute scratches, Miss Fowler. As if they were pried from their settings and not with care."

"Ah—I know nothing about their provenance." Her mind whirled. Carlyle Jameson a thief? It seemed impossible. She reminded herself that she had no proof whatsoever that the stones belonged to him. She had found them in her corset. That was all.

He gave an eloquent shrug. "Perhaps someone didn't want you to know. I think they are stolen."

Susannah turned pale. Meaning that if she were caught with them, a case could be made that she was a thief.

"Would you like a glass of tea?" Mr. De Sola asked solicitously.

"Y—yes," she stammered. Her father's old friend would not think that of course. But she needed something to calm her.

He called into an interior room, and in a few minutes, a young woman in a loosely cut dark dress came in with two glasses of hot tea. The glass was held by an openwork cup of silver that fitted it perfectly, with a silver handle.

"My daughter-in-law, Rebecca. This is Miss Susannah Fowler."

The other woman greeted her in a low, pleasant voice and handed them their glasses, going back for a bowl of rocklike lump sugar. Mr. De Sola took a lump and held it in his teeth, sipping the tea through it. He looked thoughtfully at the rubies and sapphires, and occasionally at her.

Susannah sipped her tea the way it was, not taking sugar. It was hot and strong—exactly what she needed. She had no idea what to do next.

So the jewels were stolen. Her father said that it often happened. Precious stones cast a spell upon the most reasonable of men. People would steal, even kill to get jewels they could not buy, and unusual ones had an unholy power far beyond their size.

She remembered the rare star sapphire her father had once shown her when she was very young, its six-pointed star shimmering within the blue depths of the stone. Then he had brought out a star ruby, rarer still, and let her hold the magnificent gems in her palms, cool and round.

"None of the stones in the maharajah's treasure chests compare to these, Susannah," he had said. "But they are only pretty little rocks."

To him they were worth nothing more than what people were willing to pay for them. But she had been completely dazzled by the sapphire and ruby in her hands. A little of that magic had emanated from the stones she had found in such quantity and heaped in her lap.

Susannah and Mr. De Sola finished their tea, and he helped her refold the stones in their paper envelopes.

"Would you venture a guess as to—as to what they might be worth?" she said. "I shall have to return them to their rightful owner."

The old man thought for a moment and named a sum in the thousands of pounds. "Maybe more," he added quickly.

"I see." She slipped the envelopes back into her purse and tucked it inside the light fitted jacket that matched her dress.

"Miss Fowler." He seemed to be studying her carefully. "Sometimes stolen gems cannot be returned."

"Why is that?"

He shrugged again, pushing away the tools of his trade. Then he clasped his hands together and set them on the table. "Sometimes no one knows where they came from. I last saw those two rubies fifteen years ago. They came in uncut; they went out to Argentina."

"A country I have never visited."

Mr. De Sola nodded sagely. "And somehow they got to

you. An innocent young lady who lives in London. I will say no more."

Susannah got up. "Thank you very much for your time and expertise, Mr. De Sola. What do I owe you for the consultation?"

"Only a promise."

"Certainly."

"Be careful, my dear. And keep those stones in a very safe place."

She nodded. Mr. De Sola rose a bit stiffly and rang a bellpull for his clerk. It seemed an eternity until the man arrived but she was outside soon enough, her veil drawn over her bonnet once more. She looked up and down the lane, and glimpsed the same shadow, where it had been. Susannah fought the impulse to touch a protective hand to the pocket in her jacket where she had put the gems, and walked away as quickly as she could.

Chapter Three

A few days later . . .

It was now or never. Carlyle went to Susannah's door and knocked. Mr. Patchen opened it, polishing a lamp globe vigorously with a rag.

"Good afternoon, sir."

"Good afternoon. Is Miss Fowler at home?"

Mr. Patchen spat into the globe. "She is not, sir. She will not be back for several 'ours. She and that Lakshmi 'as gone shopping." He resumed what he was doing, swirling the rag around in the globe and not looking at Carlyle.

Rude of the man. Had Susannah told the servants to keep him at bay? Carlyle had known neither she nor Lakshmi was at home. Familiar with her routines, he had waited until he saw them leave together and that was why he was here. But something about the other man's stance—Mr. Patchen nearly filled the doorway—irritated him.

Carlyle was there to get the corset, of course. He had planned to borrow a book from the library—it was on the second floor, next to her bedroom—dash into that feminine sanctuary, rifle through her chest of drawers, and leave.

He put a booted foot on the top step, countering Mr. Patchen's blocking of the doorway with a slight leaning forward of his body. The manservant leaned back a little, just enough for Carlyle to bring up his other foot and tower over the fellow.

"And what may I do for you, sir?" Mr. Patchen said, in a tone that sounded a trifle more agreeable.

"I had hoped to borrow a book—something on India. I know it is in the library, but not exactly where. If I might browse for just a few minutes . . ."

"I suppose you could, sir. Miss Fowler would know where it is, though."

Carlyle gave him a jovial smile. "Oh, I don't think so. May I come in? Thank you." He squeezed past Mr. Patchen, tempted to remind him who paid his salary.

He brushed past the new maid, Molly, who gave him a surprised look and then a tentative smile. Good. He had at least one ally within the house. He smiled back and took the stairs two at a time.

Carlyle reached the upper landing and went directly into the library, opening the door without making a sound. He shut it just as quietly and looked about. The room held thousands of volumes, shelved in double rows, the newer books in front of the older ones. Susannah came into it to read, he knew.

Her bedroom and sitting room were next to it, and the brief glimpse he'd had when he'd seen her in the corset would help him. Not that he had taken in the details of the decor on that startling night.

But she had told him that she and Lakshmi had made the round of the shops, and decorated with bright colors and pretty trinkets. He had no doubt that her rooms were as charming as their inhabitant and quite unlike the sobriety of the library.

There had been a chest of drawers and no doubt there was a closet. He hoped it would not take him long to find the corset.

He would need a book. Carlyle looked at the shelves. It

would be best if the book were large enough to hide a corset, with floppy covers and a well-worn spine. In other words, an old book.

There were many that would fit that description—he pulled a few out at random. Now in India, Dr. Josephus, the owner of both the houses, was a scholar of ancient languages and the author of several tomes on Sanskrit that only a few people had read. He had been happy to let the place to a well-recommended young woman who had penned a note of appreciation to him in graceful Hindi.

None of the books seemed large enough. Perhaps something more like a monograph, or a book of art prints. That would do to hold the thing.

He coughed and it echoed. For a room that held nothing but words, the library was profoundly silent. There was not a speck of dust in it, but the room had the faintly musty smell of old paper.

Carlyle kneeled down to the lower shelves, which held taller books, and drew out a volume bound in tattered silk brocade. He opened it carefully and saw the first illustration of lovers, quite naked, in a pavilion under the moon. He leafed through it, realizing he had found an exquisitely painted manual of the arts of love.

He could not read the ancient script but the paintings were ravishing. Tender couples entwined in dreamy bliss upon page after page, pleasuring each other in myriad ways. It was the perfect hiding place for the corset of a woman he would have loved to love in just that way.

Carlyle closed the book and walked out of the library, grateful for the thick Persian carpets that muffled his steps. He looked about on the landing, then peered down the stairwell. No one seemed to be polishing or sweeping anything. Most important, no one was coming up the stairs.

Her bedroom door was only a few feet away, but he would have to work fast. Carlyle turned the knob and took a precautionary peek before entering. He went straight to the chest of drawers, set the book on top of it, then began to open each one. He looked through the contents without leaving them in disarray, but doing it made his skin crawl. Should Mr. Patchen catch him at this underhanded business he would whack Carlyle with the poker and it would be just retribution. But he had to get those diamonds.

In the last drawer, in the back, he saw a bit of pink silk. He lifted up the rest of the clothes and there it was, limp. Something that would never happen to him if he was next to her skin, he thought, grinning.

He pulled it from the drawer and examined the ribbon rosebuds in the frill. They were still intact, tightly furled. He could feel a diamond deep inside one. Carlyle looked to her dressing table for scissors and saw a little pair that would serve very well.

He used one blade to open the rosebud, squeezed it just so and eased out the first diamond. It lay in his palm, giving off a cold light that seemed somehow accusatory. It took him less than a minute to remove the other five and put them in his pocket.

There was no time to resew the rosebuds and they looked much as they had. He folded the corset and put it back in the drawer, then picked up the book of love. He was looking forward to further study of its beautiful pictures.

Well and good. He had done it. Carlyle turned to go, but a noise in the garden made him cross the room to look out of her bedroom window.

Below him was the quince tree, near the end of its bloom, the center of a boxwood maze that had been carefully tended by the old scholar. Carlyle had wandered in it just last week with Susannah—if twenty steps down a right-angled brick path could be called wandering, especially with Mrs. Posey a discreet distance away.

Susannah and Carlyle had lingered for awhile all the same. The flowers reminded her of India, she'd said. He heard the wistful longing in her voice—ah, how he loved the sound of her voice. It was as if he was hearing it right now.

But . . . he was. Susannah and Lakshmi were standing outside the door. He was caught in her bedroom, a place he had no reason to be.

"So you are a thief," Susannah said quietly.

He was momentarily speechless. There was nothing he could say or do to extricate himself from this situation. Lakshmi looked at him, trembling all over, her doe eyes wide with fear. No doubt she could guess why he was there, but she wouldn't give him away.

Carlyle could not confess everything. He had no idea how Susannah might react and there was much was at stake. But he had to say something.

"I came up to borrow a book." He held it up but kept it tightly shut. If she saw what was inside it, he would be a dead man. Which sounded rather restful.

She barely glanced at the tattered brocade cover. "That is not mine."

"No, it isn't. It belongs to Dr. Josephus."

"Do you think I have the right to lend out his books?"

"I will ask him myself," Carlyle said boldly, then realized his mistake.

"Really? But he is in India," she said icily. "And you should not be in my bedroom. Do not try to tell me that that book was in here. I have never seen it." Susannah came into the room, putting down her things and brushing so close to him that he had to step aside. She turned around and did it again, and Carlyle realized that he was being herded out the door. If he stayed in her room a second longer, she would probably nip at his heels.

He had been bested and with a trick very like the one he had employed to get past Mr. Patchen. Humiliated by his undignified position, Carlyle told himself he was getting exactly what he deserved.

He stepped out into the hallway, nodding to Lakshmi

and holding onto the book, trying to make the best of it. Susannah put her hands on her hips and glared the nonchalant expression right off his face. He straightened up.

"Forgive me. I should not have entered your room. I can only imagine what you must be thinking, Susannah."

The look in her eyes would give any sane man pause. "No, you don't, Carlyle Jameson. You haven't the slightest idea. Get out."

He cleared his throat. "I was just going." He clutched the book as if it would protect him from her wrath, walked to the stairs, down them, and out the door. Not three seconds later, a large vase crashed at the base of the stairwell.

But you still have no real proof, Susannah told herself some hours later. Mr. De Sola had said only that the rubies and sapphires were probably stolen, not who had stolen them. And he'd added that it was often impossible to determine such things. She did not regret sending Carlyle Jameson packing, however.

How dare he stroll into her bedroom, as if he owned her house—and her. She could not calm herself, could not stop seething. Despite her agitated state, she had gently dismissed Lakshmi for the night, telling her there was nothing to worry about, but she didn't seem to have convinced the girl of that.

She could hear her in her room right now, singing something sorrowful in dialect. It was just as well Susannah couldn't understand the words.

There was another reason for her dismissal of Lakshmi: Susannah wanted to examine the corset without the maid looking on. She pulled open the bottom drawer and took it out, smoothing it open on the bed and studying it carefully. It seemed the same. The ribbon roses were a little crumpled but the corset had been folded up for days. They were very pretty—she toyed with one for a moment. It unfurled into a curling strand of soft silk ribbon and she felt a flash of irritation.

She had been spending a great deal of time fussing over this corset and now it needed mending again. Still, it was only one ribbon and it would not take a minute to roll it up and affix it more tightly.

Susannah looked about for her sewing box, then remembered that she had left it downstairs. She let out a sharp sigh, then turned to see Lakshmi at her door. She had not noticed that the singing had stopped.

The girl was looking at the curling strand of ribbon with something very like shock. And it dawned on Susannah that there had been something in those rosebuds that wasn't there now. She took a very close look at the others. The furls had been loosened and one bore a tiny cut.

Probably made by the scissors that were on top of her chest of drawers. Where she hadn't left them. The scissors had been on her dressing table, she was sure of it.

Lakshmi turned and fled down the hall. Susannah went after her. And before midnight, in bits and pieces and between sobs, she had the story from beginning to end.

So Carlyle had only been trying to help an Indian maid who might have been murdered, along with her erring mistress. Susannah was familiar with the ancient and often inhumane code of justice in India, and many aspects of it appalled her. She could not blame either party to the secret for keeping it.

No wonder Lakshmi had been unwell. She was consumed by guilt and afraid for her life. Perhaps she had left the corset where Susannah could find it as a mute plea for help. Susannah felt the maharajah did not deserve to get his trinkets back, not even his enormous diamonds, but she had a feeling that she had indeed been followed. By whom and why was a question she scarcely dared to think about.

Most likely the maid had been followed also, but she might not have noticed, especially if her shadow was English.

Curled up in an armchair in her peaceful sitting room, Susannah knew she was not safe. But she could no more go back to Jaipur and give back the whole lot of gems than Lakshmi could. At least Carlyle had not been to blame—she regretted her suspicions concerning him. Her own covetousness had made her cynical.

But Alfred Fowler liked to say that cynics did not deserve their bad reputation. They simply knew how the world worked, and said so plainly, a statement that made Carlyle roar with laughter when he'd heard it. Susannah did not know what to think anymore. London seemed suddenly more ominous than ever.

Her neighborhood was respectable, even elegant, but she found the city grim and gray. Despite Lakshmi's revelations, Susannah passionately wished to be back under the sun of India where she might read her way through a library for a week without censure, or ride about upon an elephant, or fall under the spell of a centuries-old temple, carved with wondrous beings and forgotten gods. Of course, she knew that her status as a foreigner—and the only daughter of a man who had made himself useful to a powerful maharajah—had permitted her such pleasures but that didn't stop her from wanting to return to those innocent, carefree days.

Days that were gone forever. Stymied by the problem of what to do about the damned gems, her mind returned once more to Carlyle—and that marvelous kiss. How could he have done it if he considered himself duty-bound to marry her off? Where that was concerned he had been true to his word, and she supposed he had done his best. But the men he had selected as possible suitors were not to her taste. Her half-aunt's choices were no better. All she could remember of the fellows thus far were a few physical traits—large nose, small chin, tendency to whiffling of mustache when lost in thought, that sort of thing—and nothing at all about who they were.

Mrs. Posey said the particulars of physiognomy—her unlovely phrase—shouldn't matter to a woman as long as her husband gave her pin money and a few children. Susannah found that prospect too dreary to think about. She could not become a docile wife, disappear into a dank London house filled with stuffed owls and grandfather clocks, and then just . . . procreate.

Her innocence was gone forever, too. But there were aspects of that she didn't miss. The sensation of being in Carlyle's arms and surrendering with mad joy to that incomparable kiss was well worth repeating. It would pass the time until he married her . . . to someone else. No. *No.* That could not happen.

Carlyle's teasing words came back to her: *You were the happy empress of your own domain.* Far from it. She was as nearly powerless as most women. Her brief fantasy of independent wealth was never going to come true. But it was possible that she could be happy all the same. She would have to talk to Carlyle.

Chapter Four

He settled his tall frame into the same chair that he had occupied when she had confronted him with the corset and tapped his hand upon the table in the same way.

Nervously.

Susannah was glad he was nervous. It gave her the advantage. As always, having him near seemed to muddle her wits. The man exuded physical confidence, even when he knew he was in the wrong. She had not absolved him yet. His good manners and intelligence only added to a natural charm that allowed him to get away with far too much, she reflected, willing herself not to smile back when he ventured to smile at her.

She gave him a severe stare, which required her to look up slightly. He was too tall to be truly humble, of course. Carlyle Jameson towered over people even sitting down. But she would not be intimidated or impressed by such things.

The difficulty was that she found him so attractive. But she could ignore that for a few minutes. "Shall we begin?"

He nodded. "Certainly. Should you have any questions about the techniques of interrogation, I would be happy to answer them."

That took her off guard. "Whatever do you mean?"

"It is part of an officer's training. I know that you are a novice at this sort of thing."

Susannah vowed not to show her irritation at his mocking tone. She folded her hands upon the table and kept her voice calm. "I know that you have the diamonds."

He gave a deep sigh and pulled a balled silk handkerchief out of his coat pocket. "I do. Here they are." He didn't unroll the silk, just pushed it across the table to her.

She had not expected to be presented with them. Susannah's curiosity got the better of her. She unfolded her hands and carefully opened up the balled handkerchief. Six big, brilliant diamonds sparkled up at her.

"Keep them," he said amiably.

"They are no more mine than they are yours, Carlyle." She rolled them back up again.

He took back the handkerchief and stuffed it into his pocket. "You are right."

"You cannot keep them either."

He leaned forward and looked into her eyes. Susannah was momentarily mesmerized. "Indeed, Susannah," he said softly. "From the moment I found out what Lakshmi had done, I have been on constant watch. What if an agent for the maharajah should appear in London?"

She sighed and folded her hands upon the table. "I believe that one has." She told him of her meeting with Mr. De Sola and his face grew thoughtful.

"The game is reaching its end."

She sat up very straight, every muscle in her body tense. "It is an ugly one."

"How much did Lakshmi tell you? I know she was forced to confess that she was the go-between in an illicit love affair involving the maharajah's young favorite and a palace guard."

"Yes."

He shook his head and a raffish lock of dark hair fell

across his forehead. "And did she explain that she came to me and implored me to help her? Her unfortunate mistress was imprisoned in a pretty cage of wrought iron and sentenced to death. Can you imagine that, Susannah?"

"I can. I lived all my life in India."

"Then you know that Lakshmi would have been next."

Susannah only nodded.

"I said I would help her, knowing nothing of the gems she'd concealed. She hoped to find safety and begin a new life in a distant land and she was desperate. I have ever been a fool for a woman's tears."

"Is that merely foolish?" She felt a flash of chagrin. He had often comforted her when she cried for her father, finding the right words to assuage her unbearable grief, and speaking with genuine compassion. The memory of being held in his arms, close as could be to his warm, manly-smelling chest was dear to her. Perhaps that was why she had given in so readily to the kiss.

He shrugged. "I had other concerns, of course. I knew you might be less lonely accompanied by a servant whom you knew. And Lakshmi would serve as a chaperone of sorts. My ultimate loyalty was to you, not to the maharajah, although that august personage seemed to expect all men and women to bow to his will."

She pressed her lips together, not about to argue that point.

"I suppose the woman told Lakshmi to sew them into a corset?"

"I have no idea."

Carlyle looked out the window before continuing, his mind elsewhere. Susannah's tension eased slightly. She knew he was not lying about what had happened—Lakshmi had told her much the same story. But the details he provided were interesting.

"I immediately thought that we might be followed by

agents of the maharajah—who would not necessarily be Indian. Most maharajahs keep a few Englishmen around and not for decorative purposes."

She could not argue with that either. The shadow who had appeared in the lane by Mr. De Sola's shop had not revealed enough of himself to tell. But she was troubled by a sudden question. "Yes—that's so. But how did you come to be at the maharajah's palace? You never said and no one ever told me. Not even my father."

"I was on assignment. The Rajput kings and princes think it best to keep an eye on the nominal rulers of India— us. Our old fellow limited himself to your father, whom he trusted, and by extension, me. But neither of them knew that I was also an agent in the Queen's service."

"Oh." Susannah's eyes widened. Lakshmi had not known that either.

"The monopoly enjoyed by the East India Company is coming to an end, and it is in the interests of the empire to keep the peace in India. Therefore, we spied upon maharajahs and nawabs who in turn spied on us. All very gentlemanly. Except for the occasional chap who gets found out and fed to the tigers."

Susannah just stared at him. So Carlyle had not merely been taking his exercise when he went out riding in the Rajasthan hills. And his visits to the maharajah's palace had not been just social calls.

"How very interesting."

"I would have to say that things got a little too interesting. The court and the women of the zenana expected the maharajah to punish Lakshmi as severely as the favorite, but he seemed to have decided that if the bereaved daughter of his dear friend Mr. Fowler wanted her, good riddance. The execution was put off until after our departure. I made an attempt to plead the woman's case. The maharajah was interested to hear that erring wives were no longer routinely done away with in England—at least not since the reign of

Henry the Eighth." He frowned and began to tap his hand upon the table again. "But as I have said, my chief concern was for you."

She did remember Carlyle's watchfulness. Traveling by train over the scorching plains, boarding the ship in Calcutta for the endless voyage home, even here in London, he was rarely far from her side.

"Thank you." Small words, said in a small voice. She had underestimated him.

"Susannah, I do think he will want the diamonds back. They once belonged to a Mughal emperor, and they have come down through his ancestors. They are worth more than all the rubies and sapphires together."

"Well," she said at last. "What now?"

He thought it over before replying. "It will take months for a proper exchange of letters and a trustworthy courier must be hired. I suppose I could do it. I will be sent back to India eventually."

That was not something she wished to hear. She had shared one of the best years of her life with Carlyle in India, and though she might never go back, she could not imagine London without him. She and Carlyle had been close from the day they'd met and they had drawn closer still in the months after her father's death, when she'd relied upon him unthinkingly—and somewhat ungratefully. She realized with a rush of feeling that the extraordinary kiss had been a mere taste of what might happen between them. He had never meant to test her trust. The decisions he had made concerning the gems might not have been the best, but he had not stolen them and never intended to enrich himself by their sale.

"I wish you would not go," she said tenderly.

Carlyle looked at her with surprise. "Oh?"

He stood and began to pace the room. Back and forth he went as Susannah watched, twisting her hands in her lap.

"My dear Susannah," he said. "Is there a better way to

292 / *Noelle Mack*

protect you? The gems must be returned." He had risked much. He was ready to risk more.

"I will go with you. Marry me."

"No. But I do want you. With all my heart—and if you must know, my body." His voice was a little rough around the edges. "However, I am not the marrying kind."

"Neither am I," she said suddenly.

"What?"

She stood and went to him. "Carlyle, it is you I want."

"I know it will infuriate you if I say that what you want doesn't matter, but—"

It was her turn to shut him up with a kiss. Given the difference in their height, it was not easy for her to do, but it was not impossible . . . because his mouth met hers halfway.

"My dear, my dear," he whispered into her hair, holding her head when he broke it off. "There is a way . . . but only if you let me love you as I wish."

She nodded, nestling against his chest. "And what is that?"

"Call it the ultimate kiss."

"I beg your pardon. I thought we had done that."

He clasped her waist with both hands. "Can you send the servants away?"

"Are we still keeping up appearances?"

He smiled. "For as long as possible."

Susannah was naked in her bed, alone with him, and it felt . . . glorious. Utterly glorious. He had removed every stitch of her clothing, admiring and loving every inch of flesh as it was revealed to his hungry eyes. Feeling utterly unself-conscious, she watched him take off his clothes, remembering how often and how immodestly she had imagined what his body looked like.

He was perfection. Broad shoulders tapered to a flat belly and muscular sides that went in at the hips. He stood with long, muscular legs apart, his erect cock jutting out proudly, looking down at it when she did. "No, my dear. Not yet."

"But I want to," she whispered, on fire with a heavy longing.

He shook his head and came to her, sliding between the sheets and encompassing her in his powerful embrace as they lay side by side. He kissed her forehead, her eyes, her neck, and smoothed her disheveled hair. "You will have everything you want. But you will also remain a virgin. In that way I will keep my promise—and you will be able to decide if you truly want me or some other man." He breathed a soft laugh into her ear. "Who will never be able to tell that you have been loved by another."

"What do you mean, Carlyle?"

His hand slipped down, caressing her belly, and he touched the outside of her most intimate flesh with a gentle finger. "Open your legs."

She obeyed, clutching his shoulders, but he moved out of her grasp and down as he flung back the sheet.

He pressed her thighs apart somewhat more and then . . . put his mouth where his finger had been. Susannah felt a soft sensation unfold deep within her, as his gentle tongue began to lick her there lovingly. Whatever this was called, she wanted it. She arched her back, presenting herself instinctively, craving more. He took the tiny nubbin inside the folds between his lips and sucked it lightly. Cascades of sensual pleasure made her tremble and she began to moan.

Carlyle took his mouth away and sat up, caressing her breasts with expert skill. He rolled her nipples between his fingers, tugging lightly and watching her writhe with a pleasure she had never known.

"I must confess, Susannah—I saw you in that corset by accident when I stepped out on my balcony. I wanted to do this then. You were playing with the little rosebuds on it." He let go and took her hands, placing them on her breasts. "Play with your nipples while I . . ." He said no more.

Dreamily, on fire with desire, she began to pinch her nipples rather harder than he had done. She felt his stiff cock bump her side as he sat back and watched, and she looked up in his eyes. "Like that?" she whispered.

"Yes. You are so beautiful, Susannah. Innocent still . . ." He parted the folds of the swollen flesh between her legs and touched her hymen with a fingertip. She began to shake and grabbed her breasts hard. "But wanton at heart. I am proud to be the man who touches you first. But I will not take you."

She let go of herself and reached up to him. Carlyle grasped her wrists and prevented her from holding him. Then he put his mouth between her legs and resumed his tender lovemaking. The feeling grew stronger and stronger and she held her thighs as wide as she could, desiring the pleasure that shot through her. His lovingness opened her soul—and his sexual skill made her moan his name over and over.

Susannah reached down to hold his head, then grabbed his hair when he suckled the little bud tightly between his lips and teased the tip of it with his fluttering tongue.

Oh, oh, oh . . . *ohhhhhhhhhh.* As the ultimate pleasure overcame her, she knew how much she loved him.

Chapter Five

They were sharing a postcoital dinner and conspiratorial winks. Susannah had managed to wriggle into a corset—not the dangerous one—and fasten her dress by herself. The candlelight hid her faint air of disarray, she hoped. Out by the back door before the servants returned and in by the front door when they were about the house, Carlyle was soberly dressed and impeccably groomed, the picture of upright manliness once more.

In more ways than one, she reflected, looking at him adoringly. He had not reached climax as she had, preferring to wait and putting her from him when she protested, saying with a laugh that there would be time enough for that. But he had let her explore his nakedness as much as she wished once she agreed not to arouse him too much, and she had taken her time about it, not knowing when she would have the chance to do so again.

He was attacking a chop at the moment. Something about the vigorous use of knife and fork told her that the physical frustration bothered him rather more than he would admit to her. Still, Susannah appreciated his self-restraint. Was there ever a virgin who had felt so satisfied in the history of the world?

His suggestion—that she wait and see which man she

wanted—was simply absurd. There was no other man. She only wanted him. Susannah wanted to shout it from the rooftops.

Carlyle was gnawing on the bone of his chop almost ferociously and looking at her with the same tenderness he had shown in bed. She half expected him to growl just to make her laugh—and he did.

Susannah nodded to the maid, Molly, who brought in the next course, a puddinglike lump of something that could have originally been potatoes, perhaps mashed up with beets. It was dark red, blotched with brown. "Thank you. That looks delicious."

Molly set the dish on the table and withdrew.

"It looks terrifying," Carlyle said, poking it with a fork. The lump emitted a blast of steam. "English food is dreadful. Perhaps we should hire an Indian cook."

"I would be happy to move back."

"You cannot."

She permitted herself a pout. "If you say so. But I might move somewhere else. Italy is warm."

He took a bite of the puddinglike lump and made a face, putting down the fork. "Hmm. You seem to like countries that begin with I. What about Ireland? I believe that they do not treat potatoes as badly as this in that country."

"Cold and damp."

"Go to Ifrica, then. Or Istralia. Very warm, both of them. And there is always Imerica."

"You are being very silly." She laughed. "And I don't want to go alone. Do keep in mind that we are not married." Carlyle gave her a fond look, as if that fact made him happy. Beastly of him—but he was still the beast she wanted.

He rose from his chair and tossed his napkin on the table. "I only wish to grant you the freedom you seem to want so much."

"Bah. I want—" she blushed—"more of what you—what we—just did."

Carlyle came around and put his hands on her shoulders, glancing through the open door to the hall to make sure they were quite alone before he slid his hands over her bosom. He caressed her breasts in a way that brought back every single sensation she had experienced in bed with him. "Do you now?"

"Yes."

"Not tonight, my darling." He bent to kiss the top of her head. "But soon. I don't know when."

She turned in her chair to look up at him. "That is not the answer I wish to hear."

"The empress has spoken," he said mockingly. "Well, you are in your domain. Remind me to pick up a few pea-cocks. You can give them orders."

Susannah got up, wrapping her arms around his waist and standing on tiptoe to kiss him on the chin. "They would look good in Dr. Josephus's garden." She pulled him over to the window and he went with her without a trace of reluctance.

Holding each other in a loose embrace they looked down at the maze and the quince tree at its center, which had shed its blossoms and leafed out fully. A moving shadow beneath it made her draw in her breath. "Did you see that?" she said softly, drawing him back from the window. Carlyle only nodded. "We are being watched."

He let go of her and moved to one side of the window, looking out without seeming to. "So we are."

Susannah felt sick, her body tight with tension and—she had to admit it—a measure of fear.

He studied the shadowy garden and seemed to come to some conclusion. "He will not come out into the light. And there is not much of that in any case. I must deal with this now, Susannah. And the servants must not know." He sighed. "It is a good thing your drainpipes are in excellent condition. Make sure that Mr. Patchen locks all the doors tonight."

"He always does," Susannah replied in a miserable whisper. "But the servants will remark upon your sudden absence."

"Are you not an empress? Ignore them. And stay away from the windows."

"Yes, of course."

Carlyle waited a few moments more, and she watched his eyes follow the movements of a predator she could not see, drawing her own conclusions when Carlyle looked up through the window and in the direction of the garden's back wall, shrouded in darkness. The man, whoever he was, had undoubtedly gone over it

Carlyle didn't waste a minute. He lifted the window, put one long leg over the sill, grabbed the drainpipe, which clanked, and swung the rest of himself out.

It was three in the morning when he returned. Susannah had stayed in the same room, waving away Molly, who thought she had fallen asleep in the armchair. The English girl had been easy enough to get rid of, but not Lakshmi.

Lakshmi noticed the slight disarray of her mistress's attire—and more important, the agitated state Susannah was in. But Susannah had sent her away too.

"Never mind, Lakshmi. Please go."

The Indian woman had obeyed, but with obvious reluctance.

Susannah eventually did fall asleep in the armchair and wakened with a little scream when she realized Carlyle was standing over her.

"Hush," was all he said.

She looked at his face and gasped. "Oh—what happened?"

His eye was black and a bloody scrape extended from his ear to the front of his chin.

"I became involved in a rather delicate negotiation. But in the end I prevailed."

She rose and looked about for a handkerchief to soak

and wash his face with. The cold cup of tea on the small table by the armchair would have to do for balm. "Who was he, Carlyle? What did he want?"

Carlyle shrugged. "A hired brute. His name is not important. He meant to frighten us."

Susannah dipped the handkerchief in the tea and pressed it carefully to his face. Carlyle flinched. "He hurt you."

"Indeed he did. And I hurt him back."

She cleaned away the drying blood. The task was made more difficult by the short whiskers that roughened his jaw. "Why? You should have—"

"Should have done what, Susannah? Notify the police?"

They would not understand the complicated matter of the gems. "No." She inspected his skin, seeing for the first time the faint purple bruise underneath the blood. "But should you see a doctor?"

He shook his head, looking at her wearily before sinking into an armchair. "We must keep the gems in a safer place than this house. Do you know, I had thought of putting the corset into a safe deposit box at the bank, but I could not get Lakshmi to let it out of her keeping."

"She has been so frightened, Carlyle."

He sighed. "She has reason to be, now more than ever. But there may not be much time. Where are the rubies and sapphires?"

"In the toes of my evening shoes. I took them out to have Mr. De Sola appraise them, but it seemed like as good a hiding place as any so I put them back."

"Females," he said with irritation. "Why do all of you squirrel away valuable things inside your clothes?"

"Because God did not see fit to allow women to do our own banking," she replied tartly. "A divine law to that effect is undoubtedly somewhere in the Bible, although I cannot cite chapter and verse at the moment."

Carlyle laughed under his breath. It was obviously painful for him to do so.

She softened her tone a little. "Imagine the questions I would get if I asked my father's banker for a safe deposit box. And do not forget that I had nothing to do with smuggling those damned stones in the first place."

Susannah came over to his chair, saddened that the glow of their evening together had been obliterated. She put a hand upon his shoulder and he patted it. "We must not fight. I have had enough of that for one night. I nearly killed the fellow."

"Why?" she said.

"He was in your garden. He confessed to following you."

Susannah raised an eyebrow. "And what did you do to encourage that confession?"

"I punched him in the belly and he went down. But that was after he slammed me into a brick wall." Carlyle rubbed his chin. "I shall not shave today."

"Tsk. Surely nothing is worth that. The gems be damned. We should throw them in the Thames. We can live without them, surely, and so can Lakshmi. I suspect the carpet-seller's son would take her off our hands. I shall marry her off."

"It seems to be de rigueur in Albion Square," Carlyle said wryly.

Susannah looked down at him. "What happens now, my love?"

He didn't answer right away. "What did you just say?"

"What happens now?"

He craned his neck rather stiffly to look up at her. "I decamp before the servants wake up. And then, my love, we shall see."

The next night . . .

Carlyle had extracted the name of the fellow who had hired the brute before he dropped him on his head in a Soho alley, so chasing him down had been worth it. The brute had even been persuaded by a well-placed kick to mumble a relevant address.

He raised the lion's-head knocker and let it fall. It sufficed to bring a doorman, who let him in with a silent nod when he said his name and went inside a room to the left to announce his arrival. Carlyle waited in the hall.

"Mr. Jameson." The doorman returned and accompanied him to the room on the left. He withdrew as Carlyle entered.

He had no clue to the identity of the man sitting in front of the fire, other than his Indian name: Tagore. The high-backed chair made it impossible for him to see the fellow.

"Good evening, Mr. Tagore," he said.

The man rose slightly, hands on the padded arms of the chair, and looked over the back. He wore thick spectacles and his black hair was parted in the middle like a school-boy's. His face was almost cherubic—except for the considerable intelligence that shone in his dark eyes. "Good evening, Mr. Jameson. Please sit down."

Carlyle chose the matching chair and they sat side by side in clubby warmth. But there were no other members present. Considering what they were about to discuss, that was just as well. One did not talk casually of rubies and sapphires and diamonds without expecting every ear in the room to twitch inquisitively.

"I understand you and Jack had a bit of a scuffle last night. Oh—" he peered at Carlyle's bruised jaw and black eye—"I hope you are healing nicely. How unfortunate. Jack is quite a one for fisticuffs and mayhem."

"That was why you hired him," Carlyle said.

"Of course. But you were more than a match for him," Tagore said cheerfully. "Boxing is a wonderful sport, but I prefer cricket. More mud, less blood, you know."

Carlyle was feeling rather worse than he had last night, when his injuries were fresh. "Mr. Tagore, if you could get to the point, I would appreciate it."

"Of course, of course, of course. Let us begin at the beginning. We know that you and Miss Fowler came into possession of some very interesting gems, by means which may not have been entirely illegal, but nonetheless resulted in the removal of said gems from the vicinity of Rajasthan—"

"The point," Carlyle reminded him. "You must have one."

"The maharajah wants them back."

Carlyle suppressed a yawn. He was not trying to seem indifferent, but he was utterly exhausted and feeling rather like he had been run over by a horse and wagon. "I see. I mean, I think I do. Perhaps I should not admit to a thing."

"Ha-ha. You are making a joke and I appreciate it. We meet as friends. But our position is that none of them belong to you or Miss Fowler."

"You are entitled to your opinion, Mr. Tagore."

The other man hesitated and tried another tactic. "Produce them at once."

Carlyle regarded him through his good eye. "I just might, if I had them."

Tagore relaxed, but looked at him narrowly. "Are they on your person?" He didn't wait for an answer. "If they are, I cannot take them from you. Be reasonable, Mr. Jameson. You of all people know what a maharajah can do. His sword is swift. His reach is long."

"Then kill me," Carlyle said wearily.

"A rash action. It is our feeling that the Queen's ministers might take it amiss. Although you are replaceable. Another man will quickly take your place. We know every British secret agent in our country."

"India is a thousand countries, Mr. Tagore," Carlyle said. "And they seldom agree. We are keeping the peace as best we know how."

Mr. Tagore scowled fiercely. "That is a subject that might be better left alone. But let us get back to the diamonds."

"What about the rubies and sapphires?"

The other man waved dismissively. "Valuable as they

are, the maharajah feels that it was fated for you and Miss Fowler to have them. In memory of her father, his dear friend, he has decided to give them to you as a wedding gift."

Carlyle's eyebrows shot up. "But we are not going to be married."

"According to the palace astrologer, you are. Perhaps not soon, but it will be an auspicious coupling. The maharajah extends his congratulations. He says that a good wife is a joy."

"He should know," Carlyle muttered. "His eminence has quite a few of them, as replaceable as I am. Whatever happened to the favorite?"

"She lives now in the house of the maharajah's auntie, who sees to it that she is unhappy. But being unhappy is better than being dead."

"Perhaps it is the best that could be hoped for." Carlyle sat up straight and his voice strengthened. "Then thank him for his kind thoughts regarding me and Miss Fowler. And thank him for his gift. Every new household should have an adequate supply of rubies and sapphires."

Mr. Tagore laughed appreciatively. "I enjoy your sense of humor, Mr. Jameson. I forgot to mention that the maharajah says you may also keep Lakshmi."

"In England she is a free woman."

The other man only nodded. Carlyle rubbed his aching chin with a light hand, thinking over the offer. It was more or less what he'd expected. It had been only a matter of time before someone caught up with them, and now that it had happened, he felt an odd sense of relief.

Susannah had not empowered him to answer for her, of course, but he might as well. Mr. Tagore was right enough in saying that none of the gems belonged to her. The maharajah could have his gigantic diamonds back—if the old fellow wanted to give them the lesser stones for old times' sake, who was Carlyle to say no?

"Mr. Tagore," he said at last. "Tell me what you think the rubies and sapphires are worth. We may not need so many."

The Indian man calculated the sum in his head, then named it.

"That will do very well," Carlyle said with a smile. "On behalf of Miss Fowler, I accept the maharajah's gift."

Chapter 6

They had moved from Albion Square to the Surrey country-side and set up housekeeping in a manor that was nearly new, although it had changed hands several times. There was no changing the climate, however, but the extent of their land enabled Carlyle to create a remarkable garden. For the first time since her return to England, Susannah felt that she could breathe.

He had hired the local stonemason to build her an open-air pavilion that overlooked a reflecting pool. At the moment the pool reflected nothing, being no more than a large, rectangular area of mud. But when it was fully dredged, filled and banked with stone, it would be very like the idyllic place where they had once played chess.

A pastime which they once again enjoyed, now that Carlyle could live as a gentleman. His brother, the earl, did not enjoy so grand a vista or so great a house. Carlyle's proliferating nephews had taken over every room they could, and the unfortunate earl hid from them in his library, where he was writing a scholarly book about newts and salamanders, his new passion. He had given up on his wife and women in general.

A peacock strolled by, dragging its spectacular tail over the grass. It peered at Susannah as if she did not belong in its domain, and stalked away. She adjusted the bag slung over her shoulder and looked inside to be sure that her paints and paper were inside.

She had vowed to chronicle the construction of their love nest inside and out. The interior decoration had been completed first, in light and airy colors that reminded her of India. She had insisted on avoiding bric-a-brac, heavy curtains, and excess furniture—not that Carlyle cared about such things. He gave her a free hand where the house was concerned, preferring to concentrate his efforts on the garden, drawing up ambitious plans that required an army of men, supervising the removal and replanting of trees to create the vista he desired, and bargaining at the local fair for a flock of decorative sheep to keep the lawn short.

The velvety, close-cropped grass prickled under her bare feet. There was no one to see, no Mrs. Posey to scold her for going about barefoot. She had retired with a pension they provided, and seemed quite happy to do so. But some of the other servants had come along—Mr. Patchen and Molly being two.

Susannah had even sketched their portraits as they went about their daily routines, as she wished to remember it all. Molly in the kitchen, stirring an earthenware bowl at a stout pine table. Mr. Patchen on his knees transplanting crocus bulbs, a concerned look on his face as he patted down the covering earth. And Carlyle himself, riding about his little Eden on a big bay horse he had named Tagore, for some reason. She supposed he wanted to remember India too. Perhaps he'd had a friend by that name.

She found her favorite rock to sit upon—it was very large and quite flat, rising from the ground as if it sought the sun that warmed it. Susannah settled her bottom upon it and took her painting things out of the bag. She pulled out another book that Carlyle had given to her before they moved away from London. Her father had made it for her. But he had instructed Carlyle not to give it to her right away. She was glad enough of that, because it meant much more to her now. He had told her that the heavy envelope in his hand was from her father and nothing more, and when he'd left her alone with it she'd opened it to find a scrapbook, an unexpected gift that had let her cry at last. Without her ever knowing of its existence, the book had been created over the course of her twenty-three years by her father, with a few early entries from the mother she had never known.

On its pages, he had jotted down his fond recollections of her as a very young child. Her refusal at the age of three to yield the right of way to a big white cow in a Jaipur street. The cow had prevailed, but she had called it a very naughty cow and its owner had requested baksheesh to salve his pride. Then there was the gaily decorated little wagon in which she took her dolls, Indian and European, out for an airing—he had done a wonderful sketch of it and many other drawings of Susannah.

His swift pen had captured her sturdy body and cropped hair, and a characteristic look of mischief in her eyes, as well as a definite and stubborn pout. But her father wrote that her pout that would turn quickly to a smile at the sight of an animal or bird, which he deftly sketched as well.

Once she had reached the awkward age, he hadn't stopped adding to the book. That was a time she scarcely wanted to remember—the swinging between extremes of emotion, gloom one day, glee the next—and the way she had felt suddenly and dreadfully far too tall and too, well, womanly.

The final pages were begun when her father knew he was gravely ill, and they constituted his last words to her: *So loving and so warm and so encouraging that she could not read them without dissolving in tears at first.*

By now she had memorized most of it, especially the final page: *I have lived my life and, and save for the loss of your mother, it was a happy one, because of you. And now, my Susannah, dear and only child born of our love—you must begin your life without me. I have only a few words of advice: Think for yourself and follow your own star, as I have done. Joy is elusive, but it is worth looking for. And know that somewhere, somehow, I shall watch over you. . . .*

In his way, he had. And now, of course, she had Carlyle. Wherever her father was—not in heaven, not in hell, but perhaps in an afterlife that allowed for a few pleasurable sins—he would have approved of that.

As unconventional as their love was, it was exactly what she wanted, sustaining her heart and soul. She had meant the vows she'd spoken and so had he.

Much later that night, she lay under him after their love-making, giggling drowsily as he lavished caresses on her breasts, kissing them noisily and moving up her neck to growl in her ear and make her laugh some more.

Susannah had never regretted choosing him. No one else could make her feel this way and she wanted no other man. Of late she had been considering having his child. Considering his skill at the ultimate kiss—and the similar skills she had learned to satisfy him—she had not yet conceived, but that was all to the good.

They had spent many months exploring the techniques in the old book he had taken from Dr. Josephus's library. She had even managed to decipher some of the ancient script and set it down in erotic poems, creating a pillow book for the two of them to read together. There was nothing he was not eager to try, but it had been some while before he permitted himself to penetrate her, waiting until he thought she was ready, and pleasuring her in myriad other ways.

He really did spoil her, no matter how much he complained about her imperial tendencies in and out of bed, simply because it amused him to do so. Susannah sighed with happiness when he lifted himself off and curled around her, one hand between her legs. She was slick and he—she felt the nudge from an eager shaft—he was hard again.

"Ahh. May I, my love?"

She decided to deny him. "I am not ready."

His gentle fingers probed and teased. "I beg to differ. Mmm. Swollen and soft. Made for me." He swept her tangled hair off her neck and bit her nape very nicely.

Susannah wriggled, pushing her bottom back against the curve made by his thighs and lower belly.

He groaned. "You are a tease."

"Far from it. I have not recovered from our first time." She pushed his exploring hand away. "Your lovemaking was so splendid and you—you are so virile that I have folded my petals, so to speak."

He snorted and put his hand back where it had been. "And I shall open them."

Susannah clamped her thighs around his hand.

"My heavens, what a powerful grip you have." He pretended to be unable to yank his hand out, twiddling his fingers between her legs in a way she found irresistibly exciting. It was not easy to hold off, but it was amusing.

Carlyle forced his thigh between hers to open them. At last, laughing, she rolled on her back and let him top her again. But he did not enter her body at once, just looked down at her with love in his eyes.

Susannah looked at him quizzically. "Why are you waiting? What do you want?"

"Oh . . . just give me a kiss, Mrs. Jameson."

She did.

Please turn the page for a
look at Kathy Love's
MY SISTER IS A WEREWOLF
available now from Brava!

Reaching for her beer, Elizabeth took a sip, and, for the first time tonight, felt a little normal. The atmosphere seemed to envelop her, as if she was meant to be there. A much-needed sense of contentment filled her. The talking, the laughter, the smell of drinks and salty, roasted peanuts. It made her feel oddly better. This was a good idea—a good distraction. Tomorrow she'd return to her research more relaxed and focused.

Elizabeth smiled as Jill Lewis finally took the stage. The reluctant woman shook her head, glaring good-naturedly at her friends.

"All right!" Jolee cheered from over her microphone, and much of the audience exploded into applause. Elizabeth clapped along with them.

Jolee started the music and the woman's voice filled the room almost from the first note. Elizabeth recognized the tune as a song from the radio with a happy, contagious beat. And the woman sang it well—better than well. It was little wonder that her pals were urging her to get up there. She was great.

Elizabeth looked back to the woman's table of friends to see their reaction to the woman's fantastic singing. Two of them, a man and a woman, beamed and clapped, while the other at the table, a male, just watched. He was somehow distant from the other two. The clapping male leaned over to say something to him, and the one who only watched turned toward his friend, giving Elizabeth her first full view of his face.

Elizabeth's smile disappeared. Desire, so strong that it almost made her cry out, ripped through her, shredding any trace of calm she'd found. Every muscle in her body tensed, every sense sharpening until her whole being was centered on the man before her.

Without saying a word to Christian, she rose. Carefully, purposefully, she zigzagged through the tables, her eyes never leaving the man. Just tables away, she stopped herself, fragments of her reasonable mind taking control. She glanced back to the bar. Christian watched her, but when he saw her looking, he busied himself by taking an order from one of the patrons.

Her brother could sense her desire now. Of course he could. Vampires could sense emotions—and she knew hers ran very strong. Shame filled her, but still her gaze returned to the male at the table.

The man was beautiful—dark hair, sculpted features, perfectly shaped lips that any woman would have killed for, yet on him they were sinfully masculine. He was beyond handsome.

Elizabeth had seen many handsome men in her life, but her body had never reacted like this.

She swallowed. *Control yourself! What was she doing?*

But instead of walking back to her bar stool like her brain ordered her to, she took another step toward the table of friends. Then another. She sauntered slowly past the man's chair, not getting too close, not drawing attention to herself—not just yet. She had to assess, she had to watch. Stalking her prey.

She lifted her head to breathe in his scent. The hint of woodsy cologne, the freshness of soap and shampoo, the minty traces of toothpaste. And a warm, rich scent—a scent that made her want to tip back her head and howl.

She continued around the table until he was directly in her line of sight—then she sat down at an empty table. Eyes trained on him, she studied him. Oh yeah, she wanted him.

For just a moment, she closed her eyes as her rational mind took tenuous control. Why was this happening? It was as if the wolf was in control. But that didn't happen. She didn't stay in human form and think like the wolf. She didn't allow that. Some werewolves did. Brody did. He was more wolf than man at all times. She didn't allow that. She didn't.

Her eyes snapped open. The man was looking at her. She'd felt his gaze before she'd actually seen it. Their gazes met, but even in the dim light, she could see his eyes were a mixture somewhere between brown and green.

Again her body told her this was what she needed. This was what she'd been wanting. *He* was what she wanted. She continued to stare, meeting his gaze, until he looked away. Still she watched him. Unable to do otherwise. The need was in control now.

She was acting like a bitch in heat. And she didn't care.

Take a peek at the scintillating new novel
YOUR MOUTH DRIVES ME CRAZY
from HelenKay Dimon.
Available now from Brava!

A bathroom. He walked her straight into a windowless bathroom and then into the shower stall. The world spun beneath her until her feet landed on the cold tile floor with strong arms banded around her waist.

Every cell in Annie's body snapped to life. The lethargy weighing down her body disappeared when she heard the screech of the shower curtain rings against the rod. A rush of water echoed in her ears as steam filled the room.

"Here we go," the stranger said to the room as if the nut chatted with unconscious people all the time.

He balanced her body against his. Rough denim scratched against her sensitive skin from the front. Lukewarm water splashed over her bare body from the back, making her skin tingle and burn.

A gasp caught in her throat as her shoulders stiffened under the spray. A scream rumbled right behind the gasp, but she managed to swallow that, too.

"This should help." He continued his one-sided conversation in a deep, hypnotizing voice.

He seemed mighty pleased with himself. And since he had stepped right under the water with her, a bit ballsy for her taste.

"This will feel better in a second."

He wasn't wrong.

Firm hands caressed her skull, replacing the frigid ocean with bath water. He rinsed and massaged and rinsed again. The sweep of his hands wiped away the last of her confusion. With that task done, his palms turned to her arms, brushing up and down, igniting every nerve ending in their path.

His chest rubbed against her bare breasts until heat replaced her chill. Her thighs smashed against his legs. The full body rubdown sparked life into body parts that had been on a deep-freeze hold for more than a year.

"Better?"

She didn't answer. Wasn't even sure she could speak if she wanted to.

"Open your eyes and say something," he said.

The husky command broke her out of her mental wanderings and sent a shot of anxiety skating down her spine. This was the part of the program where she ran and hid . . . and then ran some more.

Naked. Alone. Strange man. Yeah, a very bad combination.

"I know you're awake." He sounded pretty damn amused by the idea.

The jig was up. Okay, fine, she got his point.

Not knowing if her rescuer counted as a friend or foe, she played the scene with the utmost care. Only a complete madman would attack a vulnerable woman who didn't know her own name. If her stranger fell into that category she'd scream and make a mad dash into the kitchen for the nearest sharp knife. The nearest sharp anything.

She groaned in pain that was only half false.

"Your eyes are still closed," he said.

Yeah, pal, no kidding.

"You aren't fooling me."

She could certainly try.

His hands continued to massage her sore flesh with just

the right amount of pressure to bring her blood sizzling back to life. If he kept this up her eyes wouldn't open. She'd be asleep.

She couldn't remember the last time she slept through the night. In the almost fifteen months since her mother's confinement in a Washington State psychiatric ward, she'd spent most of her time looking for the man who put her mother there. She scheduled her freelance jobs around the project.

The path led to Kauai. To that yacht. To flying over the side of the yacht. To being in this shower.

"We can stand here all night for all I care," he said.

Nothing that extreme. Maybe ten more minutes.

He chuckled. "Doesn't bother me."

Lucky for her she found an accommodating potential serial killer.

"Because I'm the one with clothes on," he pointed out.

Her eyelids flew open.

And now here's Diane Whiteside's latest,
THE NORTHERN DEVIL,
coming next month from Brava!

"I must remarry and quickly," Rachel announced.

Marriage to someone else? Well, he'd always known it would happen one day. But it seemed more wrenching now that he'd carried her and known the softness of her in his arms, and the sweet smell of her in his lungs.

"There is no time for a protracted struggle against Collins, here in Omaha. It is vital that he be immediately cut off from all revenues, especially as my trustee."

Lucas immediately came fully alert, recognizing her sharpened tone. "Why is it so urgent?"

"He means to trap William Donovan at the Bluebird Mine and kill him."

"*Murder* Donovan? Why, that bast—toadstool!"

She nodded agreement. "But if he's no longer my trustee—"

His mind was racing, considering the implications. "Then he can't give orders to the men at the Bluebird Mine in your name."

Her pacing brought her less than a foot from him. She stopped with a small gasp and pivoted, swishing her train out of his way. Did she glance too long at him over her shoulder? But if so, she wasn't behaving like a woman who knew how to flirt.

"Yes. Elias bought the mine several years ago from an old friend, who needed to raise cash. He also sold an interest to Donovan, as part of a bigger deal."

"So Humphreys, the mine's manager, has always answered to Boston."

She sank down onto the settee by the coffee tray. "Exactly. I'll need to personally tell him that I've remarried so he won't help Collins in any way."

Every protective instinct in Lucas revolted. "No! You won't go anywhere near the Bluebird, not if there's about to be a murder attempt."

She raised a haughty eyebrow. Ah, that was more like the woman he was acquainted with—who enjoyed challenging his mind, not his loins.

He relaxed, ready for a pleasant round of debate.

"Mr. Grainger, it's critical that an innocent man's life be saved. That's far more important than any polite folderol about not sending women into danger. I'm certain that once Mr. Humphreys understands I've remarried, he won't assist Mr. Collins, and all will be well."

A Nevada mine supervisor would fall into line like a sheep when she crooked her finger? Appalled at her optimism, Lucas opened his mouth to roar objections but she was still talking.

"No, what I need your help for is to find another husband. Immediately—before Mr. Collins can take legal steps to regain my custody."

Lucas frowned. Rachel Davis and another man—in her wedding bed? Someone certain to be honorable, polite, and respectful even in the bedroom.

He growled, deep in his throat, and began to stride up and down the carpet.

Like hell, anyone else was climbing into her bed if she was willing to accept a marriage of convenience!

But marry her himself?

He swallowed hard.

She was right: The best way to protect Donovan's life, given Collins's malice, was for her to marry. He owed Donovan a blood debt that his life alone would not repay, but his honor would. Marrying Rachel would even the scales.

Did his old vow never to marry carry any weight against saving Donovan's life?

He grimaced and spun on his heel. No.

But Rachel was his friend. She wasn't looking for love, just protection and companionship. They could build a solid union together on that basis.

But in marrying her, there'd be the necessity of siring children. For the first time in his life, he'd have to hope that his seed would set fruit. Fruit that could grow to become a little child, vibrant and alive, beautiful, intelligent, happy to see him. A true family, in other words, and his oldest dream.

He began to smile.